RECOVER AND TERMINATE

A TOP SECRET PRESIDENTIAL NOVEL

Table of Contents

07:15 - 7 AUGUST

TIME ZONE TANGO

Rain poured down in heavy sheets. There was no other sound. Just the rain. The light from the small stilt hut was a blur. Almost impossible to see. It had been hours since he reached the edge of the jungle surrounding the village and found the designated target. He had to make sure he took out the right man, so he waited for the right moment. There were several shadows moving from light to dark and then light again. The rain was his friend, his only friend tonight. He low crawled silently through the mud and made his way past the jungle vines that tangled everything in their webs. Carefully, slowly he made his way to the bamboo stairs that led to the raised floor of the hut made from bamboo poles, mud, and vines.

He knew the only way this was going down tonight was to climb the bamboo ladder without making noise that could be heard above the low roaring of the falling sheets of rain. He pulled the silenced High Standard .22 caliber from its shoulder holster under his left arm. He pulled the receiver slide back, and in the weak rays of light coming down through the floor of the hut, he checked to make sure there was a round chambered. He climbed the almost vertical ladder using his left hand and moving his right hand with the silenced .22 up along the rail of the ladder with the barrel held down, away from the falling deluge. He made it to the top of the ladder and thought how lucky he was that the monsoon rain was keeping the village dogs lying in any dry places they could find. He knew his plan would never work without the rain.

He crouched by the only door in the hut and waited. He could hear two people talking about the plans they had made to take one of the village pigs to the outskirts of Saigon to cover for their contact with the local VC about the raid that was going to happen later in the week. The assassin drew nearer to the cloth covering at the doorway. He pulled the fabric back, located the VC collaborator, and shot him once in the forehead. The subsonic bullet dropped him like a rag doll. He stepped over the dead VC and put another round in his right eye.

Screaming like a banshee the female jumped on his back and tried to stab him in the chest with a knife. He blocked her arm as it came down, and threw her over his head, following her down to the floor next to the dead man. He pinned her arm down and jammed his pistol deep into her throat and pulled the trigger. The top of her head blew out, showering his face with blood and pieces of brain and bone.

Hawk shook his head, trying to clear it. He tossed and turned and finally started to feel the wet of the sheets knotted around him. There was a low soft mewing sound much closer to him than the pounding of the huge drops of rain that always came with a storm in the Rocky Mountains. He had trouble concentrating on the sound; the rain blocked it with the clatter on the roof of the camper where he lived. The cracking, booming sound of artillery exploding nearby made by the lightning grew to a crescendo. There was a dead weight on his chest. It was keeping him from taking a full breath. Bending his head toward his chest, he saw the problem.

It was one of the many recurring nightmares that frequented his life when he slept. They were all different, but starkly exact in every detail of the way they happened during his two tours of duty in Southeast Asia. Vietnam, Laos, Cambodia, Thailand. They had all taken their toll on his mind and body.

He pulled one of his arms from the soaked, knotted sheets and reached for Eliot, his tabby Maine coon cat that was curled up on top of him for security from the echoing, crashing thunder and lightning. He ruffed Eliot up and pushed him to the side. Eliot and Cowboy, his teammate during both his tours, were the only two friends he had. He remembered the platoon sergeant at the end of basic training telling them all to look to their right and left, and then he said, "At least one of you will be coming back in a body bag." His teammate was his only human friend, and they both came back—or at least their bodies came back. They had left their souls in the steaming hell of the jungles in that godforsaken place.

Hawk rolled out of the small cramped camper bed and said, "Eliot, let's eat."

The cat jumped down from the bunk and ran to the kitchen, which didn't take long, since the kitchen, if it could be called that, was only three feet from the elevated bunkbed. He sat with his face upturned to the small cabinet above the sink and waited, ears back and tail switching with excitement. Hawk pulled on a pair of wool socks and took the few steps to the kitchen. He opened the door of the cabinet and pulled down a can of tuna from a stack he kept there. He had been told by the vet that feeding Eliot tuna every meal was bad for him. Not one to follow all the rules, Hawk gave the twenty-pound cat what he wanted to eat. Besides, Eliot was a hunter too.

While the cat ate, Hawk put on some old sweats and running shoes, and a waist-length lightweight slicker. He opened the door of the camper and stepped out on the wood plank over the cement block patio he had put together, and closed the door after Eliot ran out. Funny thing about Eliot: he loved water. It was the lightning and thunder sometimes mixed with hail that he didn't like. He ran under the camper and wrapped his tail around himself as if saying, "You must be crazy to run in the rain."

Hawk ran every day barring a two or three feet snow. He was still built well at an even six feet, with black hair and coal-black eyes. He had been back about six months and had managed to get a job with a one-man garage and settled in to learn the trade. The camper was all he could afford. He had lived in much worse. Way worse. The camper was tied down next to a small lake fed by a creek running down from the mountains. There were fish to be caught. The quiet is what he needed. The high shear peaks surrounding the lake gave him the solitude he needed. He was quietly working his way back from the abyss. That's what he called it—the abyss. He felt like he had taken a small step back from it, but knew there was a long way to go. He still slept with his pistol under his pillow and took it with him each day as he ran, and then to work. He was certain Ray, the owner of the tiny garage, had seen it stuck at his back when his shirt lifted up too much. Hawk didn't think Ray cared. Ray had given him a job because he was a vet. Ray had his WWII Armored Division patch framed and on his wall. Hawk guessed that was called watching your six, but then Ray probably wouldn't understand that being from a different war and all.

07:45 - 7 AUGUST

TIME ZONE TANGO

He started his run down the curving dirt and rock road that led down to the town of Frisco and the Blue River. The road was a series of short switchbacks that followed Buffalo Mountain's contours. He ran a steady pace slugging through the runoff created by the rainstorm. He ran around a sharp *S* curve and cut up the mountain on a trail worn into the dirt and rock of it by hundreds of years of deer, elk, and moose making their way down to the lower valley of the Blue and the lush vegetation that ran for miles down the valley between the high mountains next to the continental divide. His father's ancestors had lived in these same mountains and lush valleys for a thousand years. They were the most feared fighters of all the Indian tribes, the Utes. His father had taught him to hunt with gun and knife and how to survive in the wilderness. That was at the core of his survival during his tours.

The trail ran across open areas of sage and grasses, through dense mottes of aspen and lodge pole pine, so thick it acted like an umbrella for him. The ground was hard packed and rocky, making the water run off quickly, and into torrents of gullies and creeks, then gulches, and finally a multitude of rivers and beaver lakes. He was slowing as the trail became steeper, running into the wind blowing hard over the tops of the mountains then rushing down toward the valleys, blowing the rain in sheets so strong it could blow a man over. He turned a sharp corner and did a fast side step to the right to avoid a torrent of water cutting across the trail immediately in front of him. He felt the whip of the bullet before he heard the crack of the pistol. Instinct took over. He dove for the cover of several pines and large boulders in the same motion of his quick jog to the right that saved his life. He slid in behind a boulder with his M1911 .45 Colt out in front of him. He wiped the mud from his eyes and scooted to his knees for a better firing position. He carried the M1911 locked and cocked with a seven-round magazine, and one in the tube. He thought the shot had come from above him and to the left of the trail. He stayed low in the mud and looked through a tiny space between the boulder and the nearest pine, trying to catch a glimpse of the shooter. No luck.

He started to worm his way slowly down and to the left of the boulders figuring on flanking him. He never was one to wait to be shot. He made it sliding through the high grass and mud to a small wash running full of water, coming down the mountain from the left. He slid into the water and crawled forward, up and to the left. The water was rushing wildly down the course of the wash.

He tried to keep his head halfway out of the water as he grabbed roots of trees and rocks in the bottom to pull his way up. Water flooded his nose and made him gag and start to cough. He plunged his head underwater and blew it out, not making any sound at all.

He worked his way slowly up the side of the mountain until he thought he was above the shooter. He crawled and pulled his way out of the torrent in the wash and rested there until his breathing was back to normal and the shakes were gone from being in the cold water for so long. Working his way to a fallen pine, he listened for any sound. During the time he worked his way up the wash the rain had stopped as suddenly as it has started. The mist that replaced it added to the quiet. He waited patiently.

Suddenly from not far off to his left and down in some Aspens near where he remembered the trail ran, he heard Spanish being spoken in soft but urgent tones. His mother was Mexican American from the Taos area and had made sure he spoke her native language.

"Donde esta el pinche gringo?" ("Where's the damn gringo?")

"No pasa nada. Callate!" ("Don't worry. Shut up!")

There were two of them. That helped Hawk. He knew what he was facing. He moved like a large lizard, one inch at a time, waiting, then again. It took him a long time to make it to the cover of a pine tree within ten feet of the two men. During his slow progress the scared one asked if they could leave. The other one, most likely in charge, said that the boss would kill them if they didn't take Hawk out. The boss wanted him dead.

Hawk was standing behind the tree trunk with his M1911 pointed at the one in charge when he said, "Drop your weapons and lay down on the ground spread-eagled."

The one in charge was leaning on a tree trunk, the other sitting on an old stump when they turned and started shooting wildly in his direction. Bark flew from the tree with pine needles flying up from low shots. Hawk leaned out and shot the one in charge in the head. The left side of the man's face blew off, and as he flew back and up, Hawk shot him in the chest to make sure. He stepped back behind the tree for a second and came from the other side of it to shoot. The scared one shot too fast, and Hawk felt the shockwave push past him, near his shoulder. He wanted this one alive. He shot him in the shoulder, tearing through muscle and destroying the shooter's scapula. The shooter's gun dropped into the wet layer of pine needles, grass, and leaves. He was thrown back and to the right side, falling facedown.

Hawk walked over and checked to make sure the leader was dead, and then went to the scared one after he picked up his pistol. He rolled the wounded shooter over and pulled him up against a tree. He asked the shooter why they were trying to kill him. The scared shooter sat against the tree and bled. Hawk asked him again, and when he didn't answer, he figured out his mistake. The guy didn't speak English!

Hawk asked again in Spanish, "Why were you trying to kill me?"

The wounded man looked at him and said, "They will kill me if I tell you anything."

Hawk said, "You and the dead one tried to kill me. If you don't tell me why and who ordered it, I will kill you. Understand?"

"I can't tell you."

"I'll leave you here to bleed to death, if you refuse."

"We didn't know you would be armed and know how to kill us. No one told us that. It was to be an easy job, and then we were to return to Mexico."

"Who sent you to kill me?"

"Carlos D'Arcy Garcia. He is our jefe. He is asked to do others favors sometimes. I do not know who; maybe him, maybe others."

"Where is your boss now?"

"Quintana Roo. There is a large villa there. In Playa del Carmen."

Hawk turned to go as the scared one said, "Please don't leave me to bleed to death."

Hawk turned halfway around and brought his pistol up. He shot the man that had tried to kill him in the forehead. The Mexican shooter's head bounced against the tree, and then he rolled over on his side, missing the back of his skull.

Hawk looked down at him and said, "Now you won't bleed to death."

He had seen so much death in the past years, it didn't bother him. That part of him, the remorse, had died over there.

O8:45 - 7 AUGUST

TIME ZONE TANGO

Hawk made his way down the mountain wondering how these men from Mexico had found him. He was back in his camper washing up when it dawned on him. Ray! They must have talked with Ray. He threw on a sweatshirt from the Army Language School in Monterrey, California, and a pair of old 501 Levi's, then ran to his pickup. It was an old beat-up Ford F-100 V8 that his dad had given him when he graduated from high school. He was afraid of what he would find. He had begun to like the old man.

He drove into the parking lot of the small garage and honked his horn. Not waiting for anyone to come from the building, he left the truck running and the door open as he ran to the office door and tried the knob. It wasn't locked. He closed the door behind him and checked behind the cluttered desk and in the coat closet. He ran over to the door from the office into the bay and looked through the dirty grease-smeared little window to the two car lifts. Both were up in the air. They were left that way with or without cars on them so the floor could be cleaned each night before stopping work. The trouble was, it was the afternoon, and the lifts should have been down while Ray worked on whichever car was due out first. He opened the door and ran around the bay looking for Ray, but didn't find him. He took the short way back to the office under the lifts, wondering if he was wrong and Ray had stayed home sick expecting Hawk to open the shop up.

He stopped and looked at a pool of oil that had dripped down from the car on the first lift next to the office door. He thought, "There shouldn't be a pool of oil draining from the interior of the car." He looked up more acutely and saw the driver's door was ajar. He went over to the air pump and turned it on. Then pulled the lever that would let the car down. It came to rest on the cement floor with a little rock side to side, and the driver's-side door swung open, on its own volition.

Hawk pushed back his ball cap and rubbed his forehead. He felt sick to his stomach, and the rain and fright and blood and guts started to return again. He willed himself to walk over and take control. Unsteady at first, his steps became steady as he made his way to what he knew he would find. Ray was on his stomach across the car's front bench seat. His head and his right arm hung over the running board, and the blood had dripped from his throat being slit from ear to ear. His face was battered, and his knuckles on both hands were torn and bloody. He had put up a fight.

Hawk wondered why the two men would have killed the old man. They could have controlled him easily enough. Maybe it was because the old man wouldn't tell them what they wanted to know. That sounded like Ray for sure. But no, it wouldn't be that. They killed him because he could identify them, once Hawk was dead. They were covering their tracks. The sorry sons ah bitches!

Why had they come here and killed Ray and tried, though it had been badly, to kill him from ambush on the mountain? What was it the scared one said, "Quintana Roo." The Mexican state next to the Caribbean Sea and up to the Gulf of Mexico. Their boss was named Carlos Garcia D'Arcy. Why would a Mexican boss want him dead? What had the scared one said: "He has many places to live." Why would a wealthy Mexican order his death, and how the hell did they find him? Somehow, they had gotten to Ray.

Hawk called the police, and for the rest of the day he told them what he knew and showed them where the two men were and was told not to leave Summit County until the coroner's inquest.

14:45 - 7 AUGUST

TIME ZONE TANGO

Hawk went back to the little camper. Eliot met him at the door and double bumped him for food. After he gave Eliot his food, he grabbed a Coors out of the little half fridge and sat in the ragged old comfortable chair that was the living room. It swallowed him in its folds and worn-out cushion with the stuffing hanging out where Eliot had used it for a scratching place. He popped the top and took a long swallow. Eliot had finished his meal and came to sit on Hawk's lap. Eliot could always tell when he was upset or down in the dumps. He was both now, so Eliot trilled for him too.

***

Hawk woke with his back hurting and a furry lump pressing down on his stomach. His beer was stale, so he moved the cat and took the two steps to the fridge. He knew he wasn't going to sleep, so he grabbed another Coors and went outside and sat on the steps that went down to the wood patio on the lake. He was working his way through the anger and sorrow and headed for payback. He thought again of how they found Ray, and through Ray, him.

Like a light bulb turning on, he knew it. It had to be his Social Security number or his serial number from the military and then the Social Security number. That would take someone in the military or the government being involved in some way. With the Social Security number, they could find Ray because he had to report Hawk's employment to the government. That had to be it. But never mind how he got the number, Hawk knew what he had to do, no matter what. He would find D'Arcy and get some answers, and then some payback for Ray. Then he would find out who had given his information out.

He finished his beer and went into the camper. He packed his duffle bag, his extra ammunition, and cans of tuna for Eliot. He took a few other things he thought he might need and put Eliot in the cab of the truck. The hell with the coroner; he was driving into Mexico and going after this guy D'Arcy. It was a good thing Eliot liked to ride in the truck!

He drove straight through to El Paso. He needed a friend to take Eliot and if possible loan him some cash for the trip into Mexico. He didn't have to ponder, fret, or decide who that person would be. There was only one man that fulfilled Hawk's definition of the word friend. He pulled into a twenty-four-hour gas station. After putting the nozzle of the pump hose in the truck's gas tank opening, he went in to pay the clerk. Once he had the gas running he walked over to the phone outside the store next to the restrooms. There was a single light on a wood pole showing yellow light down onto the phone and doors to the restrooms around the corner of the building. There was a buzzing noise coming from the light, as well as from all the bugs swarming around it. Hawk pulled a letter from his pocket and held it up so the light was on it. He picked the phone up and unwound the silver coil, then held the phone between his shoulder and neck while he dialed the number in the letter.

The phone rang several times with no answer. Then some clicking noises and a female voice said in a rather nasal tone, "This is a long-distance call. Please deposit seventy-five cents for the first three minutes."

Hawk dug into his pants and after not finding any quarters in the first pocket checked the other one where he kept his truck keys. He put the quarters he found there into the phone, listening to each one making a sound inside the phone like coins rolling down a tunnel and dropping into a box.

The ringing started again.

"Hello," said a male voice that sounded older than his friend.

"I'd like ta speak with Cowboy, if he's there," Hawk said.

"You from the army? Nobody calls Juan 'Cowboy' unless he knew him in the army."

"Yes sir. My name's Hawk. Maybe Juan told you about me."

"Why sure, son. He's out in the barn, I think. I'll go get him for ya. By the way, Hawk, thanks for making sure my boy came back."

There was quiet on the phone for a couple of minutes; then he heard the voice of Cowboy.

"Hawk, is that you? Where the hell are ya? What's up?" Cowboy yelled into the phone. It sounded like he was out of breath.

The nasal voice cut in again and said, "Your three minutes are up. It will be another seventy-five cents for another three minutes, please."

"Cowboy, I'm out of change. Can you take the charges for me?" Hawk asked.

"Miss, would you please charge the rest of the call to this number?"

"Yes sir," the nasal voice said. There was another click.

"Cowboy, how they hangin'? It's me alright. You told me when they were puttin' you in the Dust Off that you had my back. I'm in a bind, Cowboy. I'm in El Paso now. If you'll give me directions to your place, I'd like to stop by, if that's good for you."

"If that's good for me? What the hell you talkin' about, man?" Cowboy gave him directions, then said, "Get your sorry ass down here. My old man wants to meet the man that saved his boy's life."

Hawk walked over to the truck and put the pump hose up. The meter read twenty dollars. That's what he had paid the clerk, so he started the truck. Eliot came over and sat down in his lap. He headed out of El Paso, driving southwest, following the Rio Grande to Del Rio. Cowboy had told him to call when he got there, and he would come into town so Hawk could follow him out to the ranch.

***

Cowboy pulled into the Chevron gas station on the south side of Del Rio about forty minutes after Hawk called him. His truck was beat up as much as Hawk's. The only difference in them was Cowboy had a cattle pen sticking up from the bed of his. They hugged and did the dap they had made up when they were "in-country."

"You look like shit, man. What the hell is goin' on?" said Cowboy as he slapped Hawk's back.

"Man, I'm shot, been driving for two days and nights, and there may be a warrant out for me by now. Let's head to your place and let me get some Z's. We'll talk after I've had some shut-eye. Let's di di mau. Let's get the fuck out of here!"

10:15 - 9 AUGUST

TIME ZONE SIERRA

Hawk followed Cowboy's old beat-up Ford, south along the Rio Grande. The country was sandy, flat to low rolling hills, and covered in sage and cactus with an orphaned cedar here and there. They turned right from the Texas state highway across a cattle guard, and under a wood arch with "Double D" painted in white letters. Hawk figured the ranch was named for Cowboy and his dad. Cowboy's real name was Juan Luis Diaz Villalobos.

They followed the rutted dirt and caliche tracks around hills and across arid pastures, down into steep arroyos washed out by the rare torrential rains that came in the monsoon season. The two trucks crested a hill with a motte of live oaks on top and saw the ranch house and outbuildings set back in the trees following the course of the river. The ranch house was a low one-story home that looked like it was made of mud bricks with the red, orange, and yellow tile roof covering the sprawling structure.

An older version of Cowboy walked from the house and stood under the portico in the morning shade waiting for them to park the trucks and come to the house. Cowboy introduced the two men. His dad looked to be in his fifties, average build with wide, strong shoulders and a narrow waist, just like his son. Hawk was impressed with the strength the older Diaz put in his handshake— not too much, but strong. The hand was coarse and calloused from the hard life they led working the ranch.

The older Diaz smiled as he said, "My friends call me Paco, and the man that saved my son's life is my friend, so please, call me Paco. My son tells me you are known by the name Hawk. I would like to call you Hawk."

"That's great, Paco. Thanks for allowing me to come by to see Cowboy. Is it okay for me to call him Cowboy, sir? It's the only name I've known him by."

"Yes, yes, of course. Juan told me you have not slept in some time, so let's get you to your bedroom and let you catch up on your rest. Whenever you are with us, this will be your room," he said as he led the small group down a cool, shaded hallway. The room they entered was in the Mexican style with Saltillo tile and warm colors in the paintings on the walls and the covers on the big bed.

They left Hawk in his room and walked toward the large open living room that was rich in old leather furniture, with a large fireplace set in the corner surrounded by shelves of books on each side. They sat down in two well-stuffed chairs smelling of old leather, and Cowboy told his dad what he knew about Hawk's sudden visit, which was little, to say the least.

His father snapped his fingers as he recalled something and said, "Son, while you were gone to pick up your friend there was a call from the sheriff's office asking if he was here. I didn't lie to them, I told them he wasn't here. I didn't tell them he was coming shortly. They told me to have him call them if he showed up at the ranch, that it was important. I asked what it was about and they simply said a man from the government needed to speak with him urgently. Do you think we should tell him now?"

Cowboy said, "No, he needs to crash for a while. If we tell him now he will not rest until he knows what the government wants with him. He told me there might be a warrant out for him, but that sounded like a local thing, not the feds. We'll keep him safe while he rests, and he can do what he wants when he isn't dead on his feet. Don't answer the phone until he is up and around, Dad."

"Okay, Son, you know him like a brother, so we will wait until he is rested to tell him."

Hawk woke up with Eliot purring away on his chest under the covers. He could smell the bacon frying in the kitchen. He pulled on his jeans and a T-shirt with his cowboy boots and walked into the kitchen. Paco was working in front of an old gas range while Cowboy scrambled some fresh eggs he had gone to the barn and picked up from some of the nests in the hay. Hawk asked what was for breakfast. Paco answered, telling him chorizo and eggs with bacon and lots of coffee. He told Hawk that his belief was if you worked on a ranch you had to eat enough to keep up with the animals. He chuckled to himself as he turned the bacon again. Hawk got a large cup of coffee and watched the father and son work together. They worked like a well-oiled machine.

During breakfast, Paco told Hawk about the call and about it being urgent that someone in the government wanted to speak with him. Cowboy put in that it didn't sound like a local matter, and Hawk agreed.

He drove back to the Chevron to call the number that Paco had given him. He had become a cautious man during the past few years. He wanted to know if a warrant had been issued for him and if the sheriff's office in Del Rio planned on arresting him. There was no need in getting Cowboy and his dad more involved than they already were. He dialed the number.

"Sheriff's office, Officer Dugan speaking," said the gravelly voice.

"There was a request for Diego Black Hawk to contact your office. This is Diego Black Hawk."

"Aha, hold on a minute. I'll get the sheriff."

A few minutes later the sheriff came on the line. "Mr. Hawk, I have been requested to contact you, but before I give can give you the information I have, I was told to ask you what your favorite weapon was."

"M-1911A1 Colt."

"I'm to ask you to go to the main gate at Laughlin Air Force Base east of here and get directions to meet with Captain Jack. Does that make sense to you, Mr. Hawk?"

Hawk didn't answer his question, but asked another one himself. "What's the time and date for me to be at the main gate?"

"That is not in the information I have. It just says to go to the gate and ask to meet with Captain Jack."

"Okay, thanks, Sheriff. I'll be on my way."

09:10 - 10 AUGUST

TZ S

Hawk sat in his truck, still parked at the Chevron, holding the steering wheel with white knuckles, and short of breath. He knew he was headed for the abyss but he couldn't stop it. He was deep behind enemy lines doing an RDF mission in the mountains with Cowboy when the man that sent them out broke radio silence and told them to get out fast. The bird dog doing the second vector had just spotted a large-sized NVA force moving straight for Hawk and Cowboy. They left their hide, and headed for the exfil LZ about two days southeast of their position. They could hear the enemy running down the trails near them. An AK-47 opened up, and Cowboy went down. Hawk took up counter fire, and grabbed

Cowboy by his ruck, starting to drag him down the trail they were on. Hawk dropped him and slammed in another mag for his M14. Vines tore at their arms and legs, making them trip and fall. Hawk pulled Cowboy up on his back and continued his fire behind and to one side as the NVA slowed their pursuit. Hawk knew they would try to outflank them, so at the first really thick jungle he rolled Cowboy into it and pulled down all the vines and brush he could. He sat there hoping the NVA would pass around them and not work right into them. He could hear them running around the think hide he had found, and then silence came. He checked Cowboy's wound for the first time. It was a clean wound in, and out of his lower right side. As quietly as he could, he put a pressure bandage around Cowboy's waist and gave him some water. They waited until dark, and then Hawk picked him up, and slowly, as quietly as possible, headed for the exfil LZ.

Twice in the next two days they had contact with small groups of the enemy. Cowboy tried to walk holding on to Hawk's shoulder. He started to bleed again, but was able to keep up fire while Hawk flanked one group of NVA. Hawk shot the last rounds from his rifle and then threw a grenade. There was one of the enemy left standing, and Hawk charged him with his Kay-bar knife. He dove under the enemy's rifle, shoving it up and away as he drove his knife into the man's chest. It caught between two ribs and stopped. With a grunt of last strength Hawk shoved it past the NVA's rib cage and sunk it into his heart. He held the man down with his hand on his mouth until his blood quit pumping from the knife wound. He pulled the knife out and cut the enemy's throat, just to make sure.

He crawled back to Cowboy, who had used his last mag. They couldn't rest where they were. More NVA were probably not far away. Even though he was exhausted, Hawk picked his friend up and headed to the crest of the low mountaintop where the exfil should be. It was the same LZ they had used inserting a week ago. The enemy was smart. They knew that an insertion LZ would sometimes be used for an extraction. There weren't that many places for a helicopter to land. Hawk planned on hiding Cowboy and doing a recon of the LZ when the helicopter got there. Checking for new enemy positions.

The sun was going down as they lay in the jungle at the edge of the clearing that sloped off to the east. Hawk knew the dust-off would come in hot, around sundown. They heard the chopper coming, and both of them leaned against trees with their backs to the LZ in case more NVA moved in trying to shoot down the chopper. They heard a minigun start up from a cover ship tearing up the edge of the jungle around the LZ as the dust off made a hard, fast touchdown. Two medics jumped out and helped both men into the open door.

"Hey, mister, you okay? You need me to call for help or something? You've been sitting here a long time, and you're all white and sweaty. Are you having a heart attack? Mister?"

Hawk felt something rocking his body. He thought it was the motion of the chopper, but then he heard someone talking to him, loudly. He blinked his eyes, and shook to get free from the memory. He looked out the window of his truck and saw a small crowd gathering, all wanting to know what was happening. He felt alone, sad, and worn out. He didn't want anyone to see him when he was having a memory of the hell that was the past. He waved the boy off. Tried to get the truck in gear, and finally managed to drive off. To what, he didn't know, but it probably wasn't good if Captain Jack was involved.

Hawk stopped at the next gas station he came to, and asked directions to Laughlin AFB. He was too shook up to go into the shop where he had called the sheriff. It wasn't far from Del Rio, about six miles. He pulled up to the main gate and waited with his window down until the AP on duty finished with a car leaving the base.

11:02 - 10 AUGUST

TZ S

The AP private walked through the small gatehouse and asked Hawk if he could help him.

"I'm meeting an army captain named Jack Mason," said Hawk.

"Yes sir, I'll check the log and see if I can find him. I'll need some identification."

Hawk pulled his driver's license from his wallet and handed it to the young air force policeman. He watched the young airman go to a clipboard hanging on a hook in the guard shack and leaf through the pages looking for confirmation of the meeting. He stopped and used the phone for a moment. He hung up and walked out to Hawk waiting in his pickup.

"The people you are to meet came in last night and are now leaving the BOQ. They will meet you at the U-21 Ute at the ready ramp. If you'll pull over to the parking area, I'll have a jeep and driver take you to the aircraft."

Hawk pulled over to the visitor parking area and waited for the jeep to pick him up. He sat there thinking how funny it was to have his tribe have an airplane named after them. The military loved their nomenclatures. The U-21 Ute was really a Beechcraft King Air 90. It was the utility aircraft for the military with twin turboprop engines. The cabins had different configurations according to their use.

It wasn't long before another AP drove a jeep to the gate and conferred with the AP on duty. The driver waved Hawk over to the jeep and handed him his driver's license.

"Mr. Hawk, I'm to drive you over to the ready ramp at the government lounge."

Hawk jumped into the open jeep painted in air force blue and told the driver he was ready. The young airman driving drove like he was being chased by VC. After a sliding turn around a corner of a hanger, he drove down the taxiway to the very end and again did a two-wheeled turn into the airplane parking area for non-air force, government aircraft. Sitting away from several other aircraft was the only Beechcraft King Air. The door was open and the stairs were down. The airman braked to a stop so hard Hawk had to grab the corner of the windshield to keep from being thrown out on the tarmac.

He left the jeep but stopped to watch it roar off down the taxiway at top speed. He shook his head and went up the stairs and into the King Air. This one had a leather seat with its back to the cockpit and one facing it with the door between. On the other side was a long leather couch. There were men sitting in the two facing seats and another on the bench seat. One he knew. It was captain Jack Mason. Hawk knew Captain Jack when they were in Vietnam. He had military rank, but Hawk figured him for an operator out of MACV-SOG. If it was a deep, dark special operation, it was Special Operations Group. Hawk and Cowboy worked for them from time to time. When Captain Jack showed up at their base camp it always meant a really tough mission for them. And usually meant lots of enemy contact. Hawk and Cowboy didn't trust him as far as they could throw him.

The three men stood once he was inside the cabin, and Captain Jack shook Hawk's hand and introduced the other two men as Charles Richards and Philip Shillings. They shook hands all around.

Captain Jack said, "Hawk, we need to talk with you about an emergency situation that has come up. You have already taken care of a small part of it back in Colorado, but there is much more to it. This discussion will be classified Top Secret, and I have made sure that your clearance is still in effect. Do you understand that?"

"Yes sir."

"We're going for a ride so we can make sure the information we discuss stays classified. We will return you to Laughlin when we are finished with what we have come to talk with you about. That good for you?"

"Yes sir."

Captain Jack motioned for Hawk to take a seat on the long couch, and they all buckled up. Captain Jack knocked on the bulkhead several times, and the big turboprops began to turn. Their noise was enough to keep the men from talking as the plane made its way down the taxiway and turned the corner for the active runway. The aircraft rocked and pushed like a thoroughbred horse waiting for the gate to slam open. The pilot let the brakes off, and the plane charged down the runway with ever increasing speed until Hawk felt that moment of weightlessness as the wheels left the ground and the props pulled with all their force into the sky.

After the King Air leveled off, Captain Jack stood and opened a small closet in the bulkhead across from him. He pulled four sets of headsets and mikes out and handed one of them to each man. He plugged in the male connector to the comm. unit and made sure everyone had followed his lead. After everyone had placed the headset over their ears, he said, "This comm unit is not connected to the aircraft comm. unit. It is considered secure but must be used on a need-to-know basis. First, Hawk, myself, and Mr. Shillings will be on the closed net. When we are finished, Shillings will unplug and Mr. Richards will plug into the net for his part of the discussion. Is that understood by everyone?"

Hawk watched carefully as both men nodded their understanding. He wondered what these two men knew that made it necessary to build their own secure comm. room at fifteen thousand feet.

"Mr. Shillings, I think you should be first to use the net," said Captain Jack.

Shillings nodded and watched as Richards unplugged his jack from the unit and removed his headset and placed them in his lap.

"Hawk, let me complete the introductions now. This is United States senator from the state of Texas Phillip Shillings. Before he begins I want to let you know that the warrant from Colorado has been stopped by a federal judge in Denver. The man D'Arcy that you learned about from his killers will be our focus during the conversation. Senator Shillings, you have the floor," Captain Jack talked at a normal level so Richards would not hear what was said over the aircraft noise.

Hawk wasn't surprised when Captain Jack mentioned the man's name, but quickly put two and two together and figured that the way D'Arcy knew of him and for some reason wanted him dead had to do with Captain Jack or whoever he worked for and whatever they were involved in. He heard Shillings clear his throat like a teacher in school and knew to listen up.

"Mr. Hawk, I'm not going to bother you with family history and will make this as short as I can. Please feel free to ask questions as we go. I have a daughter that has had a drug problem for a number of years. Last year she was finally getting her act together at the age of twenty-four. She took a job working as a social worker in Kingsville, Texas. She was doing well apparently and then suddenly disappeared. That was about three weeks ago. No stone has been left unturned, but not a sign has been found until now. Last week we received a handwritten note from her. Dropped into my home mailbox during the night. She is a captive of D'Arcy's, and he wants ransom to return her to me. My being a senator makes that difficult, and if we do pay, there will always be the threat of blackmail. Lord only knows what he might ask for if he tried blackmail after I paid the ransom. I was put in contact with Captain Mason through a mutual friend, and he quickly recommended you for the job of freeing and returning my daughter to me."

"What's your daughter's name?" asked Hawk.

"Elizabeth Shillings. I call her Liz."

"What does she look like? Does she have any identifying marks?"

"She's tall, about five feet eight. Blond hair and blue eyes. Slim for her height and has a smile that lights up a room. She has a yellow rose and the word Texas tattooed on the inside of her left wrist. Oh, and she's right-handed."

"Are you finished, Senator Shillings?," asked Captain Jack.

Shillings nodded, and passively unplugged his jack from the comm. unit.

Richards looked over to Captain Jack, and he nodded that it was okay to plug his phone jack into the comm. unit.

"Hawk, Mr. Richards is part of the Federal Bureau of Narcotics."

"Mr. Hawk, we, as a Department of the Treasury, have no power or jurisdiction outside of the United States. I was directed to Captain Jack by a highly placed politician. After discussing our problem with him he tried to contact you but was unable to until you stopped by your friend's near Del Rio, that Captain Jack knew about. He believes you are the only man that can help stop the man named Carlos Garcia D'Arcy. He is the head of the largest drug trafficking group in Mexico. Since the Vietnam war began the amount of heroin coming into the country across our southern border has doubled, and now has quadrupled since he has taken over control of the organization. We don't know who is in charge on the other end, but we have CIA people working on that. Being part of the federal government, we can't invade Mexico with a force of armed men to stop D'Arcy. What we need is a totally dark man or men to go into Mexico and capture or kill D'Arcy and disrupt his organization as much as possible, quickly. Captain Jack will be able to take care of any logistics you may need."

"Why don't you go to the CIA? They operate outside the United States," said Hawk.

"Unfortunately, The Need to Know will keep me from giving you that information, at this point," said Richards.

Hawk turned to Captain Jack and said, "The Need to Know, is he kidding? He's asking me to go risk my life without knowing all there is to know about this man D'Arcy. Are you shitting me? And by the way, this Mexican drug guy found me quicker than you did, and he tried to kill me before I even knew what it was all about. To me, that's a red flag right there. He is so deep into our government that he knows what is going to happen before it happens. Now how's that possible? You people are crazy. Tell the pilot to land this damn plane at the next airstrip, and I'll walk home!"

Captain Jack looked at Richards as Richards pretended to pull the jack from the comm. unit. Before he pulled his jack, he said, "He's a burnt-out troop, no good to us, or to anybody else, at this point. You brought us all the way out here on a wild goose chase. I'll agree with one damn thing. Land this plane, and let him walk home!"

Captain Jack looked at Hawk and put his hand, palm out, toward him while he said, "Back off Hawk, back off. I'll talk with you after these two leave the plane at Laughlin."

The men all started to move and unbuckle their seat belts as the main gear wheels chirped when they hit the tarmac. It then taxied to the government ramp and stopped. Richards and Shillings walked down the stairs as soon as the door was opened, without speaking to the two men still seated. When they had disappeared into the FBO building Captain Jack looked at Hawk and asked him to go for a walk with him. They headed down the perimeter walk that followed the secure fencing around the base.

"Hawk," said the captain, "I know why you came back for the second tour. You were the best at what you did and you did it in your own way to help stop the war and to save the lives of the men and women fighting the NVA and VC. You didn't like or enjoy what you did; you did it for as unselfish a reason as one could have during a war. Any war. This is another type of war, Hawk. Bad guys are killing our young people with drugs both here and in Vietnam. If we stop the drugs, we save lives and our country. The only way to stop the drugs is to take out those that are involved in their transport and sales. The mission would be to recover Stillings and terminate D'Arcy.

Hawk said, "You don't need to worry. I'm going after D'Arcy. I just didn't want Richards or Shillings to know. One of them has a very dangerous person around them, leaking information like a sieve. That almost got me killed. There's no way I want anyone other than you to know where or what I'm doing. You have to give me some assurance of that, Captain Jack."

"We're watching a deputy director, but have no way to get anything on him. I will try to keep him out of the loop, as much as possible. I'm working with some ex-ASA guys, and that might help also. It will be a completely dark operation with whatever support you need."

"There'll be only one other person that will know about your assignment," said Captain Jack.

"No, absolutely not," said Hawk.

"Hold on a minute, Hawk. He's someone you can trust."

"Who is it?"

"The president of the United States. When his younger brother was killed in-country, he came to me for support. I was best friends with his brother, and he has trusted me ever since. Hawk, he came to me with this request. Some of his advisors are worried that the CIA is involved in some way with the huge increase in heroin coming into the country since the beginning of the war. He wants me to get some answers for him through you. This'll be your first contract with him. You and Cowboy will have a new clearance classification. TOP SECRET PRESIDENTIAL."

"I don't want to get down there and find out I have been set up for some political reason. If that were to happen, you know I would come after you, right? You understand that Captain?"

"Yes, I know you would. Now what do you need?"

"I need Cowboy, if he'll go. If he says yes, then I'll give you a list of stuff and where to deliver it. I'll not give anyone the plan that Cowboy and I make. Just like the Nam. No one knows, not even the president."

"That's going to make you completely dark, Hawk."

"That's what you said about the mission yourself, completely covert!"

"If Cowboy says he'll go that's all the support I need. You know he went through Ft. Devens when I did. That's where we met. After he got the O5K MOS he stayed when I left for language school. Then he picked up the O5D also. We were teamed before we went over for the first time and have been together ever since. We're like an old married couple—he finishes my sentences for me."

"Fair enough. We need to set up another meet now to keep the electronic trail to a minimum. Any ideas?"

"If Cowboy goes for it, we'll use the Double D Ranch. It's on the border, and he told me there are several easy places to cross over without being checked. I'll call if Cowboy is in with the date and time only. You know the rest, and you're the only one that knows. Our lives depend on that, and YOUR LIFE does too."

They walked back to the ramp where the U-21 Ute sat. Hawk walked over to a ramp guard and asked for his lift back to the main gate. The same driver and jeep skidded around the corner of the building and slid to a stop. The young airman said, "You lookin' for a ride, mister?"

Hawk laughed for the first time in a long time and climbed in thinking about what he was about to do and realizing that he could feel the old adrenaline rush start up. How could it be that his body and mind had gone without the fear and excitement of the hunt for so long. Was he destined to continue his life on the dark side of right? Would he spend his life in the shadows, hiding his identity, keeping few friends, and living life alone?

Even with the circus ride in the jeep couldn't stop him at the edge of the abyss. He started to think of his girl he had left when he went to Vietnam the first time. She was the special girl that he wanted to live life with. They were engaged to be married. He bought her a simple small diamond ring and made payments on it for a long time. For the first six or eight months she wrote almost every day. She stopped writing then. She stopped going by his folks' house to spend time with them. He knew something was wrong, but she wouldn't answer his letters. So he went on more long-range assignments to hide the hurt from himself. At mail call when he was back in camp there were two letters for him. A large bulky one and the normal one from his mom. He was afraid to open the other. It was from Beverly, his fiancée. His heart raced, and his hands shook slightly as he tore open the envelope. He pulled out a cutout of the local paper, and nothing else. It was the announcement of her marriage to someone he didn't know. He sat quietly at first; then the strength that had carried him through so much in-country came flooding back to him, and he threw the paper in the fifty-five-gallon drum used to collect trash. He vowed to never trust a woman again. It was the only reaction he could have if he were to remain alive in the killing jungle of Vietnam.

He walked around the compound trying to clear his head. The camp had been quiet for the last few days. No incoming at all. Several guys were in their shorts and boots, getting some rays, they said. He sat on some sandbags lining the first perimeter trench and remembered the letter from his mom. He sat there in the sun letting it dry out his clothing, always damp from rain or sweat, holding the folded letter, wanting to read it and not at the same time. The letter was full of family stuff. Then in the last paragraph she told him the news he didn't want to read. Beverly had left his engagement ring in their mailbox. No note, no nothing. His mom told him she was sorry and she would hold it for him for when he got home. She didn't need to know he would never be needing an engagement ring again.

***

The jeep came to a skidding stop next to the main gate. He stepped out and started to walk soberly toward his truck. The horn on the jeep sounded beep, beep, and the young airman waved the ball cap that Hawk had taken off when the wild ride had started. He walked back through the gate area and took the cap.

"Ya look like yur best girl just tol' ya ta go fly ah kite, buddy. Ya goin' ta be okay?" said the young man.

Hawk looked at the hat and then put it on with a tug to seat it. He looked at the young man and told him thanks as he thought, "Well, there are nice folks in the crowd."

His walk was a bit quicker, and his head was held a little higher with his shoulders back slightly. It was amazing to him what a little kindness would do for people. Just any little kindness at all.

Cowboy and Hawk were on the back patio of the ranch house overlooking a bend in the Rio Grande. After Hawk filled him in on what went down during the meeting with Captain Jack. Cowboy walked over to an old coke machine and brought out a couple of beers. They popped the tops, and Hawk said, "Here's to another good mission."

Cowboy said, "You remember every time Captain Jack was involved with our mission, the shit hit the fan, right? So, we don't trust anything he tells us. Right? We do our thing, like always, right?"

"Yeah, he might have a mole for this drug cartel guy to deal with too. We be extra cautious."

22:00 - 10 AUGUST

TZ S

"We've got the target, let's make the plan. Just like the old days, there are beaucoup variables. Language won't be a problem. We both speak Spanish. I'll go get some paper to make a list of what we will need. Are they supplying the money for this soiree?"

"That's for damn sure. I'm so broke I may have to re-up for the bonus pay," Hawk said with a laugh.

"Are we goin' in wearing civvies?"

"Yeah, I was thinking we should be regular West Texas ranch hands on a trip to visit Boy's Town."

"That'll work for me, and you can use some of my stuff. New would attract attention."

Cowboy got two more beers from the coke machine and said as they popped the tops, "Don't mention the mission to my dad, okay? Let him think we're goin' down to check out Boy's Town or something."

"Where's the best place to cross over?" asked Hawk.

"Piedras Negras is right across from Del Rio, and they see punchers crossing all the time. From there we can go east and follow the Gulf of Mexico around to the Yucatán or head to Monterrey, to Mexico City, and then down to Villahermosa and across," said Cowboy.

"You have some maps we can take a look at? We'll need to make the best speed to keep D'Arcy out of the know. A fast trip should negate the informant, whoever that is, and give us our best chance to locate him before he knows we're coming for him."

They talked and drank beer as they made a list of supplies they wanted and refined their mission plan.

When they'd had enough beer and the plan was looking like it would work, Hawk asked Cowboy if he would make up a substitution code to send the supply list to Captain Jack. Cowboy told Hawk that he would have it for him in the morning. Hawk planned on sending the list from Laughlin and calling Captain Jack from a gas station with the code.

They went to their bedrooms, which were off the patio, telling each other how tired they were. Both bedroom lights stayed on until the first rooster called loudly at the new morning coming.

20:12 - 12 AUGUST

TZ SIERRA

Things went off as planned, and two days later a chopper with the supplies went wheels down just off the patio, as the last rays of the day faded into darkness. In less than ten minutes it was pulling for altitude and heading in a half circle to the east, landing at Laughlin from a different direction than they took to the Double D.

Paco walked out to the patio with three fingers of scotch in a short tumbler. He said, "Boys, I hope you don't think you're putting anything over on the old man. I just stopped by to wish you a good and safe trip and to tell you to watch out for those girls at Boy's Town. He grinned and patted Cowboy on the shoulder and told him to keep his head down, and the same to

Hawk. He walked back into the ranch house without saying anything else.

"My old man never was much for long speeches, but when you see him with that much scotch and no ice, you know he's concerned about what's going on," said Cowboy.

Hawk watched Paco enter the house and said, "He's a hell of a good man."

They had separated the supplies and made up rucks for things they might need immediately and loaded up Cowboy's truck. It was newer and in better shape than Hawk's. He had changed out the cattle stall on the bed to a cover on it that locked. They felt locking the majority of the equipment in it was the best idea. It was late in the night when they shook hands with Paco and Hawk rubbed Eliot's ears one last time. Paco was going to feed him twice a day, and Hawk had supplied him with enough tuna for a long time. They wanted to hit the border crossing around midnight when traffic would be non-existent and the Mexican border guards tired.

They crossed the old wooden and iron supported bridge about one in the morning. There was a small guard house just off the bridge with a short strip of gravel and blacktop, to stop on. Past that a metal pole acted as a barrier. Before they stopped, Hawk took a bottle of Jim Beam from the case sitting at his feet, and with it open, placed it on the bench seat between them.

One of the two Mexicans at the border crossing, wearing dirty, poorly fitting hand-me-down GI issue uniforms, asked Cowboy what they had in the back of the truck. Cowboy told him ranch supplies for a friend's ranch in Tampico State. He looked toward Hawk, but his gaze stopped at the open bottle of liquor.

"It is illegal to bring liquor into Mexico, senor."

Hawk screwed the cap back on the bottle and said, "It is for you and the other soldier to keep the night chill away, amigo."

The disheveled man stood straighter and said, "We can't take it from you, senor. You should leave it on the ground and drive up to the pole gate to press the button for green or red light. Hawk opened his door and sat the full bottle of Jim Beam on the ground, away from the track of the wheels. He closed his door, and without looking, Cowboy rolled forward and stopped at a cement block structure with a metal box in a covered hole. Cowboy pushed the button that operated the signal light. The green light came on. The mission was starting out right. The green light meant they would not be inspected. He put the truck into gear, and as the pole rose he drove under and passed the Mexican guards on the side of the road. They did the inspections when the red light came on. The gravel and oil strip turned into a narrow dirt road barely wide enough for two cars to pass.

14:32 - 13 AUGUST

TZ SIERRA

Two men sat in the dark facing an elevated dance floor with floodlights lighting it, like daylight. Everything was painted black, except the polished steel poles that were placed to give the men sitting in the dark, smoke-filled room the best view possible. The bar was off to the side, curving with the dance floor, so the male patrons could sit at the bar and still see the dancers. The dancers were twisting and turning, curling and sliding, sometimes up and sometimes upside down. There were small two-person tables sitting around the curve of the dance floor, making it easier for the dancers to have money tucked or stuffed into any available opening by the drunken or stoned, and sometimes both, raucous men that had paid an exorbitant amount of money to watch, touch, and get lucky, if they paid even more to the bouncers scattered around the bar.

This afternoon was special, though it happened on a regular basis. Once, each month. The short, plump Mexican with combed-back slick hair, eyes bulging out, a flattened nose, and bulbous lips that made him look like a puffer fish, said to the taller, muscled man with severe pock markings covering his face and neck, "There are three this time, Nacho?"

"Yes sir. The first two are from Houston, and the third we got from Reynosa. I have her coming on last. I think you might like to keep her for your own pleasures and not show her for sale tomorrow when the buyers are here," said the pocked-marked man.

"They are all using drugs or addicted?" asked the puffer man.

"Yes, jefe, they are much easier to handle as long as they have their drugs to keep them content."

Music started to play loudly, and the first girl came through the opening in the background curtain. She had dark hair and very white skin. She wore thong panties that showed off her full round butt with a black panda bear tattoo. The white of her skin made up the white of the bear. She started to move slowly with the music and grabbed the pole with a leg and hand, showing off her rather large breasts to the men. The men talked over the music and both agreed quickly that she would be sold to the highest bidder the following day. "Some men like them with more meat on them," said Puffer Fish.

A cruel-looking man came out when Nacho whistled, and took her away. The next woman came out and started to dance with a poll. It was obvious she had been a dancer before. She moved around the floor in a slow swaying movement, making her way to the men's table. She swayed to the music and in a practiced motion, slipped off her bra, releasing her breasts, and bent over so both men could touch them or kiss them, if they wanted. Neither man moved or said a word. She bent over in front of the two men and pulled down her panties, exposing her butt for them to admire. There was no response. She walked back to the curtain, angrily parting the curtain and giving the men the finger.

The third girl came out and tripped over the edge of the curtain. She was more screwed up than the other two. She had long blond hair put up in a ponytail. Her breasts were held in by a too-tight bra, and her panties were a light shade of blue. She walked carefully out to one of the polls in her high heels, and held on. She stood there and stared back at the two men. Nacho told her in accented English to move around with the music for them. When she started to move about, her breasts moved in unison with her hips. Her face was narrow, with pronounced cheekbones, a soft, angular line to her jaw, and a small central cliff in front. It was hard to tell from the distance, but her eyes were probably blue. She had a small yellow rose tattooed on the inside of her left wrist with the word Texas under it. When she didn't remove her bra, Nacho had the stage man rip it off. The head man let out a low groan as her large pink nipples rose up hard, making him think about the erection he had and what he would make her do with it. Even though she was unable to stand with the help of a poll, the cruel-looking helper yanked her panties off and turned her around, trying to bend her over with her butt facing the two men. She hit him with her elbow and shoved him off balance long enough to get a high heeled shoe off. She threw it awkwardly at the two men sitting at the small table.

The two men ducked as the shoe went flying by, and Nacho asked the other man what he thought.

"She's the best of the lot. I like 'um feisty. I'll keep her. Make sure she gets to the villa in Playa, Nacho. I don't want any bruises on her, understand? Do you know what her name is yet?"

"Her name is Liz, Senor D'Arcy. Liz Stillings."

"Take her back to Cozumel in my plane, and then send it back to Mérida for me. I don't want her being discovered by some damn government roadblock. I'll plan on coming back two days from now, after I have the money for the two we are selling tomorrow," said Carlos D'Arcy.

"Do you want me to keep her at the house in San Miguel, or take her to the villa in Playa, sir?"

"Take her to the villa, but have the boat waiting for me when I get to Cozumel. I don't want to wait in San Miguel while it comes from Playa. You got that, Nacho? Send the plane back for me, take the girl to Playa, and have the boat waiting when I arrive in Cozumel," D'Arcy said in a way to make his aid feel stupid. He liked being able to keep the peons under his control, or they might try to turn on him. He always kept his bodyguards near him, but he was still paranoid.

09:44 - 15 AUGUST

TZ S

When D'Arcy and his two bodyguards arrived at the small wooden pier near the middle of San Miguel, Cozumel, his thirty-one-foot Bertram sport fisherman was waiting for him. The crew and captain were standing by the gangway in a line, wearing crisp, clean uniforms, waiting for inspection like sailors in the navy. D'Arcy walked across the gangway without apparently noticing them and went down into the cabin. His bodyguards went to the open deck and sat in the fishing chairs, while the captain and crew removed the short wooden gangway and got underway. They were glad the jefe had not noticed them. When he did, it meant one of them would be punished severely when they reached the pier in Playa. The captain backed the Bertram away from the wooden dock and swung her around as she picked up speed. He loved the boat and ran up her engines to listen to her throaty rumble on the short trip across the Yucatán Channel, to the mainland and Playa del Carmen.

Playa del Carmen was a sleepy little fishing village that acted as the mainland contact for the island of Cozumel seventeen miles offshore. Carlos D'Arcy Garcia's villa was away from the beach in a grove of coconut palms, and next to several ancient Mayan ruins. It wasn't far from the rickety old wooden pier where boats of various types came to off-load people from the island, and load food and other supplies to take back.

D'Arcy walked the short distance down a narrow sand and dirt track to the exterior wall that surrounded the courtyard, pool with a large palapa, and bar connected to the back of the villa. The top of the wall was covered in broken shards of different colored glass to keep who or whatever out. The entrance had two large thick doors curved at the top that normally were open, and the similarly made metal gate doors were normally locked with an armed guard on each side of the arch, over the gates. The guard on the right welcomed his jefe back and opened the smaller door gate to allow him and his personal bodyguards to enter. The staff: a gardener, cook and assistant, pool man, and several maids were lined up on the veranda that surrounded the villa, like the crew of the boat. D'Arcy walked past them without acknowledgment, and into the villa. The staff, like the crew, were relieved that there had been no recognition from the jefe. It was always bad when that happened.

Nacho was waiting for him, past the two-story entry, near the bar by the floor-to-ceiling glass doors. They made up part of the larger floor-to-ceiling glass wall leading out to the pool area and palapa. He had a drink in his hand, and there was one on the bar waiting for Carlos—a large tumbler filled to the brim with Chivas Regal scotch, and ice. He nodded to Nacho, took a long drink of the scotch, and wiped his mouth with a bar towel.

"Where is she?" he said.

"Upstairs in the room with bars in the windows, senor. Like the ones before," said Nacho.

"I need to clean up from the trip and rest. Then I would like music and the girl by the pool for drinks. Have one of the maids bring another drink to my room," Carlos commanded.

"It will be down as you ask. How would you like the girl to dress for the evening, jefe?"

"I think a small revealing bikini. I don't plan on either one of us remaining clothed later in the pool," D'Arcy said.

"*Para servirle*, senor."

19:17 - 15 AUGUST

TZ A

The heat of the day had cooled slightly with the breeze coming from the Caribbean. The sun was down, and Carlos sat near the palapa in his swim trunks. The soft lights from the pool and palapa gave out the ambiance he wanted. He was relaxed and had a little thrill going through him in anticipation of the girl—he thought her name was Liz—and what he would do to her later that night. A crystal bowl sat behind his drink on a small table along with a thin knife made for cutting rows of cocaine. He had finished a row and was enjoying his second tequila of the day. He couldn't remember being so excited about a new girl, in a long time. This one would be special, he thought.

The white cotton curtains moving in the breeze at the entrance to the villa separated ever so slightly, and the girl, Liz, walked out in a tiny yellow bikini. The bra showed just a margin of pink from her nipples, and the bottom was cut so small she could have left it off. He watched her walk to him in yellow high heels, a little unsteadily. By the time she came to the lounge chair next to his, he had a huge erection pushing at the top of his swimsuit.

He stood, somewhat awkwardly himself, and offered to share the one lounge chair with her, and asked her in passable English what she would like to drink, or if she would like a rail of the coke that was on the glass-topped table.

"I want the coke and then a tequila shot for a chaser," Liz said.

After she was sitting on the edge of the lounge and had crossed her legs, she started to do the rail with a thin straw made of pure gold. She held the left side of her nose—she was right handed—and snorted the white powder in one long expert hit. She leaned back and wiped her nose with the silk hanky at her side. Carlos had been admiring her tits while she was bent over doing the coke and was near to having a climax. He hadn't been so excited for a number of years. He thought back, remembering a girl that had been able to do that to him. She was a real beauty too. He couldn't remember her name, but he knew where she was buried.

A man came through the curtains of the house with a large silver serving tray loaded with frosty gold shot glasses filled with tequila shots, with slices of lime and salt on the side. He sat the tray on the side table and moved it over in front of them. She took one and tossed it down. Carlos then did the same. She heard him call the man that brought the tray "Nacho."

Liz stood up in front of Carlos and said, "I'm going swimming in the pool before I get too wasted to enjoy it."

She took off her top and showed him her perfect breasts—not too large, not too small, the pink nipples erect and shaped perfectly. Her lips were almost full and had an angelical look that made her appear childlike, even with her beautiful adult body. Her blue eyes were red, so was her nose. She turned and walked to the shallow end of the pool and carefully walked down the steps into the pool.

Carlos was stunned. He was so weak in the knees he thought he would fall if he stood up to go into the pool with her. He turned carefully and used the table to lean against as he pulled his trunks down and walked over to the steps leading into the pool.

Liz was standing waist deep, watching him come into the pool. When he was halfway down the steps, she said, "I hope that's not all you've got, shorty."

Carlos charged down the steps and tried to grab her just as she moved off to deeper water. He had gone from excited to enraged in a second. If he could catch her he would kill her. His other passion, besides raping young girls and women, was killing them with his hands. He no longer cared about sex; he wanted her begging him to let her live, and then he would choke her to death, or use the coke knife to gut her and shove it up her vagina as a final insult.

She swam to the aluminum climbing stairs and stepped out of the pool quickly, laughing and moving carefully to the lounges, as Nacho came near her with two large beach towels. She grabbed one from him as she went by and used it to lightly dry her hair. She stood by the chairs and took another shot of tequila, laughing all the while. Carlos walked deliberately up the steps and out of the pool. He was shaking with fury and limp like a wet rag. He charged her, but was blocked suddenly by a huge arm reaching out and pushing against his chest. Someone was yelling for him to think, to stop; this was about business too.

D'Arcy stood for a moment braced upright by Nacho, the only man that D'Arcy would let touch him. When he had calmed down Nacho went under the palapa and sat down. D'Arcy went back to sit down as Liz said, "I know your first name now. The man that stopped you called you Carlos. What's your last name, cutie?"

D'Arcy almost fell for it again. She was baiting him for some reason. He would find out soon enough, one way or another.

"D'Arcy is my last name, Carlos D'Arcy."

Liz said, "That's not Mexican, is it? Your last name sounds French."

"It is. My father."

She drank another shot without talking more and then picked one up and took it to Nacho. He told her thanks, but he was working and could not drink. She went back to Carlos and sat down, giving him the shot. He did it and then suggested they had started off badly and should start over again. Liz nodded her consent and Carlos made two more rails. After several more shots he was getting excited again. Liz was lying back with her eyes closed when Carlos had Nacho move her over to his lounge and lay her between his legs. His erection immediately became larger as he pulled her head up, and then while he held his erection, he pushed her head down toward it. She suddenly pulled her head away from him and spit in his face. She stood and then fell down, unable to move.

D'Arcy's rage returned dual-fold as he got up and kicked her in her side. Nacho was suddenly on him, holding him back telling him to stop, this was business. He finally calmed down again and wiped the spittle from his chest and face.

"Nacho, throw her in the pool to sober her up. In the morning, you can take her to Mérida to dance, strip, and have sex. No, only oral sex, if the price is right. I need her for the plan to work. I will write the note to the father about the ranch, and tell him I require a ransom too," said D'Arcy.

Nacho took her into the villa and had a maid clean her up and put her in bed. Early the next morning Nacho and the young woman left by car for Mérida.

10:17 - 16 AUGUST

TZ S

The private phone rang in D'Arcy's study after the girl had left with Nacho for Mérida. Very few people knew of the phone or the number. If it rang it was important. He walked into the study and picked the phone up.

"Who is this?" he asked.

"Rodrigo."

"Why are you calling?"

"I have heard indirectly that the men you sent to kill the man picked to get the girl back, have themselves been killed," said Rodrigo.

"Who killed them?"

"The man you sent them to kill killed them both. Your men killed his friend, and now he is angry," answered Rodrigo. "There is another man with him now. One also from Vietnam."

"So the number of men the United States thinks is enough to kill me is only two?"

"The number I heard mentioned was two," said Rodrigo.

"That isn't enough. I will be expecting them. No problem. Gracias, Rodrigo."

13:37 - 14 AUGUST

TZ A

Hawk and Cowboy had made it through the oil town of Tampico and were headed toward Veracruz along a narrow road that followed the Gulf Coast through volcanic hills and valleys, twisting and turning, up and down, like a roller coaster. The next town of any size was Tuxpan, a river town with a large deep-water inlet that the growing oil industry used for oil-field work boats and tugs to tie up for supplies and repairs. They decided to stay over there. It would be a good run all the way from Piedras Negras to Tuxpan in one day, with all the tank trap holes there were in the roads.

The next day was a continuation of the day before. Cowboy was still driving when they came around a curve heading into a sharp climbing series of curves. Hawk's side was covered in jungle and volcanic rock, and on Cowboy's side was a steep cliff falling hundreds of feet into a rocky gorge. There was a volcanic black-sand beach along the shore of the Gulf of Mexico. They skidded around a sharper than usual curve leading into a sudden downhill turn. A short straight section of the road was blocked by a large tope, and a few feet beyond that the trunk of a tree. Two men standing on the jungle side holding shotguns, and one with what looked like a single shot rifle on the cliff side were waving and yelling for them to stop. It didn't look right to Hawk.

He said, "Drop the gear down and hit the gas, Cowboy. Let's jump that sucker."

Cowboy heard Hawk rack a round into his pistol as he dropped the truck suddenly into second gear and floored the gas pedal. The truck lunged forward, gaining speed like a fox running from the hounds. Hawk leaned out of his window as they hit the front of the tope. The front end of the truck flew high into the air. He shot several rounds into the air, and the three bandidos ran for cover. It was too late for the truck. Its front end went farther up in the air, like the truck was about to switch front with back end. The back end jumped into the air making the whole truck fly forward in the air. The front end landed first, hitting the narrow road after passing the tree trunk. The front bumper tore from the mounts and flew off into the jungle. Hawk and Cowboy were thrown into the dashboard and then into the windshield, sending two separate spider webs crisscrossing the glass. Cowboy hung onto the steering wheel as the rear end hit the ground and knocked Hawk from his seat down into the floor, and his head into the dashboard again. Cowboy regained control of the truck in time to make the next curve, throwing the gearshift into drive, and hitting the breaks to slow it down. The outside wheels came off the ground, and the jungle vines and tree limbs started banging into the truck making Hawk cover his head as leaves, sticks, and vines tore past his window.

The road was so narrow there was no place to stop and check for any damage to the truck or themselves. Hawk was bleeding from the forehead, and Cowboy was holding his chest because of the sudden impact with the steering wheel. When Hawk tried to pull and push his way from the floor of the car, he looked over at Cowboy, and they both began to laugh.

"What the hell, you think you're in a demolition derby or something?" Hawk shouted out between laughter.

"Well, hell, you're the one that started banging away with that cannon of yours," laughed Cowboy. "Kind of reminds you of the old days, huh, Hawk?"

"Yeah. Well let's get this thing to the next town and check the damage. While we're at it we need to steal some Mexican plates for the truck so we fit in better."

The next town had a gas station, but no gas. They left the gas station and parked the pickup on a narrow, hard packed-dirt street that had no street lights. The small houses and shacks that were put together with used boards, tar paper, and corrugated roofing sheets were also all dark. Hawk figured there was no electricity in that part of the village. He dug into his pack and found the flashlight he had stuffed in with the spare ammo and everything else he thought he might need in an emergency.

20:14 - 14 AUGUST

TZ S

As Hawk was getting out of the pickup to search for some type of car or truck that had plates on it, Cowboy told him he was going to hook up the transmitter and check in with Captain Jack. He pulled a small Morse code key and battery from his kit along with the day pad codebook and started to send a quick coded message to Captain Jack. He found a wire hanging down from a pole and clipped a connector from the antenna on his unit to it, making the antenna able to receive from much farther distances. He sent in Morse code: "NEAR Poza Rica. NO PROBEMS. ANY INFO?"

Captain Jack had several Morse intercept operators from the Army Security Agency standing by in shifts to monitor for his signals. A message came back quickly. It was in five letter groups, and Cowboy used the same sheet of the day pad he had used, to decode Captain Jack's reply: "Shipment due Mexico Caribbean Port. French ship."

Cowboy then sent back a five-letter group for "understood": "MWLGP."

The day pad was used for absolute security. It was totally unbreakable. He tore the small sheet from the pad and burned it in the ditch by the side of the dirt street. The next sheet would be for the next contact, normally the following day. He put the key, battery, and pad back in his ruck and waited with the lights off and the truck at idle for Hawk to return with the stolen Mexican plates. It wasn't long before he saw a pinpoint of light down the street: "dit dah, dit dah." Cowboy nodded his head. Hawk was in recon mode. The two dit dahs were the recognition code they had used when returning to a camp, or LZ, after a mission at night. In Morse code, it was double A. During the day, they popped a pre-arranged smoke grenade. There was no way Hawk was going to come up on Cowboy while he was in potential enemy country. If he did, he'd die.

Hawk came up to the truck and threw two Mexican plates through the window as he said, "Man, you don't know how hard it was to find a set of plates. There aren't many cars around here, and the ones that are here either have only one or more likely none. I walked three blocks before I found these. He got in the truck, and Cowboy had it moving by the time Hawk closed the door. Cowboy told him about the message from Captain Jack.

Hawk said, "Let's get back on the highway and out of town, then pull into one of the little jungle cart paths to look at the map. Now that we're in-country, we need a more finalized plan."

They followed the highway designated number 180 for about twenty klicks and pulled into a rutted cart path leading back into the jungle. The jungle was a solid wall on each side of the truck. Cowboy left the truck running in neutral while they studied the map with the flashlight Hawk had out from the search for Mexican plates for the truck.

With the information from the message, it was decided they would keep to the Gulf Coast instead of cutting across the Yucatán Peninsula by going to Villahermosa, Escárcega, and Chetumal; they planned on heading to Mérida, known as the Paris of Mexico. It was only a few kilometers from the maritime loading and unloading docks for the northern part of Southern Mexico, and only hours by truck to the state of Quintana Roo. They put the stolen Mexican plates on the truck and agreed to stop for gasoline when the gauge on the truck reached half a tank. During the trip down, they had tried to buy gas at two stations that were totally out of gas. When they were near Veracruz, they soon found another station that did have Magna gas. Running out was not an option. The next large city would be Mérida. It was late in the evening and they were tired. They found a small hotel outside of Veracruz.

18:35 - 15 AUGUST

TZ S

After another day of hard driving they came to the outskirts of Mérida. It was a sprawling city with a beautiful central plaza and a main boulevard named for the Spanish conquistador that settled the area, where the Mayan people had once lived. The Paseo del Montejo had street lights glowing when Hawk and Cowboy made their way to it through the back streets and past the hovels of the peones. There were many fashionable hotels, and shops on the *avenida*. It was busy with auto traffic and horse-drawn carriages, as well as streetcars down the middle.

The two men decided on a hotel that had the same name as the beautiful street that was near the Zocalo or central park of the city. It was beautiful, with a large entryway and open reception area stretching to the back, where there was a pool surrounded by flowers and tropical plants, with coconut palms as well. They got separate rooms overlooking the garden and pool area that connected by a private door.

They agreed to meet in the lobby at nine o'clock that evening and walk the paseo, getting a feel for the city and the people. When Hawk came down the curving marble steps, he saw Cowboy at the bar talking with several younger men. They all seemed to be having a good time. Cowboy had a huge frozen margarita standing in front of him, and the other two men appeared to be drinking shots. There was a saucer between them with cut limes and salt. The two young men were dressed for the evening, and both were smoking American cigarettes. Hawk had a cream-colored guayabera Cowboy had loaned him and dark blue linen pants. Cowboy had on similar clothes, but his guayabera was peach and his slacks were a light tan. Both men were dressed for an evening out; so, they fit in with the crowds but did not draw undue attention to themselves.

Hawk walked by the bar catching Cowboy's glance and walked out to the paseo, where he waited for him to join him. When he came up, he told Hawk that the two men he was talking to at the bar were new to the area and didn't have a clue where there might be a men's club or strip bar. Hawk stood looking out on the paseo, and without turning his head told Cowboy that he wanted to split up, to cover more ground this evening.

"You catch a cab out to the town of Progresso where the pier is and find out if any French ships have been coming there. I'll grab one and see if I can locate a Boy's Town, or something like it. Maybe I can get a line on the woman we're looking for, on that side of our mission. It's a little after nine now. Not much starts until ten. It'll take you a while to get out to Progresso and back. Knock on my room door when you get back. If I'm not in, I'll wake you when I get in."

Hawk caught a taxi and asked the driver where he could go to have some fun. Somewhere that had both bars and women. Something like a gentlemen's club or a strip club.

"I know where to take you, senor, but I must warn you, it is frequented by bad men, and dressed as you are will make them think you have money with you. Do you still want to go to such a place, senor?" asked the driver.

Hawk reached under his shirt to his back and felt the reassurance of his M1911 colt nestled there. He nodded his head up and down in the universal yes and sat back in the seat watching the buildings and people go by. The taxi headed south away from the heart of the city. The odd numbered streets ran east and west in Mérida, and the numbers grew larger the farther they went from the town center. The street lighting grew dimmer gradually with fewer and fewer large, high modern buildings. The taxi stopped, and the driver pointed at a cross street crowded with people.

He said, "This is the place, senor. Anything and everything you can want is there."

"Why don't you take me to the street?" asked Hawk.

"If I drive you to the street, senor, they will break the windows of my taxi. They have done it before. Please pay, senor, and go, before they see my taxi."

Hawk paid the driver. The taxi turned and drove up on the small sidewalk, backed up, and drove off with a cloud of smoke blowing from its tailpipe. Hawk started to walk toward the crowded street and could hear the laughter and shouting a block away. He spent some time being carried along with the moving swells of young people and old. There were shops for tourist and cantinas for food, but most of all there were bars everywhere. Any type of bar imaginable, but no men's clubs. Hawk asked a young man where the strip clubs were, and he pointed ahead and said down the next street to the left.

The buildings started to fade out, and the areas between them grew darker. The residue from the heavy partying started to appear in the alleyways and doorways. There were bodies in every shape and form, some flat on the ground, others hunched over vomiting. Hawk saw one boy curled up on the edge of a sidewalk, with a needle in his arm. He could feel a panic attack starting to work on him. He had to maintain; it could mean the life of the girl he was looking for. He had to maintain. He cut through the garbage and up an alley, willing himself to stay focused on the mission

An arm came from a dark doorway and reached out for him. He was still focused enough to throw his arm up and block the arm from reaching him.

"Hey, man, where you goin'? I think you need a drink. You want some junk, man? That's it, isn't it? You want some junk or a girl to pass the time with. Yeah, how 'bout a girl, man? This is the best club around, no paying as you go. Pay me one time, for you only fifteen hundred pesos. Com'on man, I know you got it."

The arm came out again, trying to catch the sleeve of his shirt. Hawk blocked it and hit the man in the chest with his elbow, knocking him back against the door he was protecting.

Hawk slurred his speech, "Ya got any gringas in there, man? I want to fuck a gringa. Ya know what'ah mean, man? Ain't never had me a gringa. You got a gringa, I've got the *efectivo*."

The doorman looked at him and said, "Ya don't talk like no gent to me. Who're ya anyway? What ar'ya on tha make for, a man?"

Hawk reached into his pocket and held out the money. "You got a gringa, man? I give you money now, and then more if I git ta bang her tonight. Don't fuck with me. Ya got the girl or no?"

"Yeah, there's a gringa in the club. Ya give me money now, *pendejo*, and I'll let you in. I'll need ta search ya first."

"Tell me what she looks like first. Is she tall, fat, what?

The doorman said, "She's tall, as tall as I am, blond hair, and she's skinny. That meet yur needs, man?"

"She got any tattoos, man? I like women with tattoos."

"Yeah, she's got one. A rose on her arm here." He pointed to the inside of his left wrist.

"She sounds special. I'm goin' ta go an sober up then come back. Will she be here tomorrow night?"

"She's here every night, man. Com'on in. Give me the money, and she'll take care of you."

Hawk shoved him back into the door again, turned, and started to stumble away, retching as he went. Before he turned the corner, he managed to turn back and say, "Later, *pendejo*!"

Hawk walked around the block, checking if there was a back way out of the club. He found a door in the alley that ran down the middle of the block. The door had the name Club del Gallo—the Rooster Club. He walked back to the street at the corner of the block and looked across the street at an old two-story building. The windows were broken out, and the front door hung on only one hinge. He stepped around the partially fallen door and into a dark canyon of despair. It smelled of human waste, rotting garbage, and years of old sweat. The floor was littered with empty beer cans, wine bottles, and tequila bottles. Every step he took toward what he saw as the remainder of stairs going up to the second floor, crunched from the sound of breaking syringes and pieces of broken glass, from the windows, and the bottles that were thrown through them.

He made his way to the second floor, careful of all the debris scattered on each step. There was an old stained mattress against one wall with used condoms lying around it like a wreath of rubber flowers on a dead man's door. He walked over to each window on the side of the old building that faced the alley and the front door of the Rooster Club. He was unable to get both doors in view at the same time. He walked around the entire second floor looking for some way to get to the roof of the building. He found no interior stairs or ladders going up. No drains, no latticework, nothing. On the back side of the large room he found his only chance, he thought. There was an old thin rope hanging between it and the adjacent building, away from where the club was. He pulled and pulled again until it broke free from its attachment to the other building. He was unsure of the rope and the attachment to the roof of the building that remained. He broke out the rest of the glass left in the window and leaned out, putting the weight of his upper body on the line. It gave an inch or two, and dust, dirt, and old crumbling cement fell all over him. He tried again, and the rope stayed in place. He climbed up on the sill of the window, put his weight on the rope, and climbed up.

The roof of the old building was in bad shape too. He walked around the roof, bent over with his hands on the cement blocks making up the exterior wall. The climb was worth the chances he took. On the side facing the Rooster Club he had a clear line of sight to both doors. He would use it as his hide for the time being.

He watched both doors, never letting his mind slip away from his mission. Men and women came and went from the front door. No one from the back door. When the first ray of daylight cast over the buildings and trees to the east, the women that worked there started to come out. Singles, doubles, and one pair holding up a third woman, but no blond. For the first time, Hawk wondered if the bouncer had lied to him about the girl. He could have done that just to try to get his money and get him inside, and once inside, he or his henchmen could have done almost anything to him, including trying for ransom from him. He touched the handle of his .45 at his back and shook his head. No ransom from him, he thought.

A lone man came out the back door and checked around. A guard of some kind. Hawk had lost focus and had almost lost a possible contact with the girl. The door closed and opened again with the big Mexican guard pulling someone out by the upper arm. It was her! A tall, slender blond. They walked down the alley toward the old building, the man always keeping contact with her. Hawk ran straight across the roof and slid down the rope all the way to the ground, and stood by the corner as the couple emerged from the alley. They walked across the deserted street and continued up the alley. They were going to pass right by him. He kneeled on one knee and pulled his pistol out. He didn't need to check it or rack the slide to put a bullet in the chamber. He knew it was cocked and locked.

This was a great opportunity. Maybe he should take it. No, all his training and his past missions told him to hold off for backup. He needed to make sure it was the girl he wanted, first. They walked past him and continued on down the alley, and Hawk got back to his feet to follow, when he heard the chink of glass being kicked. He kneeled again behind the corner of the old building as a second guard pulling drag duty came walking up the ally. He had an AK-47 slung across his chest in the ready position. The AK-47 changed everything. He waited until the man in the tail was out of sight, and followed.

The two men and the girl continued to walk farther south out of town. The drag guard joined the two in the lead when they reached a dirt cart path lined with barbed wire and a post of cement. Off in the distance, on a low hill was a house with a veranda that went around the front three sides. There was a low fence with broken glass on top that ran around the house. The open fields surrounding the house had shade trees here and there for what Hawk thought was a horse ranch. He could make out several horses close to a spring-fed water trough through the fog of early morning, rising as the sun rose, in bright oranges, yellows with red mixed in. He stayed back from the cart path behind a big old oak and watched as the two men talked with two other guards that were walking around the courtyard in front of the veranda. They seemed at ease for a guard unit. The two new ones were both smoking, while the two mobile guards sat and relaxed with drinks in their hands. Hawk figured they would be easy enough to take, but there could be more in the house too. He and Cowboy would return during the afternoon to check it out better. He turned and made his way back to the club, and then to the area where the taxi had dropped him off. He walked about a block north and hailed a cab, telling the driver to take him to the Montejo Palace on the paseo.

Hawk stopped by the reception desk and ordered fresh coffee for his room. He went up to his room and knocked on the door the room shared with Cowboy's. Cowboy answered in his tactical clothes and jungle boots.

Hawk turned as he said, "Sorry for being so late, but I've got some good news. Coffee's on the way, and I need a shower. How'd you make out?"

"It took some time for me to locate a worker that could tell me what French ships came and went for the Progresso pier. He told me my question was easy to answer. There have been no French ships docked at the pier in the two years he has worked in the office of the pier master. I asked him if there were any ports along the Caribbean that were deep enough to handle international shipping. He told me there were two. One at Chetumal which also serves the northern part of Belize. The other one is about thirty kilometers north of Playa del Carmen. He also told me there was an airport on the island of Cozumel directly across from Playa."

"What're your thoughts on the two ports along the Caribbean shore of Quintana Roo state?" asked Hawk.

Cowboy was about to answer when there was a knock on the hall door to Hawk's room. Hawk stepped to the side of the door and asked who was there. It was the bellboy with the coffee. He told him to come in and set the tray on the low table in the center of the room. The young boy made his thanks for the tip and left the room, watching Cowboy, wondering why he had been standing behind the door when he entered the room with the coffee, and wearing combat clothes and boots.

Cowboy poured two large cups of dark black coffee and gave one to Hawk.

"I'm going to jump in the shower. I'll be out in a couple of minutes."

"I'm heading for the balcony. I just saw a Mexican beauty walk out to the pool and I don't want to miss out on the local attractions," Cowboy said with a wink and a nod.

Hawk walked out to the balcony in a pair of 501s and a tight T-shirt that showed off his lean upper chest and back. His arms were lean and muscular. Cowboy noticed him when he stepped in front of the small table and blocked the scenery Cowboy had been admiring.

"Okay, lover boy, tell me your thoughts on the ports."

Cowboy looked up at him and said, "The way I figure, the port at Chetumal is too far south for D'Arcy to do business. I'm thinkin' the other one near Playa and Cozumel, called Puerto Morelos, is the one to check out first. It's close to ground and air transportation, and it would be easier to get the stuff across the Gulf than to take it up through the whole country."

"Makes sense to me," said Hawk. "When we're finished here we'll head that way. Let's look at the map again for a road to Playa, and then I want to go out and recon a couple of places. I found the girl last night and followed her and her guards home after the strip club closed up. This guy D'Arcy isn't playing for chips; at least one of the guards has an AK-47."

Hawk told Cowboy he needed to get some shut-eye, and to wake him up around two or three in the afternoon.

15:05 - 16 AUGUST

TZ S

They rented a couple of old beat-up motorcycles from a shop on the east side of the Zocalo not far from the US Embassy, and began their planning. They rode in and out, up and down all the streets and side streets around the Rooster Club, and then Cowboy followed Hawk out to the ranch where he had last seen the girl. With the sun at mid-afternoon it was easy to tell the place was being run as a horse ranch. Horses were out in the pastures and relaxing in the shade of the big oaks. There were two guards walking the veranda, and several other men working around the ranch. They could be guards too.

They rode past the main ranch area in hopes of finding a back trail or road. There was an even steeper hill behind the ranch house that would give them an even better idea of what they would be up against if they took the girl from there. They rode down the road looking for a trail or road up to the steep hill, but didn't find one. With no luck, they rode back to the shop where they had rented the bikes.

They sat in a shaded area of the bar at the hotel and had a couple of beers while they thought over what they had seen. They left for their rooms to make final plans and rest up before the mission started.

They packed, paid their hotel bill, and went to the truck parked in back of the hotel. It was still early in the evening, so they drove by the embassy to make sure they knew where it was. The marine guard at the front of the embassy would be there through the night and early morning, when they planned on bringing the woman named Liz there. They circled around and drove slowly to the last block before the building Hawk had watched the Rooster Club from. Cowboy parked the truck close to the corner of the alley so Hawk would be able to see around it while keeping undercover in the truck. Cowboy would take up the position that Hawk had used the night before, at the corner of the building.

They walked a few blocks away from the club and began a last recon of the entire area. It didn't take long for Hawk to sense something different. He couldn't put his finger on it, but let Cowboy know the hair on his neck was standing up. Hawk had his M1911 Colt in the small of his back and his Kay-Bar under his shirt in front, by the buttons on his 501s. Cowboy was wearing the same thing he had on the night before. No one would recognize his clothes, since he was in Progresso checking on French freighters.

The Mexican bouncer wasn't at the front door when they walked by the Rooster Club. Hawk thought he was probably inside doing something there. They walked several blocks past the old building with the windows broken out, and circled around to the alley to check the back of the club. All seemed like it was the night before.

Still, something had Hawk on edge. What was it? Something was gnawing at him. He could sense it. It was starting again. He could feel the extra awareness, the tingle of things to come. It was early in the morning, and he and Cowboy were on the hill overlooking an NVA camp. Cowboy had given him the go-ahead for the shot. He took up the slack of the trigger of his M21 sniper rifle and stopped. Something wasn't right: the guards were gone, there was no one milling around the camp. Someway they knew. He rolled over, grabbed Cowboy, and said their prearranged escape word.

"Vaya! Go!"

Cowboy didn't think, he just went. The same with Hawk. They met up a klick back from their hide and quietly talked things over. Hawk was sure there was something wrong. They waited until the next night and went back to the hide. The camp was gone, the high grass they were in had been cut down and searched. The NVA had figured out they were there. The only thing that saved them was Hawk's awareness. They followed the trail of the enemy movement, called in an airstrike on the new camp, and got the hell out of there. Cowboy thought, "Live to fight another day."

***

"Hawk," whispered Cowboy, "you got that look in your eyes again. You think something is wrong here?"

Hawk did a little shudder and grabbed Cowboy's shoulder. "Let's make it back to the truck and talk there."

They were quiet while they walked up the alley and around the corner to the truck. When they were in the truck, Hawk said, "You remember that mission to take out the NVA general, and we didied before they came and searched where we were? It's that feeling I get, buddy. When we walked the *avenida*, the people were quieter and there weren't as many tonight. The bouncer/guard at the front door of the club wasn't there. Let's change and put on our gear and then start the misson as we planned it, but let's take the prick-six radios with us tonight. That good for you?"

"Roger that."

As Cowboy turned the corner to walk down the alley to the old building, they did radio checks with the prick sixes, whispering, "How you read?"

"Five by five. You?"

"Five by."

06:15 - 17 AUGUST

TZ S

They waited several hours before Hawk saw a few men walking the streets coming from the direction of the Rooster Club. He clicked his RT once, telling Cowboy it was time. A double click came back, and he knew Cowboy was ready. He heard a what he thought was a backfire of a vehicle, but then more of the same sound—pop, pop, pop—then more.

"Hawk," came Cowboy on the RT, "it's a raid. The club is being raided. No uniforms that I can see. I think it's a rival gang or something."

"Hold tight. I'm on my way. I'm bringing the truck. Hop in as I go by, and we'll sit tight until the smoke clears."

"Roger that."

Cowboy jumped on the running board and hung on as the truck ran down the alley and turned onto the avenida scattering what few people were still hanging around, as the sun gave first light to the area around the club. Hawk braked to a stop at the corner of Rooster Club's street and the avenida, waiting. There were several more gunshots, both sounding like pistols, and then silence. There was some banging on wooden doors, and then metal doors, after. They continued to watch and wait. Then several small car or truck engines started, and the roar grew louder as they came down the Rooster Club's street past the avenida where Hawk and Cowboy waited.

It was two small beat-up trucks. The engines were straining with everything they had. The load they were carrying was probably over the load capacity of the two little trucks. Both trucks were weighted down, almost to the street. The beds were filled the with women that worked at the strip club, and an armed man in each to keep control of them. Two men in each cab made a quick count of six total armed men. Hawk pulled out after the trucks passed and started to follow with their trucks lights off, using only a few rays of light as morning tried to get going.

"I saw some blond hair in the first truck bed," said Hawk. "Let's follow along and see where the raiders take them. I don't hear any sirens, so the cops don't want to get involved, no problem there."

The two little trucks went roaring through the early morning, down two-way narrow dirt roads and onto cart paths cut into the jungle. Hawk dropped back as the sun came up. It was easy enough to follow the two trucks' dust cloud as the dawn became day. When the dust cloud stopped, Hawk pulled over into the jungle deep enough so the truck wouldn't be seen from the path.

They geared up and started to work their way through the dense thickets of brush and scrub trees in the direction they last saw the dust cloud. In about an hour, both men sweating and bleeding from multiple scratches of limbs and thorns, they broke out of the jungle enough to see what happened to the two trucks, and the women that rode in them. There was a large compound cleared in the jungle, with its backyard running to a sand beach and what must have been the Gulf of Mexico.

Hawk pulled the strap of his binoculars over his head and checked out the compound. It was set up like a ranch house, but larger. There was a low stone fence with a large two-door curved-top entrance. Broken glass lined the top of the gate and fence. It had a veranda around the house, a large patio in back facing the beach, and a swimming pool. He could see the two trucks parked in front of the house, with a tall, dark-skinned man talking to several guards that were much shorter and carried what looked like AK-47s. The women were probably in the ranch house. Hawk gave the binoculars to Cowboy and let him get a feel for the compound.

After Cowboy took a look, they spent some time clearing the immediate area of brush to make a better hide. Hawk told Cowboy they needed to take a day to count heads and see what traffic came and went before making a definitive plan. Cowboy agreed, while pointing out two big oak trees on each side of the main gate that leaned into the compound at an angle. They talked about finding high ground that would allow sight directly into the compound, and decided that Hawk should make his way toward the beach to check that area out. He would get what they needed to assault the compound from the truck, and return to the hide they had prepared. Cowboy keeping watch over the compound and taking count of the warm bodies with guns.

The jungle had been cleared a few feet away from the stone fence all the way to the beach. Hawk stayed inside the edge of the jungle and worked his way toward the beach. He started to hear the surf rolling down on the beach when he came up to another stone fence. This one had been left to the jungle. Totally covered in vines and brush, it looked much older than the fence around the house. He discovered it was a wall, not a fence, and his heart started to beat faster: he had run into walls like this in the jungle in Vietnam. He hoped he would find this one to be similar. He continued on until he reached some stone steps leading up. He took his Kay-bar out and started to hack his way up. At the top was a small square room with a stone table in the middle. It had to be a Mayan temple. The top was shaded by another large oak that looked centuries old. He climbed up to the top of the stone room and looked toward the compound. This was the answer. He could see clearly over the top of the low-growth jungle into the compound, from across the compound at the front gate to the patio in back, the pool and the beach beyond that. He made his way back to the temporary hide and told Cowboy what he had found. They worked out a plan, and they both went back to the truck to get what they would need. They planned on spending the rest of the day getting ready and making sure they knew how many men were in the compound.

As the sun was setting, one of the trucks rolled out of the compound, one man driving and one in the back carrying a weapon, with five women standing or sitting uncomfortably in the bed of the small truck. The blond woman wasn't with them. That made two less men to deal with when they assaulted the ranch house in the morning. They counted eight, including the tall better-dressed man. Cowboy decided he was a leader or head of the group, because whenever he talked with the other men they always seemed to stand more rigidly and pay attention better than when they talked among themselves. With the two gone in the truck, they were down to six armed men in the compound.

That night the guard at the front gate started to walk slowly around the compound. He would meet the guard that stayed in the back guarding the beach area, and then return the way

he had originally walked. Cowboy slowly low crawled to the gate and waited for the guard to return and then leave again. He opened the gate and went to the stone corner where the gate and fence joined. He took a Claymore mine from his pack and set it up. Then he took another one and did the same at the other corner of the gate and fence, placing green weeds from the jungle to cover each one. He closed the gate and waited until the guard had come and gone again, before he crawled back to the hide where Hawk was waiting.

They chewed on some deer jerky that Cowboy made each year, after hunting season. Hawk left with his M14 sniper rifle and two ten-round mags plus some loose rounds and his prick six. Cowboy left to crawl over to the big oak on the left side of the gate. He had two lines to pick up at the gate and two electric clackers with him. He made his way up the leaning trunk of the tree and connected everything up.

Hawk made his way to the Mayan temple and worked his way up to the roof of the small room at the top. He set up his M14 sniper rifle and laid out his extra mag of ammo. He pushed the other ten-round mag into the weapon, put down his poncho, and waited for the morning to come.

When dawn was breaking and Hawk could see the front gate and the guard well enough to shoot, he picked up his radio and clicked once. Two clicks came back. Cowboy was ready. Hawk settled in after checking for wind direction and found the guard standing a few feet inside the gate through his three-by-nine scope. He took a breath, let part of it out, and slowed his heart and breathing rate. He took the slack off the trigger and set the crosshairs just over the jaw joint of the guard. He let the trigger break. The guard fell like a wet rag and stayed there. The sound of the shot had the lights going on all over the compound and in the house. There was yelling from all around the compound. The guard at the beach left his post and ran to his fallen comrade. There was another shot, and he fell within two feet of the first guard. The rest of the guards ran into view but were staying away from the area where their comrades had been shot. The head man came from the veranda and urged the men to do something. They began firing into the jungle, without any targets. As they gained more courage, they advanced on the two dead men. The commander followed a few steps behind with a pistol in his hand, shouting orders that could not be done.

Cowboy let them get midway to the dead guards and pushed down hard three times on the clacker of the first Claymore. The sound was deafening. Dirt and dust flew up in a cloud around the area where the mine went off, and up to cover the dead and dying men it had ripped apart. He was the closest to the carnage, so he worked his way down the tree and made his way to the gate. The gate on one side was blown off its big hinges. He stayed behind the door and checked the area for possible fighting wounded. Two were wounded and in no way able to fight. All the rest were dead. He stayed behind the door until Hawk made his way up the cleared space by the fence and then went in with him to finish the assault.

Hawk walked up to the commander that was down with multiple wounds in his lower torso and one arm mangled and twisted under him. He was dying, but Hawk wanted information. He splashed water from his canteen into the commander's face and kneeled down.

"Why did you raid the strip club in Mérida?"

"My boss wanted the girls to work in his club."

"Who is your boss?"

"He is the leader of the Yucatán Cartel."

"So, this is about drug gangs?"

"D'Arcy and his gang raided our Villahermosa club before."

"Where is D'Arcy now?"

"Maybe in Playa. We heard about a big drug delivery soon."

"What is your boss's name?"

"Raul, ahh, Raul . . ."

"He's dead, Hawk," said Cowboy.

Hawk stood up and looked at the carnage. He shook his head and said, "Let's go clear the house, find the girl, and get out of here."

They went together into the ranch house, one on each side of the main hallway, clearing each room as they went. They cleared back to a wall of glass in a large room facing the pool and beach, without finding anyone. Hawk was certain the woman had not been in the truck that left the compound. He felt she had to be here in the compound somewhere. He and Cowboy opened the huge sliding-glass door to the pool. The heat was overwhelming in the morning sun. The sound of the surf hitting the beach drowned out all other sound until Cowboy grabbed Hawk's arm and said, "Listen, listen between the rolls of sound from the surf."

Clink, clink came a muffled noise. Hawk walked to the pump house, a small stone room set next to a large palapa, with a sitting area and bar under it. Cowboy came up beside him, both waiting for the quiet lull between the rolls for the Gulf's waves. There it was again: clink, clink. There was a combination lock on the door. The clink, clink came again. This time he was sure it came from inside the pump room.

He pulled his Colt and said loudly, "Liz Stillings, if you're inside back away from the door." Hawk shot a round from his M1911, and the lock flew into small pieces of junk. He stepped past the latched side of the door frame, slowly opened the thick wood door, and pushed it in with his foot, staying safely away from the opening, and called out again. This time there was a soft sobbing sound from the dark of the small pump room.

"Who are you?" said a quiet feminine voice.

"We were sent by your father to find you and take you home," said Hawk.

Liz Stillings came to the door and peered out at Hawk. Her blue eyes were large and frightened. Her long hair was hanging down to her shoulders in loose curls. Her full lips were trembling slightly, and she had a small tack hammer in her hands. Her hands were wrapped around the handle, with her knuckles white from clenching it so tight. She wore the same outfit he had seen her in walking up the alley the night before. The pants and top fit her everywhere they should.

Cowboy came up and stood outside the door where she stood. He held out his hand, and she dropped the little hammer that she had been making the noise with and took his hand. She moved out of the door and stood between the two men and said, "I heard explosions and rifle fire. Can we get the hell out of here?"

Hawk said, "We'll lead the way, in case more men show up before we make it to our truck. You need to prepare yourself for the mess out in the courtyard. Do you need help walking?"

"No, I can do anything necessary to get out of this nightmare. Let's go," Liz said, and she gave a little shiver.

She walked with Hawk and Cowboy around the torn bodies of her captives with her head up and eyes fixed toward the remains of the gate entry. They hurried down the dirt track to the truck.

Cowboy took the driver's seat as Hawk and Liz Stillings went to the other side. Liz took the middle of the bench seat, and Hawk took shotgun. The truck started up the first try, and they were speeding down the jungle road at a breakneck speed, hoping to get back on the old oiled road before more cartel came to check on the explosions and the fires burning at the beach house.

07:54 - 18 AUGUST

TZ S

They had reached the narrow oil road that led to Mérida, and started to relax. Liz asked who they were, and Cowboy told her his name was Cowboy, and Hawk was the name of the man on her right.

"Where are we going?" asked Liz.

"We're headed to Mérida to drop you off at the embassy," said Cowboy.

Hawk sat quietly looking out the windshield watching for traffic coming from Mérida. He reached down to a pocket on the thigh of his utilities and took something from it. He reached across his chest with it and dropped it into Liz's lap. She picked the booklet up and looked at it, then wondered how he got it. The kidnappers had taken it when they searched her near the border.

"How did you get my passport?"

Silence met her until Cowboy said, "Your father had a new one issued with your old photo and sent it to us before we left the States. We figured they would have yours and you would need a passport to get out of Mexico and back into the States."

She turned halfway to Hawk and asked if he had any other surprises for her. There was silence again.

"He doesn't talk much to women. Give him time and he'll probably come around," said Cowboy.

Dusk was coming as they went around the curves made necessary by some mangroves near the Gulf of Mexico, but Cowboy drove on without turning the truck lights on. They swung through the beginning of an S curve, and Hawk caught a low flicker of light coming toward them through the mangrove brush and reflected off the brackish water it grew in. He reached behind him and pulled out his Colt. It was cocked and locked like always. Cowboy and Liz saw the gun come out at the same time.

"I saw the flicker. What's the plan if it's the bad guys?"

"We better turn the lights on and act like locals going into Mérida. Anyone seeing us will think we are Mexicans with the plates we put on the truck. Miss Stillings, you better duck down out of sight until the vehicle passes," said Hawk.

Liz ducked down toward the truck's dash, her head at the same level as the Colt. She turned her head so she could see Hawk, and told him she was glad that he could talk, and that he carried a big gun. Hawk looked down at her with his don't give me any shit look as he rolled down his window and put his arm and pistol along the edge of the window hidden by the rearview mirror. Hawk decided he would have to be careful around her; she had a quick mouth on her.

It was a small pickup that went past them in the middle of the S curve. Hawk thought it was the one that left earlier in the morning. The other one had been destroyed by the Claymore blast at the gate of the ranch house. Cowboy continued driving at the same speed. Liz sat up and pushed her hair back in place while Hawk watched in the rearview mirror.

"Goose it, Cowboy. They're turning around."

"Eeeeee haaaaa!" said Cowboy as Hawk and Liz turned at the same time to look out the rear window of the cab.

Hawk didn't think they could catch up with them. The Datsun had a four-cylinder engine, and Cowboy's truck was an eight. It would outrun the little truck in a heartbeat. Hawk turned Liz around and shoved her back down below the rear window as a round hit the glass and shattered it into a million cracks. The bullet hit the windshield just above Liz's head and made a spider crack the size of a half dollar and fell somewhere on the floor.

Hawk leaned out the window and fired a couple of rounds to let them know they were in a free-for-all. He turned and hit the back window with his elbow as hard as he could. The window bowed out where he had hit it. He braced his feet and pushed up and out with his shoulder. The whole window let go and flew back across the bed cover, and crashed onto the road sliding to a stop.

More rounds came from the truck following them, ripping holes in the back of the truck. Hawk told Cowboy to weave the truck, the bad guys were trying to hit the rear tires. Hawk kept firing out the rear window keeping the two trucks well back. The mangroves began to thin as they neared Mérida, and more dirt roads started to intersect with the oiled road they were on. Hawk thought about taking one but decided against it. He had no idea where they went, and if they were blocked off at a dead end, their chances of survival were slim to none.

"Cowboy, have you got a gun too? I can help out by increasing fire," Liz said.

"Sure, I do. Have you fired a pistol before?"

"I grew up on my dad's ranch in South Texas. I was hunting before I started school. Give me your pistol."

Cowboy reached down to his side and pulled up the Smith and Wesson .357 Combat his dad had sent him while he was in Vietnam. It was worn with some of the blue rubbed off from the countless times he had cleaned and oiled it. Its balance was perfect, and the grips were worn to his hand. He handed the pistol to her, grip first.

"It's got six rounds in it. You can pull the trigger or cock the hammer and pull the trigger," he said.

"My dad had one like this except the barrel was a bit longer," she said as she turned in the seat and got a good shooting grip and glanced over at Hawk, wanting to make sure he knew she had a pistol and was going to start shooting. He glanced at her with a look of disbelief then turned back to fire another round. His ejector slammed back. He ejected the mag and pulled a new one out of his pants pocket and rammed it into the 1911 and put a round in the tube. Liz was amazed at how fast he did it. She fired slowly, expertly hitting the truck on the driver's side, and then fired one trying to hit a tire, but missed. She was surprised at how good it felt to fire a pistol again. The kick, the smell of gun oil, the blowback of gunpowder made her lose concentration for a second, when she remembered how much she enjoyed being with her dad out hunting or sport shooting.

Small buildings and houses started to flash by as they sped toward Mérida. They were made with the tree limbs from the mangroves for the walls, some with open spaces where doors should be and palm fronds for roofs. Barren dirt surrounded the stick huts, with chickens and pigs running around. They were fenced in by more sticks from the mangroves. There were no cars or trucks. Some carts and with a donkey or small skinny Spanish horse were near the huts.

Liz and Hawk kept the fire up, but the little truck kept pace at a distance. The .357 Liz was shooting clicked on a spent casing.

"Cowboy, you have more ammo?"

Cowboy reached into his utility pocket and brought out an odd-looking round object with six bullets sitting around it.

He said, "Hold the wheel and I'll load it for you."

Liz glared at him as she pushed the release button so the cylinder rolled out, ejecting the six spent shells in one motion, then put the odd-looking holder to the cylinder. She pushed in the six new shells and flipped the loaded cylinder back into the frame of the gun, ready to fire again.

She said, "I've known what a speed loader was since I was ten," as she cracked a smile at him.

This time, when she turned with the gun held steady in her shooter's grip, she saw Hawk give a couple of short nods like he thought she had done good at what she just did. For some reason, it mattered to her that he thought she was okay. She shook it off and fired another round.

A stray bullet hit the driver's-side mirror and glanced inside the cab hitting Cowboy in the left shoulder. He reached up and grabbed at his shoulder, losing control of the pickup. Liz reached over and grabbed the steering wheel, but wasn't having any luck with one hand trying to control it. She dropped her pistol and pulled him toward her, at the same time moving on top of his lap and scooting past him, until she was against the driver's side door. With her foot on the gas pedal and both hands on the wheel, she was able to control the wild gyrations and continue down the narrow road as fast as before.

Hawk pulled Cowboy over and out of Liz's way checking the wound by ripping the buttons off the front of his shirt and pushing the left side down his back. There was a ragged-shaped furrow across the top of his shoulder. The wound was too high to have broken any bones. It looked like it involved the muscle only.

Cowboy was conscious, but in a lot of pain and cussing at his bad luck. Hawk took the left side of his shirt and pulled it up, under his armpit and over the wound. He tied it off on the right side of his neck, making a sling to hold his left arm in and keeping pressure on the wound to stop the bleeding. Cowboy was lucky. Two or three inches to the right and the bullet would have torn up his carotid artery, and he would have bled out in minutes.

The huts had turned to small adobe houses, and then to narrow oiled streets only big enough to allow one car to pass in either direction, while Liz continued to evade the gang members and Hawk worked on Cowboy. Liz started to turn right and left trying to lose the trucks. When least expected, a small *glorieta* with six streets running off it came up. Liz went around the circle part way and headed down a narrow street. The people in the small truck had stopped shooting, as she had started speeding down the narrow streets turning this way and that until they were no longer behind them.

They kept driving along the narrow streets until they came to Avenida Montejo. There was a lot of traffic on the divided street, that looked like the Champs-Élysées in Paris. They drove by the hotel they had stayed at and pulled into the underground parking in the back. They had to get a different car. The truck looked like it had been driven through a war zone. Hawk quickly found the medical kit and started cleaning Cowboy's wound. When he had finished, he gave him a double dose of antibiotics and a strong painkiller. While Liz kept an eye on Cowboy, Hawk went to find better transportation.

18:15 - 18 AUGUST

TZ S

By the time Hawk came back, Cowboy was asleep. He had paid an old man cash for another Ford pickup. It was covered in dried mud with the left front fender partially off and the hood bent up, but it ran well and there were no bullet holes in the body. Liz and Hawk loaded what they could from Cowboy's truck into the bed of the older truck and took off down Avenida Montejo toward the gulf town of Progresso. They needed to be out of Mérida and in hiding while they figured out what their next move would be.

Liz continued driving so Hawk could keep a close eye on Cowboy, who was passed out between them. The road from Mérida to Progresso ended in a T intersection. The crossroad ran parallel to the beach and between small shops and stores that had to be the town of Progresso. There was a painted sign on a wood telephone pole indicating the port was to the left. Liz turned right and passed through town. They drove down the road until it turned into a packed sand track, and Hawk told her to pull in beside a beach house just off the sand track. She pulled in and parked in a clump of palms to hide the truck. Hawk got out, walked to the front door, and knocked loudly. No one answered. He walked back to the beach side of the house, around a pool and patio, up to large glass patio doors. All the lights were out, so he hammered on the glass panes to no avail. Stepping back a step he kicked out with his right leg hitting the latch between the two doors. There was a loud bang as the latch broke and the two doors swung into the room beyond, knocking over several pieces of furniture that sat close by. Hawk walked into the house with his Colt out and in front of him. He quickly cleared all the rooms and went back out to help Liz bring Cowboy in through the shattered doors and up a set of stairs to one of the three bedrooms.

Liz left Hawk to take care of Cowboy and went down to the kitchen to see if there was any food. They hadn't eaten all day, and she needed some broth or something light to give to Cowboy. She flipped a light switch, but nothing happened. The power was off. By moonlight she saw a candle lying on the floor, where the doors had knocked it off of a small table. She searched the kitchen and found a box of matches on a shelf over the counter. The candle gave off a yellow flickering glow to the room. She went to the refrigerator. With the power off, she figured there would be no food there, but she had to check. It was empty. There were a few cans of beans of various types in a small pantry. She found a can opener in a drawer and went to turn on the range. Nothing happened when she turned on the burner. She checked to see if the pilot light was going; it was not. From the years at hunting camp with her father, she knew to check outside for a gas line or container. Outside against the kitchen wall she found a storage tank. She turned the valve on and ran back inside hoping there was gas in the tank. She lighted the pilot and then the burner. A flame went whoosh and started to burn. She opened the cans and mixed several different types of beans in a pot she had found under the counter, and started to warm them. She was sure Hawk and Cowboy had eaten worse.

Hawk got Cowboy undressed and into the bed. It was made up like someone was expecting to come back at any time. He could smell something cooking downstairs, and his stomach growled loudly. He left Cowboy, still asleep, and went down to the kitchen where Liz was just putting some beans into two bowls. They sat at a table near the patio windows and ate in silence. Hawk got up and asked Liz if she wanted more beans. She shook her head. He filled his bowl again and sat looking out the floor-to-ceiling glass. With the doors open they could hear the surf rolling on the beach, not far off.

"Thanks for making the beans. They're the best I've ever had," said Hawk.

"It's funny how good they taste. Must be because we're so hungry," she said, trying to make a smile.

"Did you have a chance to see if we have water?" he asked.

"Not yet," she said as she went to the kitchen sink and turned on the water to rinse her bowl.

"There's cold but no hot," she said.

"That's okay. We don't need hot water right now. I'm going out to the truck to get the medical kit. I need to sew up Cowboy's wound so it will stop bleeding and heal better. I'll be right back. Do you have the gun he gave you?"

"No."

"I'll bring it in too. We need to be prepared in case they find us somehow," he said, and walked over to rinse his bowl. He headed out the doors that were hanging at an odd angle, to the trunk. When he came back in, he handed the .357 to Liz, along with another speed loader.

"Just in case," he said.

She nodded her head and watched him go upstairs.

Hawk cleaned Cowboy's wound again and put a crude ladder-stitch suture in to close the wound. He thought of the medic that had told him how to do it: "It's like lacing up a boot," he said.

"Ya never know when some little thing you are told will become very important to you," Hawk thought.

Liz took the first watch of the night and let Hawk get some rest. Cowboy was still sedated, but moving around in the bed from time to time. He must have still been in pain, even as he slept. Hawk tried to sleep, but he had too much on his mind with all that had gone on with their recovery of Liz. It was disturbing to him that two different drug gangs had been involved in her abduction, and later taking her to the ranch on the beach. For what reason? Was it as simple as drugs and sex, or was there some hidden purpose to it all? He wondered what the best way would be to get her to the embassy in Mérida, and then sent back to the States to reunite with her family. She seemed alert and capable. What about the drugs that got her into the position of being taken by the D'Arcy Cartel? After they got her to the embassy, they would need a plan to make sure D'Arcy was taken out. He hoped Cowboy would quickly recover from the flesh wound in his shoulder. He didn't want to think about trying to complete the mission they had been given without his help.

Hawk heard a soft knock on the bedroom door. He rolled off the bed and pulled his .45 from under the pillow. He stepped to the hinge side of the door and waited. There was another knock, louder this time.

"Who's there?" he asked.

"Liz. It's time to relieve me."

"Come in slowly."

The door handle turned and the bolt clicked open. It began to open slowly. Hawk raised his pistol over his head and put his eye to the crack as it became larger. There was no one else at the door or down the hallway. He lowered his gun and stepped out into the room just enough to stand at the doorknob and pull her into the room while slamming the door and locking it.

Hawk noticed immediately that she had taken time to clean up. The dirt that had covered her face and arms was gone, and it struck Hawk for the first time that she was a beautiful woman. He shook his head slightly to get back in his thought pattern as she told him it had been quiet while he was resting and Cowboy was still in a restless sleep.

"Thanks for taking over the first watch. I really needed the time to rest and try to think of what our next move should be. Now we have two gangs after us, and they'll want you back and to finish it with Cowboy and me. I still need to figure out how we're going to find this guy D'Arcy, and how to get to him when he has a gang to protect him, plus get you to the embassy and back to your parents. I'll work on it while I'm standing watch. You better get some sleep while you can."

Hawk went to check on Cowboy when the sun had first made the edges of the cotton ball clouds turn to the red and orange of morning. He opened the door carefully trying not to wake him. The new morning was streaming through the open window making the curtains billow into the room. Cowboy was sitting in a chair looking out the window at the beach and gulf water.

"What's for breakfast in this joint, pardner?" he asked with as much a grin as he could manage.

Hawk knew not to ask how he was doing. He was up and dressed in dirty, tattered clothing and trying to be funny. Cowboy was as tough as any man he had ever know, and twice as mean, when he had to be.

"Beans. Unless we take a chance and go to one of the little shops down the way. You want anything special?"

"If there is a café, see if they will make some chorizo and eggs to go. Coffee, lots of coffee. The strong black kind from around Veracruz. Where's the woman?"

"I'll make a run, and she can stay with you. Maybe there's coffee here, I don't know. I'll go check on her now. You stay put."

There were subtle noises coming from the kitchen when Hawk stepped out into the upstairs hallway. He thought he knew who it was, but he pulled his Colt to be on the safe side. He went halfway down the stairs and bent over to look into the kitchen from the angle of the lower ceiling and the staircase.

It was Liz looking in the cabinets again for food. It didn't look like she was having any success. She turned as he finished coming down the stairs.

"I was wondering where you had gone off to," she said. "I looked around the property to make sure everything was okay then started to check on Cowboy. That's when I heard you two talking and came down here to figure something out for breakfast."

"He's up and wanting something to eat. I'm going to make a quick run to the intersection we came through to see if there's a café that I can pick up something to eat."

"I need to go with you. I need to pick up some clothes to wear— these are torn and dirty—along with stuff to shower and clean up with. You and Cowboy look like you were dragged through a city dump and it all got on you. In fact, it kind of smells like that too."

"Okay, let's make a fast run to the intersection. Take the .357 Magnum upstairs and tell Cowboy to lock himself in the bedroom until we get back."

"Will do."

Liz and Hawk walked out to the new old beat-up pickup, and Hawk pulled a suitcase from the bed of the truck. He pulled an oil-cloth wrapped package from it and several boxes of .380 ACP ammunition. He handed the package and ammunition to Liz.

He said, "I know you can handle a pistol. This Walther PPK is for your personal protection. It should be easy for you to conceal. The magazine carries six rounds with one in the tube, and there is a second magazine for backup."

Liz unwrapped the pistol, ejected the magazine, and checked the load. She checked the barrel to make sure there was a shell there, and then rammed the magazine back home. She worked the safety off and on and used a shooter's grip to try the balance and weight.

She smiled at Hawk and said, "I've heard of this gun, but I've never held one. It feels like a dream. Thanks, Hawk, I feel safer now."

08:17 - 19 AUGUST

TZ S

They drove the sand road to the oiled one-lane pavement that went on to the intersection that was Progresso. Hawk drove past several cafés and clothing shops until he reached the *glorieta* in the intersection. He drove around the traffic circle and back to a small café with a clothing shop next to it. He parked the truck in an alley on the side of the café. Hawk placed the order for food, telling the woman at the counter it was *para llevar*. They walked into the small clothing shop to look for fresh clothing. Liz went over to the women's area, and Hawk walked to the men's. It didn't take long for them to find and purchase new clothes for all of them. The shop was too small to have an assortment. Hawk got two sets of work clothes, and Liz came to the checkout counter with what looked the same as what Hawk had picked out, but made for a smaller-framed individual. She had a pair of blue jeans and a blue shirt with short sleeves. Hawk had two pairs of jeans and two guayabera shirts, one white the other light blue. Hawk paid, and they walked back to the café. The little Mexican lady had two sacks waiting for them. One with food and one with a large *jarra*, a jug filled with coffee. Hawk paid again, and they walked out of the café and around the corner to the truck in the alley.

Hawk backed into the street and drove off toward the beach house. They were midway through the small collection of shops and run-down houses when Liz let out a scream and threw herself down onto the bench seat almost hitting the steering wheel. Hawk accelerated from habit, as Liz pulled the PPK from her waistband at her back. Hawk heard the safety click off, he put his foot to the floor on the gas pedal, and they left pavement for the packed sand road heading for the beach house. Liz scooted closer to Hawk as they raced down the road and said in a strained voice, "I saw one of the men that held me at the ranch walking toward the café as we left, and then another one across the street going into a shoe store. They must be looking for us, Hawk."

"Damn, I thought we'd lose them by coming to the middle of nowhere. We're in a bad spot now. We have to get Cowboy and try to make it back to Mérida before they figure out where we are. That little Mexican lady at the café knows the way we left and how much food we bought."

The truck was sliding around on the loose sand and was hard to control at the high rate of speed Hawk was driving it. He slowed barely to get better control. He told Liz, "I'll get Cowboy and the medical supplies. You gather up what you can at a run and meet us at the truck. We have to get out of here before they bring a gang down on us. Are you good with that?"

"No problem," she said as they slid to a stop by the swimming pool of the beach house.

Hawk left the engine running, and both of them hit the house like a hurricane. Hawk up the stairs and Liz behind him.

"Cowboy," Hawk yelled, "pick up what you need and let's didi. We've been made, and they are probably right behind us."

He ran into the bedroom and found Cowboy grabbing the medical kit and his bloody, torn clothes from a chair by the bed.

"I've got new clothes for us in the truck. Drop those and head to the truck as fast as you can. I'll check around for anything we really need and pull drag. Liz is doing the same and will meet us at the truck. Get in the middle. I'll drive, and Liz will pull shotgun."

Cowboy didn't say anything. He ran out the bedroom door in his briefs carrying the medical bag and rushed down the stairs. Liz came right behind him and took the bag as they hit the pool door and headed for the truck, still idling beside the pool. Cowboy got in, and then Liz on the right side as Hawk came bursting out the pool doors and threw another small kit bag in the back of the truck as he jumped in the cab. He threw the gearshift into reverse and spun sand and shells wildly about as he tried to get traction leaving the beach house. He hit the packed sand road and spun the wheel, downshifting into low to gain more traction heading toward the little village of Progress, and what might be waiting for them.

When they came into the little village, Liz was looking from side to side watching for the two men she had seen a short time ago. The small shops were all open, and there were people walking along the side of the partially paved road. There were stick lean-tos with cooking fires going, and others with fake watches and music tapes for sale. She didn't see either of the men that had been searching for them. She relaxed for the moment, but continued to search the sides of the narrow street.

Hawk and Cowboy were still alert and checking out any cars that approached them. They made it to the intersection and traffic circle with no problem. They went around the *glorieta* and took the road back to Mérida.

Sitting off the side of the road headed toward the intersection was a new black Mercedes sedan. There were four men sitting in the car talking and arguing about something. It was unusual to see such an expensive new car on the roads of Mexico. The back window rolled down as they were passing the car. A man's face appeared at the window as he flipped a cigar butt onto the road.

There was an audible intake of breath from Liz, and both men turned to check on her. She was white as a sheet and trembling.

"What's happening, Liz? Are you okay?" asked Cowboy.

She didn't answer at first. She put her head down to her knees and rocked back and forth. Cowboy could see her working her fists: first open, then to a fist, and back again. Then suddenly she looked up, like she remembered Hawk and Cowboy were with her.

She said with a trembling, angry voice so low it was hard to hear over the truck and road noise, "The man in the car window back there is the one all the men at the beach ranch called jefe. He's the head of the Yucatán Cartel. The one that had me taken away from D'Arcy's men's club in Mérida right before you rescued me."

Hawk said, "I've been trying to figure out why they stole you away from D'Arcy. We know you're beautiful and all that, but there must be something else. They wouldn't start a war with D'Arcy for the ransom money or for one young, good-looking American."

"Maybe we should return the favor and abduct him so we can ask him a few questions and clear up some things that are bothering us," said Cowboy with a crooked smile.

"Sounds like a plan. Let's run on down the road to a side road with good cover, eat cold chorizo and egg tacos, and wait for the Mercedes to pass. We'll tail them till they stop for the night, and make our move then," said Hawk.

"We need to get some clothes on too. It's a little windy with the windows down," said Cowboy.

"What should we do with Liz?" said Hawk. "We can't take her with us, and we can't drop her off at the embassy and still follow the Mercedes."

"I'm going with you. You're not dropping me anywhere. These people have drugged me, stripped me, beat me, and treated me like a sex slave. I can help you guys get this SOB, and you know it. I can drive, I can shoot, and I can follow orders. Besides, I may be good bait to get this guy alone so we can take him without a gunfight. Now find a place to hide this piece of junk and let me change clothes."

Cowboy and Hawk looked at each other, and Hawk said, "Okay, but you go to the embassy after we have all the information we can get from el jefe."

Liz didn't say anything, but there was a Cheshire cat smile on her lips.

They pulled off the main highway onto a cart path that had an old tire leaning against a tall stick. There were several empty jugs tied to the top in different colors. All the junk was used as the address for some pole house with a palm leaf roof back in the jungle. Hawk backed in for a quick exit. Everyone ate cold tacos and changed their clothes and waited. The coffee was cold, but Cowboy drank it like it was a cold beer on the Fourth of July.

While they watched for the Mercedes, Liz told them about her abduction, about her drug use, and that one good thing had come from being kidnapped. She told them she had discovered she was a strong person and that she didn't need the shadow of the drugs to hide from reality. She had faced reality in the middle of the hell she went through, and came out a stronger, more mature person for it.

The sun was going down and the mosquitos were trying to drink their fill when the Mercedes flew by. The road was pitted with holes that would blow a tire out if it hit right, so the car was weaving from side to side trying to miss the big ones, with the suspension working overtime. Hawk took off after it and tried to stay back, just close enough to see the Mercedes in the distance. The newer car slowly left them in the dust. They were all disappointed until the lights of Mérida came into view. There was a Pemex gas station on the right with its lights on. The Mercedes was parked next to a gas pump, with the attendant pumping gas. Hawk drove ahead until they found a side street with no lights, and waited.

They followed the Mercedes with lights off until they hit traffic in Mérida. The street lights along the Paseo Montejo were enough light to follow by, but Hawk let several cars get between them and the Mercedes and turned on the truck's lights. It would do no good to have an accident now—driving without lights on a crowded street—and lose the car they were following. At the central park, the Mercedes turned east, and Hawk followed until the lights of the city grew less intense, and then turned the truck's lights off again. He followed close enough to maintain a visual on the red pinpoints that were the car's taillights. He watched as they turned into a drive that stopped at a gate in a tall wall large enough for the car to enter what appeared to be a walled compound.

They went by fast enough not to arouse attention, but slow enough to gather good information on the wall surrounding the compound. It looked like it was made from concrete block and a veneer of stucco. In places, the stucco had buckled and fallen off. The top of the wall was covered in spikes of sharp broken pieces of different colored glass. There was a guard at the gate that opened it for the car to enter, and then closed it again. It looked like the guard simply closed a large metal latch to secure the gate, no lock.

The lights in the compound went on after they had passed and pulled off the road. They were going to wait until early in the morning to make their entry and used the time waiting to plan out the entry. Hawk would use a pile of rubble that was a few feet high on the side wall as access, and take out the guard at the gate. Cowboy was still too stiff, and the wound too fresh to try the wall. He would wait near the gate until Hawk neutralized the gate guard and opened the gate for him. Liz would be with Cowboy. They needed her to eyeball el jefe as the two men cleared the house room by room. The three of them continued to work over the plan until they felt they were good to go.

Hawk looked at Cowboy and then at Liz on the far side of the bench seat, and said, "The best-made plans all fall apart when the action starts. Keep your eyes and ears open and follow our lead. No talk, no hesitation. Our lives depend upon it. You are with us to ident the jefe only. Is that clear?"

Liz looked him in the eye and with a firm voice said, "Clear!"

20:12 - 19 AUGUST

TZ A

They waited two more hours before working their way through the thick jungle surrounding the compound. Hawk worked his way up the pile of rubble, careful not to knock loose any pieces of block or stone. The pile was tall enough for him to see the sharp pieces of glass on top of the wall. He pulled out his Kay-Bar and started to quietly work the point into the stucco to loosen and remove the glass in an area large enough for him to slip over the wall without cutting himself or making any noise. The night was clear, and the quiet was deafening. When he eased over the wall, that was the signal to Cowboy and Liz to start working their way to the gate. The opening was made, and Hawk slipped over the wall. He landed like a ghost on the manicured lawn inside the wall and waited a minute for any response. He could see a cigarette glowing close to the front of the villa, but there was no response. He kept a large palm between him and the gate guard as he moved like a dark shadow toward the unsuspecting target. He took his time at the palm and listened. He was close enough to hear the guard breathing heavily. He was squatting beside the gate asleep. Hawk worked his way up to the guard with the Kay-Bar still in his right hand. In one quick motion, he forced the man's head back and up, and thrust the knife up under his chin, through the soft tissue and thin bone into his brain, twisting as the blade guard hit flesh. The guard made no sound and was dead in a second. Hawk wiped the blade on the guard's shirt and low crawled to the gate. He opened the latch, and opened the gate only enough for Cowboy and Liz to crawl through. He motioned for Cowboy to go to the right and for Liz to stay at the gate while they got rid of the guard near the front door.

Cowboy worked to the right near the wall, and Hawk went in a low crawl straight at the guard. When he was close, he waited for Cowboy to make a noise to draw the guard's attention. There was a simple click of metal on stone, and the guard reacted as expected. He turned to look in Cowboy's direction. Hawk came up behind him, grabbed his chin, and pulled his head back as far as it would go, then drove his knife deep into the side of the guard's neck, cutting his carotid artery and forcing the knife forward cutting through his throat. When the knife stopped he pulled the blade across his neck from the inside and his head lay back supported only by his spinal cord. He was dead without a sound.

Hawk slipped over into the abyss suddenly. They were watching the guard at the front of the tent where the target was sitting at a small table eating. They had been out for ten days, working their way into NVA country. Using direction finding by crossing radio signals picked up by a bird dog in the air and Cowboy's in the jungle, they had pinpointed where the commander of the NVA force was located. It had taken another day to work their way to the camp. Cowboy made a click with his knife on his helmet, and both the guards moved away from the tent and toward him. Hawk came up behind the closest guard and killed him with his knife. Cowboy took the other one with his knife as he turned to see what happened to the other guard. No noise. Hawk walked over to the tent flap and drew it back exposing the commander. In two steps Hawk pushed the commander's chair back and killed him with his knife. No noise. They were leaving as quietly as they came.

***

Someone grabbed Hawk's arm and shook him. Again, the shake. "Come on, man." In a whisper. Hawk shook his head and held on to Cowboy's shirt to steady himself. "Come on, man. We've got to get find this guy and di di mau."

Hawk saw Cowboy first, and then Liz. She looked at him like she was scared to death. Hawk told them he was good, and they moved around to the side of the villa looking for an open window or door. They had no luck until they reached the back patio. The sliding door was open, and only a screen was closed. Cowboy thought, "This guy must not like AC."

They moved the screen only enough to slide through and entered the living area. Off to the right were a dining room and a kitchen. A long hallway led away from the living room. When they had cleared the front rooms, they started to go down the hall where the bedrooms had to be. Hawk stopped with his hand up, listening to very soft Spanish. He pointed to Cowboy to follow him to the first door on the right. They both had their guns out, working down the hall one on each wall. They reached the door, and Cowboy took a quick look. He held up two fingers and pointed left and right, then to himself. Hawk nodded. Cowboy went into the room in a crouch firing two times. Hawk followed him in and found a television playing a porn DVD playing. There was a dead man lying beside a small bunk bed, and another on the floor near a sofa. Cowboy cleared a closet, and they both went to the hall again. Liz was waiting at the door with her Walther in her hand.

The next room looked much larger than the first. They peeked in and saw a king bed, and clothes on the floor, a single soft light in the bathroom, and two lumps in the bed under a silk sheet. Cowboy stayed at the door while Liz and Hawk went to throw the sheet back. There were a middle-aged man and a young girl in her early teens asleep in the bed. The man sat up in the bed and yelled for help. Hawk dragged him out of bed by the hair and told Liz to hit the bedroom light. When she did, she gave a gasp.

"This him?" asked Hawk.

"Yes, that's him," said Liz.

The young girl had sat up in bed and started to scream bloody murder, until Cowboy quieted her by telling her in Spanish that they were taking the man, not her, and she was free to go home. That seemed to calm her down. Cowboy went back into the hallway and cleared the rest of the rooms in the house. By then, Liz and Hawk had the jefe tied with pillow slips, with one around his head and a sock stuck in his mouth. They moved out the front door in a group with the jefe in front. No one was there. They hustled him down to the truck and put him between Hawk and Cowboy. Liz rode in the back with the sliding rear window of the cab open so they could communicate. Hawk turned around and headed back into Mérida.

22:10 - 19 AUGUST

TZ S

Hawk drove to the Zocalo and turned south heading out of town on a highway that led to the city named Valladolid. At the first jungle cart path that looked like it might have a shack of some sort at its end, he drove till the path stopped, and then pulled the truck over into the jungle to hide it. Cowboy pulled his flashlight from his backpack, and they all followed him to a shack made of sticks, with the inside of the walls covered with tar paper. The door was on leather shoe-tongue hinges. The floor was packed dirt with a few stones and a grate over them to cook on. There were two windows in the small walls covered with old burlap sacks. Candles were on a narrow shelf near the stone cooking area. One oil lamp was set back behind the cooking area where two rickety chairs sat, on either side of an old shipping crate marked with pictures of oranges and the Spanish word *Naranjas*, stamped on it in ink.

Cowboy and Hawk pushed the man down to the dirt floor and tied him to one of the main poles of the roof and took off the pillow slip around his head that held the sock in his mouth. The oil lamp was lighted, and it cast a flickering, spooky light in the little one-room shanty. Liz took the other chair and sat behind the man called jefe so he couldn't see her. She kept her Walther in her hand.

When the man's eyes began to adjust to the light after taking the pillowcase off his face, he said, "Whoever you are, you are dead men. Who are you, and what do you want?"

Hawk sat on the remaining chair and looked at him. After a few moments, he asked the jefe what his name was. There was no answer. He waited again, and he told the man he could make it easy on himself or they could do it the hard way. He reached over and slapped the man's face as hard as he could.

For the first time, a hint of concern and fear started to show in the man's eyes.

"Who are you, and what do you want?" he said again, this time with a hint of fear in his voice.

"What is your name?" Hawk asked again. He waited and then hit the man in the face with his fist. It broke his nose, and blood flushed from it like red paint pouring from a bucket.

The man started to slightly move his body back and forth in a rocking motion, and his lips started to quiver. Tears started to flow down his face.

"My name is Phillipe Carillo Peneda. What do you want of me?"

"That's better. I am going to ask you questions about a woman you kidnapped from a man named D'Arcy. Her name is Liz Stillings. If you answer my questions I will not punish you more. There is something more important about this woman than just being a dancer and sex slave in your clubs. I want to know what that is."

"Her father has been told we want a ransom for her."

"I know that," said Hawk. "There is more. Why is she important enough to you to start a war with D'Arcy?"

"Her father's ranch borders the Rio Grande, and we want to use it to pass our drugs into the United States. No one will suspect a senator of allowing that to happen. It would be perfect."

Hawk nodded to himself and asked, "How did you find this out about her father's ranch, and how did D'Arcy know when to kidnap her?"

"I have a man working for D'Arcy. He came to tell me all this and that I should take her away from him. He told me the girl's boyfriend contacted D'Arcy's cartel and told him about the ranch and when she would cross the border. When the ransom is paid she was to be kept as insurance for the safe passage of my drugs in the US."

"And what was this boyfriend getting for his part in all this?"

"He is going to handle my cartel's business in South Texas."

"What was your plan for her after the ransom was paid?" Hawk asked.

"She's a troublemaker. I would have made her dance and do sex for as long as my drugs were going into the US, and if that stopped she would have been disposed of like all the rest."

"I am finished with you, but there is someone here that may not be," Hawk said.

"I have answered your questions. Please don't kill me," he sobbed.

"I'm not going to kill you," said Hawk.

Liz stood and walked in front of Peneda as Hawk stepped away. The look on Peneda's face grew to one of terror.

"I have one question. Did my boyfriend make this deal before or after he met me?" asked Liz.

"Before, I think. He told D'Arcy's man that he would be able to control you with the drugs."

Liz Stillings leveled her Walther and pulled the trigger. A hole appeared in Peneda's forehead as it slammed back against the pole he was tied to.

"You asked the wrong person not to kill you. Dumb ass!" said Liz Stillings as she walked through the stick door of the hut, never looking back.

They were quiet as they made their way to the truck hidden off the road in the jungle. When they were back in the truck and on their way, there was some quiet talk between Hawk and Cowboy about their next move. Liz was still quiet. When the next cart path came up on the other side of the road Hawk pulled into it and backed out, heading in the direction of Mérida.

"Where are we headed? I thought we were going after D'Arcy now," Liz said.

"We're heading back to Mérida to take you to the embassy now that it is safe to do so," Hawk said.

"I'm not going back until D'Arcy is taken care of one way or the other."

"Oh yes you are, and no arguing will change that," Hawk said.

"Okay, try this," she said. "I know the way to Playa del Carmen. I know where his villa is in Playa del Carmen. I know what he looks like. I know what the men guarding and working with him look like. I know where he keeps his boat, and I know what his plane on Cozumel looks like."

Hawk pulled off the side of the road. He waited until the truck had come to a halt, and asked Cowboy what he thought about Liz going along with them as only a recognition person. Cowboy shrugged his shoulders as he told Hawk that it would make sense to have someone along that could identify the people they were looking for and knew the places they lived.

Liz was sitting in the middle and moving her head left and right listening to the two men talk about her like she wasn't there. Hawk looked at her and told her she was in, but no work as part of the operational team. At this, she pulled out her Walther and jacked out the empty casing from the barrel and said, "Sure thing, Hawk," with a wink to Cowboy.

"First chance we get, Cowboy, send a message to Captain Jack and tell him she's okay."

"Will do. We'd better find a place to stay on the way to Playa del Carmen to go over the plan and have Liz clue us in on the people and places we'll be going up against," Cowboy said.

"Liz, do you know of a place that we can do a planning session?" asked Hawk.

"I saw a little beachfront village between Playa del Carmen and Tulum where the road joins with the beach road. Its name was Paamul, I think. There should be a place to stay and make plans. It's only fifteen minutes from Playa."

Hawk started the truck back on the road and did another turnaround at the next path leading into the jungle. They passed through numerous small pueblos along the way. All were dirt poor with children in ragged clothes or no clothes at all running in the same weeds and hard-packed dirt as the pigs and goats. There was a burnt bus halfway in a deep ditch along the road and half in the jungle. No people were near it. The jungle had burned with it. Not far from the bus there was a series of curves going through a swamp area. A car was off the road half submerged in the water and reeds. Since they had driven into Mexico, both Hawk and Cowboy had near misses with the speed-crazed Mexican drivers. The wrecks they had passed in the mountains and along the curving roads near Veracruz were too numerous to count.

09:17 - 20 AUGUST

TIME ZONE ROMEO

They rented a small beachfront house for the night near a small restaurant in Paamul. The water was crystal clear on the beach and turquoise colored in deeper water near a small reef. They hadn't eaten since the tacos last night, so they locked up the truck and went into the open-air café and ordered beer and freshly grilled seafood. The Montejo beer was cold, and the seafood platter was served on a huge platter for the three of them. Beer and seafood seem odd to them for breakfast, but the little café didn't offer breakfast. They were so hungry the platter was soon cleaned off. The owner of the little café on the beach came for the platter with a smile and another cold beer for each of them. The little beach house had two bedrooms and a bath. There was a hammock between two posts that were holding up the palapa roof, where the beach ended and a tile floor started for the house. There was also a screen door. A fan in the small sitting area in the house kept it cool, and the screened door let the air in, but not the mosquitos. They turned on the fan hanging down from the palm frond ceiling, and even though they were tired they began making a plan for finding D'Arcy and taking care of him. Cowboy suggested that the three of them enter Playa del Carmen together.

"Do you remember if there are other villas or apartments near his so we can set up surveillance?" asked Cowboy.

"There are other villas near it that have two stories. You should be able to see his villa and the pool area if the right place can be rented," answered Liz.

"Okay," Hawk said, "you spot his villa, and one of us will go with you somewhere that you won't be recognized, while the other one will find a suitable place to rent for the surveillance. We will also use it for our operational hide. Liz, once we get into the rental, you will have to stay there. We can't take a chance on you being seen, and you have to spot D'Arcy for us."

Cowboy said, "What about the big deal that is coming into Puerto Morelos. Don't we need to keep track of that at the same time?"

"Let's say you take the truck to Puerto Morelos and keep eyes on the incoming shipments after we rent a place. Liz will keep eyes on D'Arcy's place, and since no one knows me, I'll be moving around the area where the villa is or in town watching for anything out of the ordinary and noting any weak places into his compound," suggested Hawk.

"Liz, you'll need to keep track of all the warm bodies in the compound at any time so we know what we are up against. The rental will have to be close so you can watch the front for people coming and going also. You good with that?" added Cowboy.

"What about some type of still camera like a Polaroid or a movie camera so I can make a file of his men so you can learn what they look like as well as D'Arcy himself?" Liz asked.

"Great idea. I'll check for camera shops while I'm out. There must be a Polaroid of some type in Playa. This may not happen on the first day we are on watch. I'll get food and use a cab to bring it all to the rental. No one will suspect anything with it being a new rental."

Cowboy suggested they get some sleep, and they all agreed. He went out to re-lock the truck and close up the front door. Liz took one of the small bedrooms, and Cowboy the other. Hawk figured Cowboy needed rest more than he did. Hawk unhooked the hammock that hung outside and hooked it to two supports on the roof near the little kitchen area. He was sound asleep in no time.

Cowboy took over the driving the next day, with Liz in the middle of the bench seat. The sunrise was spectacular over the Caribbean water. The owner of the café had coffee for them. It was black and strong. There were tortillas, fresh and handmade by the owner's wife. The pathway out from the beach was filled with holes that would swallow any vehicle coming close to them. Cowboy worked the truck right and then left and right again trying to reach the road with the truck in one piece. After some final jolts and creaks and cracks from the truck being twisted in weird positions, they made it to the blacktop highway and headed north to Playa del Carmen.

09:12 - 21 AUGUST

TIME ZONE ROMEO

Carlos D'Arcy sat in a large leather chair, smoking a Cuban cigar and drinking Chivas Regal scotch with ice. He had been informed of the raid by the Yucatán Cartel and the taking of all the women at the club, including the blond American woman, that had been so much trouble earlier in the month. He was in a murderous mood, knowing that his plan for easy access into the US for his drugs had suddenly been taken away. He had ordered his best man, Nacho, to find out what had happened and where the other cartel may have taken her. Nacho had just returned telling him that the Yucatán Cartel leader Phillipe Carillo Peneda and his cartel were the ones that took the women from the club.

"I found out from the police you bribe that there was another raid of some kind that night at a beachfront villa west of Mérida. Peneda was the owner. There were four or five men killed by an explosion and gunfire at the ranch. Peneda wasn't one of them. All the women were gone including the American. Two nights later, a body was found along a narrow road to the east of Mérida by an old man making his way to a nearby abandoned shack he had been using. When he opened the door, he found the body. It was well into the morning by the time he made it back to the police in Mérida. The identification on the body was that of Peneda," Nacho told him.

D'Arcy stood up and threw the tumbler of scotch at Nacho barely missing him. "So now you are telling me some unknown group has killed Peneda's men that did the raid, and then found Peneda and killed him, and they took the American woman too. Is that what you intend for me to believe?" He stomped his way to the floor-to-ceiling windows looking out on the pool and kicked them as hard as he could. The glass in the tall door shattered into a thousand pieces.

Nacho stood very still, his eyes wide open and mouth agape. He knew when el jefe was wild and angry at the same time, anything could happen. He waited quietly until Carlos shuddered and shook himself, half turning his head to look at Nacho.

Nacho looked down at the tiled floor. He knew el jefe didn't like people making eye contact with him after one of his moments. He said quietly, almost to himself, "That is what the police believe, jefe. They have no idea where they may have gone."

Carlos turned, still fuming. "I want you to take our best men and go back to Mérida and make a deal with the remainder of the Yucatán Cartel to join us. That will make us in control of all of the peninsula and make it much easier to move the product from Cuba to the Gulf of Mexico for transport to the US. I want all our informants, both here and in Mérida, to look for anyone that may be connected to the group that hit Peneda. It could be a new group, or maybe one from the Veracruz area trying to take over. And I want that girl back, or my plan will fail."

"As you wish, jefe. I will leave immediately."

"Kill all of our people that let the raid on the club happen and the girl be taken."

"It will be done as you want, jefe."

"After you take care of things in Mérida, leave the men there to continue taking over, and come back here. The shipment is due in a few days. This new group may know about it. They may try to intercept it someway. I will need you here to oversee its transport to the villa when it is unloaded from the ship at Puerto Morelos. Now get out of my sight."

D'Arcy went to the wet bar and got another tumbler and filled it halfway with scotch and a couple of ice cubes. He went out to the palapa next to the pool and tried to figure out what was happening to his plans and who the people were that were trying to destroy everything he had built through the years. He was only forty years old but had been moving or selling drugs since he was eight years old. He knew from past experience he had to find the group tearing apart his hard work and plans. He would find them and kill them all. Then he remembered the phone call from Rodrigo. He walked into the study and called the private number in the United States. It was answered on the first ring.

"Who is calling?"

"This is your friend down south," said Carlos.

"Why are you calling?"

"I think maybe the two men you told me about have the girl now," Carlos growled.

"I was going to call you today. I have more info for you."

"And what is that?" Carlos asked.

"The mission also includes you."

"What do you mean, me?" asked Carlos.

"To take you out."

"I will add more layers of protection. My men are much better than the ones they faced in Mérida. If they come, they are the ones that will be taken out," he shouted.

D'Arcy hung the phone up.

He yelled for Mario, a man that he trusted as much as he trusted anyone. Mario was a Mestizo by birth. Taller than most mixed-blood Mexicans. His Caribbean ancestry was obvious. He was of slender build, with only lean muscle on his frame. His eyes were cruel, black orbs, and he had a knife scar running across his right cheek to his ear, where the top part was missing. He walked to the palapa and stood before his master without saying a word.

"Mario, I am concerned there will be an attempt to take the shipment from me when it arrives. We must make a trap to stop those who would take it from me. I want two men to go on board the ship and get in the cab of the truck before it is offloaded. They should remain hidden. There will be another man on the dock to drive the truck. We will have a car waiting between Puerto Morelos and here. Men hidden along the road also. You will follow in a car well back from the truck. We will need one ready to speed toward the halfway point from Playa. Can you think of anything else?"

"Jefe, that will take all the available men, to do what you want. There will be no one to guard it when it arrives at the villa."

"Have all the men involved in getting the shipment here stay here to watch over the shipment during the time it is waiting to be transported by the airplane to Mexico City."

"I will select the men to take with me carefully, jefe. You pay the army to stay away. I will get some of the best they have to guard with me."

"Perfect, Mario. Go now to start laying the trap."

D'Arcy leaned back on his lounge chair pleased with himself and took a deep drink of his favorite scotch.

Hawk turned right off the highway, where a sign indicated the ferry pier to Cozumel was located. Liz told him to go to the crossing street nearest the pier. She watched the surroundings closely as they drove down the unpaved street toward the pier and beach, looking for things she remembered from when she was a captive being brought to D'Arcy's villa. When they drew closer to the beach it became apparent to them all that there was no pier at the end of the dirt and sand street they were on. Instead, there was a wood dock long enough for a small passenger ferry to tie up and load and unload people, luggage, and small commercial items. There were a few small fishing boats pulled up on the beach. Small huts where the fishermen lived were strung out along the edge of the jungle and beach. The water was crystal clear, and farther out from the beach the water turned from turquoise to a deep purple, almost black color.

Liz asked Hawk to stop when they reached the beach road in front of the dock. She looked past Cowboy, and then the other direction, past Hawk. The sand tract that served for a beach street ended in the jungle several hundred yards to the north past Hawk.

"Turn to the right," she told Hawk, there is a small group of villas on the beach, and D'Arcy's villa is just off them in the jungle down this road. There is a right turn that leads deeper into the jungle. That is where D'Arcy's place is. It is near the beach, but secluded with a narrow car path leading to it and some other villas, in a circle. Each with a high-security wall and jungle around it. Liz scooted down on the bench seat, low enough so her eyes cleared the dashboard. The sand tract angled away from the beach and through the slightly cleared jungle past a small Mayan temple, and then back again to the beach. When the tract came near the beach again it ran between and around tall palms bent or leaning from the wind that blew in from the east.

Up ahead they could make out the first of the beach villas built of stone, mortar, and block. They looked for signs of people staying in the villas as they went past, but only one had a car parked in the palms behind the villa. They came to a narrow tract leading away from the beach, and Liz told Hawk and Cowboy that D'Arcy's villa was down the narrow palm and jungle-lined tract.

Hawk pulled off the tract into some low-lying brush, and stopped. He didn't want to go off the tract too far and end up stuck in the sand, but needed to have it out of sight.

"How far up the trail is his villa?" asked Hawk.

"I don't know exactly. Maybe a hundred yards or less, and before you get to the villas there is a slight bend to the left in the trail, then a turnaround area, with a trail running in a large circle for access to all the villas."

"Okay, Cowboy and I will recon the area. Which villa is D'Arcy's?"

"It's right in front of the cleared turnaround. It has a high gate large enough for large cars or trucks to enter, with an arch over the top. I remember a guard standing on some type of ledge or platform on one side of the arch, watching the turnaround and the circle to the other villas."

Cowboy went to the bed of the truck and lifted a tarp. He pulled out two M-16s, two ammo pouches, and two prick sixes. He handed one of the walkie-talkies to Hawk, who was standing by the driver's-side door, and walked off into the jungle. Hawk paused for a minute and told Liz to hunker down in the cab and keep her pistol cocked and locked.

"When we are close to the truck again, I'll call out TEXAS so you know who we are."

He walked off into the jungle with the M-16 at the ready position, and hooked up with Cowboy a short distance away. They made a plan and split up as they had done many times before in a different jungle, not so long ago. Cowboy slipped across the trail and out of sight in the jungle. Hawk worked his way slowly through the low brush from palm to palm, watching the ground and his front for anything that was not normal or shouldn't be there. He figured D'Arcy might have placed trips and pits similar to what the VC used in Vietnam.

Cowboy had his prick six's volume turned down so only he would hear it. When he heard a single click, he knew Hawk had the open area in sight. He clicked twice and moved on watching out for the same things Hawk had. When he had the clearing and the front of D'Arcy's villa in sight, he did one click and waited.

Hawk checked the top of the wall, and the arch, looking for the guard Liz had told them about. He didn't see the guard at first, but then on his second sweep of the arch, he saw the barrel of what looked like an AK-47 sticking past the arch on the right side. After checking out the front of the villa, he clicked three quick clicks and moved off to his left in the brush along the circle trail to the other villas. He knew Cowboy was doing the same, but going to his right. They would meet up around the middle of the circle.

Hawk and Cowboy joined up and worked their way back to the truck, being as careful as when they were going to the clearing.

They saw the truck sitting in the same place. Hawk called, "TEXAS."

"Come in slow, and you better be the boys," Liz called back.

Hawk got the truck back on the sand tract going toward the beach. It was quiet in the cab. He turned back toward the dock, but then turned into the second beach villa. He had seen a Se Renta sign tacked to the one-car garage as they passed it the first time.

"Let's check this place out and work out our next move."

They walked around to the front of the house where a freshwater pool took up the entire length of the villa. There was a small palapa for shade, and beach chairs and a table with chairs around the pool area, facing the beach and the Caribbean. They checked to make sure there wasn't anyone staying there. Under the shade of the palapa Cowboy and Hawk talked with each other, telling Liz at the same time about the recon. The guard was still in place at the front. They had discovered another sentry at each side of the wall. They couldn't see the back of the wall for the jungle and the other villas blocking the line of sight. A smart assumption would be a fourth guard was there. The walls appeared to be nine or ten feet high with the same type of broken glass as the walls around the beach ranch villa. Cowboy saw the palapa as he circled to the right side of the villa.

Hawk and Cowboy agreed there wasn't any good place to set up the surveillance post. Too much jungle and too many other villas with high walls to see down into the compound. They figured getting into the compound could be done like the beach ranch house when and if they needed to enter the compound. Hawk told Cowboy and Liz he felt the best option for the surveillance would be to rent the villa where they were. If he could rent it for a month, Liz could use the upstairs windows and balcony over the garage to keep track of the movements to and from D'Arcy's. Liz would know how many men were there, what type of vehicles were used, and when D'Arcy was at the villa.

Cowboy went around to the garage and wrote down the name and address of the local agent renting the villa. Hawk and Liz stayed at the villa while Cowboy went into the village to find the rental agent. Cowboy parked the truck near the ferry dock and asked a young woman sitting in the ticket sales box on the dock where he could find the agent on the sign. She gave him directions of a block north on the jungle side of the beach track. When he found the office, it was closed for siesta. There was a man in a hammock strung between two palms at the edge of the beach. Cowboy took a chance and walked over to the man and asked if he knew when the rental office would again be open. To his surprise the man rolled out of the hammock, and with Cowboy in tow walked over to the office telling Cowboy he was the agent and was always open for a rental. Cowboy haggled with the agent and came to a reasonable fee for a month-long rental. He left the rental office and headed to a grocery store the agent had told him about. He brought the basic food groups: hot dogs, buns, mustard, an onion, and hot sauce. He had a bag of potato chips and a bag of Mexican deep-fried corn chips.

Cowboy walked around the corner of the villa carrying two boxes. He smiled at the two under the palapa and said, "I'm home. Anyone hungry?"

Cowboy opened the patio door and walked into the tiled living area facing the pool and the beach. Liz went in and started to check what was in the boxes of supplies Cowboy had purchased at the small grocery. Liz and Cowboy set about unloading the boxes and filling the fridge with bottled water and other perishables. Liz walked over to the stairs and went up. Cowboy was close behind, with Hawk following, after he had found a snack he liked. There were a large master bedroom and bath facing the Caribbean, and two smaller ones facing the sand track and jungle at the back of the villa. Both had private baths. All three agreed this was the best hide they were going to find close to D'Arcy's compound.

Hawk went down and started to unload the pickup. He brought in and started to set up the spotting scope and binoculars. He moved a small nightstand to the double window in the back bedroom, to put the scope on. Then he brought in most of the guns and ammunition from the truck, stacking them near the stairs for easy access. He took one of the prick sixes, and left one in the cab of the truck under the seat, and locked the doors.

By the time all this was completed, Cowboy and Liz had food warming up on the gas range. Hawk looked in the fridge and took three cold beers out. He put the bottle caps against the kitchen counter one at a time and hit the top with the palm of his hand. The caps dropped to the tiled kitchen floor. Each with a clicking noise. He took the bottles out to the patio and waited for the others to bring the hot dogs, buns, and hot sauce. Liz had a bag of chips in one hand and the mustard in the other. They talked about what needed to be done next, between bites and swigs of cold beer.

By the time the American meal was finished and a second beer for each was sitting on the table with pearls of moisture dropping down the bottles, Hawk and Cowboy had worked out who was best fitted for which job. Because Cowboy was Mexican and looked the part, he was going to take the pickup each day and watch the dock in Puerto Morelos for the shipment that was expected by D'Arcy. Liz, of course, would keep track of the men coming and going, and when D'Arcy was staying at the compound. Hawk was darker and could pass for a Mestizo. He would spend his days in the village and pick up any information he could from people coming and going around the ferry dock area.

That night with a full moon and clear skies, Hawk helped Cowboy string antenna wire between several palms on the beach and connect it to the transmitter in Cowboy's bedroom. He and Hawk worked out the wording of the message to be sent to Captain Jack. Cowboy got busy with the day pad and encrypted the message.

Liz heard a muffled noise coming from Cowboy's room and walked to the door to see what was happening. She had never heard or seen anyone sending Morse code. She wanted to watch what was happening, because of the discussion earlier about stringing wire and sending a message to someone. Cowboy was sending Morse code so rapidly she thought it was one long noise as she watched his hand work the key. He was looking down at a paper he was holding in his left hand, and working the key at the same time with his right hand. She didn't understand all there was to it, but it was a sight to see Cowboy sending the message while reading it at the same time. Cowboy ended the transmission, then reached up to the transceiver and adjusted a dial.

Liz leaned near Hawk's ear and whispered, "What's he doing now?"

Hawk answered in a whisper, "He's changing the frequency. Even though the message is encrypted, he sends on one frequency and then receives on another predetermined frequency to make it impossible to intercept both ends of the transmission. There will be an answer to his transmission later at a predetermined time. It gives the other operator time to gather any information requested, and make sure the operator that sent the message is available to receive the answering transmission."

"So for now he's finished. How long will it take to get the return message?"

"It varies. That's always set up in the first message. It will be a long enough time to contact anyone other than the operator that can answer questions in the message or give instructions. If the time is hours away, he knows he can do other things, and return to the transceiver just before the time for the return message."

"Okay, I'm still a little confused, but think I understand the basics. Thanks for walking me through it," she whispered.

"You can talk normally now. I'm finished until midnight," Cowboy said with a wink and a smile.

Liz was asleep when the two men sat down by the radio to wait for the incoming message. Cowboy put on his headset and plugged it into the transceiver so no outside noise would keep him from hearing or concentrating on the code being sent. He usually had a typewriter called a Mill, which had only capital letters to copy with. He was writing on a pad of paper that would be burned later, since it wasn't possible to haul a Mill with them on the mission. When the transmission ended he signed off and reached for the day pad to decrypt the message.

It took an hour to decrypt using the day pad. When he was finished, Hawk stood over his shoulder and read the message:

GOOD WORK. WILL TELL FATHER. FEDS WILL WATCH BOYFRIEND.

D'ARCY'S BROTHER IN FRANCE, NVA GENERAL ALL CONNECTED.

D'ARCY, GENERAL, UNIVERSITY AT SAME TIME. PARIS.

BROTHER, CARLOS, OWN ALTAMAR SHIPPING, FRENCH PORT MARSEILLE.

"Great, we are tasked to find and terminate Carlos D'Arcy, who is down the road from us in Playa del Carmen, Mexico, and Captain Jack is giving us information about his connections around the world, and in particular France and Vietnam. This information is about as useful as what we used to get before heading out on a mission in Nam," Cowboy said angrily.

"We'll have to do exactly what we did back then. Make our own assessment, gather our own intel, and make our own plan, because the stuff we get from Captain Jack will get us killed," Hawk suggested.

07:20 - 22 AUGUST

TZ ROMEO

All three were up with coffee on the patio watching rays of red, orange, and yellow as the sun rose in the east. Cotton ball clouds picked up the colors on their undersides, making a kaleidoscope of colors, twisting and turning, shooting lances out from east to west.

Cowboy fixed one of his favorite breakfasts for everyone. Chorizo and scrambled eggs with hot sauce on the side. After finishing breakfast and cleaning up, Hawk and Cowboy headed out as planned. Liz was already at the desk with the spotting scope in her room when they left.

Cowboy dropped Hawk off, away from the dock. Hawk walked around the block, then to the dock area.

Cowboy parked in an alley not far from the pier, that was used as a trash dump. He walked around the small central square area until he saw the lighthouse at the entrance to the port. It was leaning sideways, like the photos he had seen in history books of the Leaning Tower of Pisa in Italy. He spotted an old woman selling tamales and asked her why the tower was like that. She told him a hurricane came through the year before and blew it over. He bought six of the spicy pork tamales, thanked the lady, and continued his walk around the port. There was a car ferry at the dock getting ready to go over to Cozumel, and a small tug to help maneuver ships coming into the port. There were a few *pangas* already back from the morning fishing, floating in the quiet waters of the port. The port water had trash floating all over it. There was a film of oil and fuel floating around with the trash. Cowboy thought, "With one flipped match the whole port would go up."

Hawk spent the morning watching the traffic moving along the main road to the ferry dock, and checking out the various stores along the hard-packed dirt road. He walked by a small wine and liquor store where a display of Chivas Regal scotch was in the glass storefront. He had never had that particular scotch, but knew of it by its reputation. He wondered how much it cost in Mexico, and decided to go in and check. He asked the store owner, who was behind a small counter, how much a bottle of Chivas cost. He was surprised at how much it cost. The owner told him there was a big import tax on foreign liquors. Then the owner pointed out two cases of Chivas sitting over in the corner and told Hawk it was cheaper to buy the case, but the two sitting in the corner were a special order for a very rich local man. It seemed like a long shot, but Hawk asked the store owner for the name of the rich local man.

"Senor, his name is Carlos D'Arcy, and I always keep two cases in the store for him. Do you know him, senor?" said the liquor store owner.

"No, I thought I might, but no, I don't know him. What about selling me one of the cases?"

"No, I can't sell them, senor. He has asked me to have it for him. He is to pick it up for a party at his villa in the next few days. It is always the same. His car pulls up to the front door, and his driver opens the trunk, senor D'Arcy comes in and pays, and the driver takes them to the trunk. They drive off. If he is in a good mood, he always gives me a *propina*. Sometimes the tip is big, and if he is not happy about something it is little, but there is always a tip."

Hawk couldn't believe his luck. He and Liz were watching every car and truck moving in and out of Playa del Carmen trying to locate D'Arcy and make sure he was in his villa so they could take him down, and here was the perfect place to finish the mission. All he needed to do was watch this little liquor store to locate Carlos D'Arcy. They could take him out at the store, or wait for the party. Hawk quickly discarded taking him out at the store. There would be too many possible witnesses in the area. Better to do it during or right after the party. He could hardly wait to tell Cowboy and Liz about their good fortune.

He bought two six packs of Dos Equis beer, to have their own little party, and as he walked out of the store he asked again, "Senor D'Arcy comes to pick up the scotch himself, always?"

"Si, senor, always."

Hawk decided to walk back to the rented villa with the beer. There was no need to keep surveillance on anything but the liquor store. He kept running the new information over and over in his head trying to see a problem with waiting for him there. Then when the people for the party started driving up to the villa, they would know it was time to start the take-out plan. When he reached the rental villa, he put the beer in the fridge and walked upstairs calling out "Texas" so Liz wouldn't shoot him. He was back hours before he was planning on returning.

Liz met him at the top of the stairs, with her Walther at her side. She said, "What the hell are you doing back so early? You scared the crap out of me."

Hawk quickly told her about the man at the liquor store and what he had told him about D'Arcy. When he finished, Liz looked at him with a smile a yard wide on her face.

"What're you smiling about? You look like a Cheshire cat."

"The party, it has to be the shipment everyone is waiting for. It must be coming in and he is having a party to celebrate. All we have to do is keep watch for the shipment, or watch for him to pick up the liquor, and we'll know when to work the plan. It seems so simple it's kinda scary."

Hawk told her she was right about the party being connected to the liquor store. They would talk it over with Cowboy when he came back in the late evening, and start working the new plan. She told him not much had happened while she was watching for cars to go to or from the villa, but she did see a car with four men in it, and the one sitting in the front right seat was the man called Nacho. They decided she should continue watching the beach trail. They needed to know when and if Nacho came back to the villa. He was figured to be in control of D'Arcy's security.

They waited for Cowboy to come back from Puerto Morelos, to have an evening meal. When he drove in and parked near the garage, Hawk went out and told him what had happened at the liquor store. He hopped up and down several times and asked if Hawk had remembered to buy more beer. Hawk popped the tops on the longnecks, and all three enjoyed the cold beer after getting a break that no one could have known was coming their way. Dinner was hot dogs again with chorizo sausage and beans from a can.

Cowboy said, "This is a gourmet meal compared with the stuff we ate in the Nam. Yes sir, a real party. Cold beer and warm food. What we need is a little music to top the party off." Cowboy went to his room and dug out half of a cedar shingle with some wires screwed to it. He went back to the palapa and told Hawk to run a wire to the palm next to the palapa where the antenna had been strung. He told Liz it was a homemade radio that he made. It was called a *foxhole radio*. Hawk had the antenna hooked up, and Cowboy moved the point of the safety pin on a razor blade that was fixed to the shingle, with a small speaker sitting to the side.

The little homemade radio came to life. "This is Wolfman Jack from XERF radio in Ciudad Acuna, bringing you the best in cool music all night long. We're using 250,000 watts. Everybody get naked and party." There was a long wolf howl then. The first song they heard was "Magic Carpet Ride" by Steppenwolf. Liz couldn't believe it. She said, "I used to listen to Wolfman when I couldn't sleep." Then came the CCR and "Suzie Q." Liz and Cowboy danced around the pool, laughing all the time. Hawk thought, "No one would believe those two were on a terminate mission for the president of the United States."

07:43 - 23 AUGUST

TZ R

Liz started the new day counting the number of people coming and going from the villa, and watching for D'Arcy's or Nacho's movements. Hawk, dressed in the new Mexican work clothes with a swimsuit under them, was going to spend the entire day moving from place to place, always keeping the liquor store in view. He found a hammock tied between two palms on the beach near the dock and spent most of the day there, with periods along the street, and in stores acting like he was shopping, and at several *luncherias* drinking coffee or having a beer and sandwich for lunch.

Cowboy went to the central square that had a view of the port entrance, moving around the port, the village, and along the beach to the north of town. The small shop and café owners started thinking of him as a local. The ferry came and went on a loose schedule, but no ships reached port and docked. There were ships that moved up and down the Yucatán Channel going to Central America, or to countries along the northern part of South America. The ships moving north through the channel were going to Mexican and American ports around the Gulf of Mexico, and a few docked at ports in Cuba. When a ship appeared on the horizon headed into or out of the channel, his heart rate picked up with a short surge of adrenalin, but soon returned to normal when they didn't make the turn to Puerto Morelos.

This continued for three days. They didn't allow themselves to become bored or lazy about the mission, or their individual assignments. They knew they were dealing with a ruthless cartel leader that would kill them in a minute. They always kept the edge.

10:12 - 26 AUGUST

TZ R

The morning of the fourth day things began to pop. Liz watched as Nacho came back to the cartel villa mid-morning. She couldn't let the guys know, but she felt it might be the start of the shipment coming and the party to celebrate its arrival. She had finished a late lunch in her bedroom when a car came down the jungle trail from the cartel villa and turned onto the beach trail headed for town. Carlos D'Arcy was in the back seat, with Nacho in the front passenger seat. A man she recognized as the one that drove her from the dock to the villa was driving this time too. Now she felt sure something big was about to happen.

Carlos was having a late breakfast on the patio when Nacho came through the floor-to-ceiling glass doors to the patio. He had his hat in his hand as he walked over to Carlos and began his report on the trip he had made to Mérida. Carlos noticed that he was turning the hat in circles and keeping his eyes to the ground. He figured Nacho was afraid that something he was going to tell him would make him angry.

"Jefe, I have done as you requested. I met with intermediate leaders of the Yucatán Cartel, and they have agreed to a temporary truce with us, until we can work out the finer points of them joining you. There was some dissension among them, but they finally realized that if they went to war with us, they would lose. The reason they raided your club was to get the American woman. I had the ones at the club that allowed the raid to happen killed, as you wanted. It seems that there is an informant within your cartel that told them about your plan to move product into America through the father's ranch along the border. They wanted to get the girl and use her in the same way."

"Did they tell you who the informant is in the cartel, Nacho?"

"Yes, jefe."

"Well, who is it, idiot?"

"It is the mother of your son, jefe. They told me she wanted money to take your son to America and to get away from you, jefe."

Carlos's face flushed red with anger. "When we are finished talking, I want her brought to me with the boy. Do you understand, Nacho?"

Nacho nodded his head up and down, not wanting to bring el jefe's anger down on himself.

"Continue your report."

"The men from Peneda's cartel told me they were in a running gunfight with a truck leaving his ranch house, after everyone there was killed. The American woman was seen in the cab of the truck. There were only two men with her. They were lost in Mérida and a search was begun. Somehow these men found Peneda's Mérida compound. They killed the guards and took him to a small unused hut where he was tortured and killed. They believe there are only two men doing this, and the police have confirmed that as well."

"Not a group! It is only two men doing all this to Peneda and his cartel! How can that be? I want to know who these men are and where they are, sooner not later! I will take great delight in watching them die a slow death."

Carlos suddenly remembered what the traitor Rodrigo had told him: "The United States sent two men to get the girl, and you too."

Then Carlos got a devilish look on his face and said, "They did me a favor by killing Peneda. Now I am going to be head of the Peninsular Cartel. That means more money, more drugs to sell, more power. I will be like the leaders in Mexico City, Juárez, and Veracruz. No one will be able to stop me, and you, Nacho, will follow with me. Is that the end of your report?"

"Yes, jefe."

"I have been informed that the shipment will be in Puerto Morelos tomorrow. I am going to give a party tomorrow night. Have the villa staff make ready for it. I have two cases of Chivas at Chema's liquor store. Go with me to pick it up, and then we will go to the house of the woman who betrayed me. I will have much to celebrate at the party. As you will too, Nacho."

Hawk was swinging in the hammock after spending the morning watching the liquor store from every angle he could without being noticed by the local traffic. He had to make a special effort not to fall from the hammock when the large black sedan pulled up by the liquor store and parked parallel to the boardwalk. The driver opened his door and walked back to the rear passenger door. The passenger front door opened and a tall Mexican man stepped out and closed the car door. Hawk was very disappointed. The owner of the store had told him it was always the same. The driver and D'Arcy came by themselves. Then the driver opened the rear door and D'Arcy got out. Hawk knew it was him from Liz's description. The two men from the front seat carried the two boxes of Chivas

Regal to the trunk of the car. D'Arcy came out with a case of champagne and put it in the trunk with the other cases. The driver closed the door for D'Arcy, and then both men from the front seat took a last look around, got in the car, and drove off. Hawk watched as the car went down the unpaved street, and started walking back to the villa.

Liz had the prick six in the bedroom, and Hawk clicked it once to see if Cowboy was monitoring the channel. No click came back. Liz and Hawk went out under the palapa, with the handheld radio and cold soft drinks, to talk over what had happened during the day. Liz felt that with Nacho showing up and the liquor run happening, the party was imminent and that meant the shipment was due in the afternoon or the following day.

"I agree totally. We'll have to figure out how we are going to spot the shipment and what we will do then to take out D'Arcy. If it comes in today, Cowboy will let us know with the radio," said Hawk.

"I'm glad it is coming to an end. I am so tired of staying in this villa. I understand that a blond American woman walking around Playa del Carmen would be a dead giveaway, but it doesn't make it easier to sit in one spot for hours watching a trail in the sand," said Liz.

"It takes time to learn the patience to stay still and control your breathing. To keep your eye from fixating on one thing. You're doing a good job for a newbie," said Hawk.

"What the hell is a newbie?"

"You know, someone new to the game."

"Okay, oldbie, I'll keep checking the trail. Let me know when I've passed the time test," she said, and walked back into the villa and up the stairs.

"Now what the hell did I say to piss her off? I just don't get it. You tell a woman something nice about them and they turn it all around and make an ass out of you," thought Hawk.

13:01 - 26 AUGUST

TZ R

The big black sedan stopped in front of a small house on the far side of the highway. It was made of cement block. All the rooms were small because the house was small, more like a miniature condominium complex. The driver stayed in the car, and Nacho got out and opened the trunk. He handed Carlos a baseball bat as he walked by. Nacho followed him to the front door. The door was locked. Nacho reached around Carlos and unlocked it. He had a copy of the key made when she moved to the little house, in case Carlos wanted to visit.

The mother of his son stood in the little kitchen. When she saw it was D'Arcy, she threw the pot of beans she was stirring at him and tried to run past him to the stairs. Nacho blocked her.

"Where is the fucking boy?" Carlos asked, with his face savagely contorted and the ball bat slapping up and down in his palm.

The young woman was so frightened she couldn't speak. She saw him bring the bat up like he was about to hit a baseball, and she screamed hysterically. There was a sound like a watermelon being dropped on the floor as he hit her on the side of her head. She fell in a lump right where she was standing, dead. Carlos continued to hit her face and head until he could no longer recognize her as a human. He stepped back and wiped his face with his hand. It came away covered in blood and brain matter and small pieces of bone. He leaned against the bat until his breathing went back to normal.

"Go up and see if he is upstairs, Nacho."

"Yes, jefe."

Nacho went up the short flight of stairs. He came back to the head of the stairs and said, "He is here, jefe, taking a nap."

"Cut his throat, Nacho."

"Yes, jefe."

When Nacho came down the stairs, he said, "It is done, jefe."

"All those that would betray me need to know that I will do the same to them. No matter who they are, Nacho. Let all the men know what I did today."

"Yes, jefe."

The two men walked out to the big black sedan and drove away. Carlos D'Arcy didn't look back.

14:32 - 26 AUGUST

TZ R

Cowboy came back as the sun set in the west. He told Hawk and Liz that the shipment hadn't arrived, but there were a lot more men around the port. Most had pistols of one type or another, and a few were dressed in fatigues and berets, with AK-47s. Hawk told Cowboy about Nacho coming back and about the liquor run by D'Arcy. Cowboy cheered up at being told what had happened while he was at Puerto Morelos. They talked about the shipment. If Liz's idea about the party was right, then there would be a large number of people at the villa. That might help them.

"Now that we know the shipment is coming in, why do we care where it goes? Our mission is to terminate D'Arcy," Cowboy told Hawk.

"If we get lucky and the shipment is taken to the villa, maybe we get two birds with one stone," Hawk said.

"Wait a minute, so now the two of you are talking about crashing a party with who knows how many killers there, and destroying a load of drugs at the same time. I knew there was something off about you guys, but now I know what it is. You're both CRAZY," Liz said loudly as she got up and stomped off into the villa.

"Wow, that's twice today she's been pissed at me," Hawk said as he shook his head like he really had no clue what made women tick.

Cowboy looked at Hawk like he was a lost soul, and told him, "She's just concerned about us. Don't let her get to you just before we go into action, Hawk. Let's take time now to make our assault plan and then carry it through. We'll have all day tomorrow to refine it, but right now we need to get a basic mission plan completed. We have a party for cover and a shipment of drugs to keep the guards interested."

"Okay, Cowboy, let's make the final plan before the actions starts!" Hawk said, knowing Cowboy would react to it.

"The best plans are only good 'till the first shot is fired. Let's do this, Hawk!"

Liz calmed down after hearing the plan they had made, but was still anxious. She stayed at the villa to keep a count on the people coming and going to the cartel villa, while Hawk and Cowboy went to town to find some suitable clothing. They returned with another set each of guayaberas, and two pairs of linen slacks, a size too big.

The shipment still hadn't shown up at the cartel villa mid-afternoon. Hawk and Cowboy drove to Puerto Morelos to check it out. After Cowboy parked in the trash alley, they made their way to the port. No ship had docked since the evening before. Cowboy talked with one of the locals he had befriended, and was told for sure no ship had come to the port. That concerned them both. Maybe Liz's idea about the shipment coming in and Carlos having a celebration party was wrong. Maybe the shipment was coming some other way. They figured it wasn't possible to cover all the possible bases, so they decided to hang out near the port, until the sun dipped below the horizon.

Toward the evening, the port started to bustle with workers along the dock. Cowboy asked one of the men heaving heavy mooring rope closer to the edge of the dock, what was happening.

"The Altamar ship, *Maria Celieste*, has called in for docking. You should be able to see her turning in the channel from the north."

"How long before she docks?" Cowboy asked the longshoreman.

"Not long, senor. The port *capitán* has given them permission for immediate entry to the port. We must hurry and get the mooring cables ready," said the Mexican dock worker.

Cowboy and Hawk walked to the seawall, by the leaning lighthouse, and searched the channel to the north. Hawk saw it first. It was headed right for them and was hard to see with only the bow and superstructure pointed at them, out in the middle of the channel, about ten miles out.

After the *Maria Celieste* was docked, crewmen started opening the huge hatches on the deck. Hawk didn't notice any Mexican customs agents board the ship and thought they must have been paid off. A large crane rolled on its rails to the side of the ship. It lowered its loading cable and hook into the hole at the bow, giving slack until a deckhand signaled to stop. A few minutes later a white Dodge van was lifted from the hole and slowly moved across the ship to the unloading area on the dock. It had no windows in the back, and Hawk saw as it was lowered that there wasn't a window from the cab to the back either. The van had Texas plates on it. Two men hurried over to it and changed the plates to Quintana Roo, Mexican plates, and got in the cab. The driver had a pistol on his hip, and the passenger was carrying an AK-47. No customs agents appeared, and the truck moved off the dock and crossed over to the road, leading out of Puerto Morelos. Another car moved in behind the truck as it passed out of the small town.

Hawk and Cowboy went to their pickup and backed out of the trash alley in time to see the white van turn south on the coast highway, heading toward Playa del Carmen. Cowboy floored the gas pedal and quickly got on the highway. He slowed when they came to the trailing car. They quickly decided to move ahead of the little convoy, as if they were in a hurry to get somewhere. He changed to passing gear and went around the car. There were armed men in it. He continued in the left lane, running quickly up on the van and passing it. When they were past it, Hawk held the prick six in his hand and hit the squawk button. Liz heard the click from the one the boys had left with her. She almost jumped out of her chair. The shipment was docked and moving toward Playa. Hawk and Cowboy stopped at a gas station at the junction of the highway and the dirt road to the Cozumel ferry, and waited to see if the van was going to turn and head for the cartel villa. It did. Hawk winked and smiled at Cowboy as if to say, "It's going the way we hoped."

They spent the evening cleaning their guns and making sure they didn't show when they put them on. Both men had their silenced .22s strapped to their legs. When they put on the oversized linen slacks, Liz checked and made sure the guns didn't show. Hawk put his .45 ACP in the front of his slacks down by his crotch, and Cowboy did the same with his .357 Magnum. They figured if someone patted them down they would be okay. They spent the night sitting in Liz's room watching people go to the party. The music was loud enough for them to hear it from where they were.

03:00 - 27 AUGUST

TZ R

The three of them left at three in the morning. The count of people there had gone down as the night wore on. They stayed in the jungle by the side of the trail leading to the cartel villa, until they reached the circle road and the opening area where a few cars were still parked. Liz checked her Walther that she had cleaned one last time. She would be backup if all hell broke loose in the villa.

Hawk and Cowboy walked past the parked cars and casually waved at the guard on top of the wall behind the arch. The guard watched the men come to the large double door gate, and said something, looking down. The right-hand side of the gate was opened by another guard. He asked them to step inside, telling them he had to search them. There was a very casual pat down for both of them. It had to be less than a minute, and they were told to go ahead and enjoy themselves. They made it past the entry that opened onto a large living area with the back opening onto a patio and swimming pool. Floor-to-ceiling glass doors were open, with a nice breeze moving the silk curtains around softly. A waiter walked by with drinks on a large tray. Hawk grabbed one as Cowboy walked directly to a bar that took up the entire wall adjacent to the patio doors. He asked for a whiskey with ice. Most of the people still at the party were really drunk, or stoned, or coked out. Marijuana filled a large crystal bowl on a low table in front of a sofa. There was another bowl with rails of cocaine already laid out next to it. Bodies were lying around on the furniture and some on the floor, unable to walk. Some were asleep, some passed out.

Hawk and Cowboy began to carefully clear the house, one room at a time. The kitchen, off the living room, had a few cooks and servers sitting around waiting to be dismissed for the night. The two bathrooms were clear except for one stall where a couple had decided to have sex and ended up partially dressed on the floor, both passed out. The study was empty. Cowboy went to the desk where there were papers scattered around. He looked through them and came back to Hawk at the door, showing him a piece of paper on which he had written down a phone number. It was for the United States.

"I copied this from a phone list by the phone. Might be interesting to check it out later."

Hawk nodded, walked out the door, and started up the curving staircase to the second floor. They found all the bedrooms with people in various stages of undress and passed out on the floor, on furniture, and on the beds. The bathrooms had people hugging the toilets, and the same in the showers, which were running full blast. It looked like a hurricane had hit and left everyone in weird positions of rigor mortis. They talked quietly so they didn't wake any of the sleeping beauties up. Hawk was the one to identify D'Arcy since he had seen him at the liquor store. The last place to look was the pool area and garden. Both of them dropped their slacks and got the silenced .22s, pulled their pants back up, and walked down the stairs looking at the open doors to the pool.

"Stop where you are and put the weapons down, now." It came from a man standing in the open front door, dressed in camouflage, with an AK-47 pointed at them. Hawk stepped down to the next step and bent over as Cowboy was doing the same thing, one step above. They fired under their left arms, across their stomachs, hitting the soldier in the head and chest. The soldier must have had the safety off. He was knocked backward by the impact of the two rounds, but the AK went off, firing a string of rounds in the entry ceiling.

Cowboy said, "Oh shit, there goes the plan."

Yelling came from the pool area. Several men drawing their guns came running through the open doors. Hawk and Cowboy shot at the same time, hitting the two men—one in the head, the other in the neck. Cowboy ran over and put a round in the head of the one hit in the neck. There were several women lying on lounges, passed out by the pool, but still no Carlos. In fact, they hadn't seen Nacho either. There was gunfire from the wall, at the front of the compound. Several AKs firing and single shots from a pistol. Cowboy went to check the gunfight out, while Hawk went to the palapa area looking for one or both of the men. No one was under the palapa, but there was a big Cuban cigar burning next to an empty tumbler. Hawk picked the tumbler up and smelled it. Scotch. Carlos had been heard a minute ago.

Liz and Cowboy both said, "Texas," as they walked out the open doors to the pool.

Hawk said, "He was here a minute ago. He's got to be in the compound somewhere. Spread out and be alert. Nacho is missing too."

Liz went around the villa toward the truck. She carried her pistol in both hands, sweeping right and left. She had killed the two guards at the gate when the shooting started, and then the two guards that came running to the gate from the Dodge van parked at the side of the villa.

"I found where they went," yelled Hawk. "Over by the side of the pool deck and garden."

The two others ran over to where Hawk was standing looking down. A cover made of bamboo was thrown on the cement deck. There was a gaping hole in the ground. It had a stone and cement staircase leading down to the bottom of a dry cenote.

Hawk stuffed his silenced .22 at the small of his back and started down the steep twisting steps into the cenote. He looked up as he reached down and pulled his .45 ACP from the front of his pants and told Cowboy and Liz, "Do something about the Dodge van before any of the people awaken from their drugged, alcohol-induced sleep, or the local police show up." He didn't think the latter would happen. He hadn't seen any police since they had arrived in Playa. He went down the steps, where only a candle lighted the way from below. When he reached the bottom, a dry underground river cut by fresh water in the local limestone made him remember the VC tunnels that were all over South Vietnam. He had gone into some with Cowboy covering his back. They had used some of the tunnels to reach enemy camps that would have been impossible to reach through the jungle. He shook the memory off and checked out the cave from the bottom of the stair. There were huge stalagmites reaching for the ceiling, and stalactites growing from the ceiling. His pistol was cocked and locked when he took it out and moved out slowly, following the cave as it twisted and turned. He thought it was going east toward the beach, but wasn't sure. There were lights, with wire strung along the floor. They were spaced so the light faded to dark before another one broke into the darkness to show the way. He moved from stalagmite to stalagmite, clearing the cave as he went. He watched for trip wires. There were limestone rock falls closing off half or more of the cave, from time to time. Soon, there were pits of water that he had to work his way around. He tasted the water; it was salty. He could hear the rolling surf now. A sharp turn to the left made him slow down even more. He dropped to his knees, and in a quick in-and-out check he saw another set of stairs climbing to a dark opening. There was a large stalagmite on the other side of the cave, near the opening. He stood and ran for it, when a shot rang out. He made it to the towering stone cone, and returned fire in the blind. Another shot rang out. Hawk made the shooter near the stairs, maybe behind them. He fired where he thought the shots were coming from. Another shot, this one chipping limestone in Hawk's face. He wiped his eyes and stood with his back to the limestone cone. He had to think. How to get to the shooter. He knew he would have the angle on the shooter if he ran back to the corner of the cave he had just left. He figured there was no use thinking it over. He crouched down and ran for the corner. Two shots this time, one hit the cone and the other whipped by, inches from his head. He threw himself flat on his stomach and scrambled around the corner. There was another shot. He waited for the next one. He knew the shooter, at that angle, would have to expose himself to fire.

When the next shot came he reached around the corner and emptied his clip in the area of the stairs. Hawk heard a grunt like a shot had hit the other shooter. Hawk changed mags and waited. There was a groan from the area of the stairs. Hawk sprinted to the cone again. No shot. He ran to the nearest side of the stairs, went down on his belly, and rolled to the other side, ready for a shot.

Nacho was curled up on his side, holding his lower stomach. Hawk kicked away his pistol, then pulled him to a sitting position.

"Is your boss, D'Arcy, waiting outside?" asked Hawk.

Nacho didn't speak.

"I don't have time to waste. I'll leave you now, and go after D'Arcy."

"I don't want to die like this, senor. I will tell you what you want to know. I have lost respect for el jefe."

"Is D'Arcy outside the opening?"

"No, senor, he is a coward. I hate his guts. He beat his young son's mother to death and made me kill his son. He is no man. He is a sickness, affecting everyone and everything about him. He is evil," said Nacho.

"Tell me what his escape plans are, and I will leave you alive."

"He keeps his boat at a small wooden dock at the beach. He will run away. He has much money in Switzerland. He will leave Mexico and go to France, his father's country, or to Switzerland, I think."

"I am leaving you now." Hawk stood up and started for the stairs.

"Senor, please. Don't leave me like this."

Hawk stood over Nacho and blew the top part of his head off. He thought, "You're a sorry son of a bitch. You killed a little kid on purpose. You're no better than he is." Hawk went up the stairs to the cool breeze off the Caribbean Sea. He stood there for a second calming himself. He wouldn't solve anything by going off half-cocked.

Hawk began to run through the fringe of the jungle and onto the beach. He saw the dock right in front of him, but no boat. Far out on the water he could see the shape of a boat, and the sparkle of the wake as it ran through millions of phytoplankton. Hawk looked desperately up and down the beach. A *panga* fishing boat was pulled up on the beach and tied to a palm tree a short distance away. He ran to it, cut the rope with his Kay-bar, and pushed it out into the low surf. He pulled out the choke on the engine as he dropped the shaft and prop into the water. He started the motor and went up to the bow where a steering wheel had been placed with a simple gear control of forward and reverse, along with a speed control. He spun the wheel and pushed the throttle to the stop. The engine answered with a roar and flew over the low surf and out into the low seas, chasing D'Arcy on his fishing boat.

Liz and Cowboy ran to the white Dodge van. Cowboy opened the driver's-side door and looked at Liz as she sat in the shotgun seat.

"I don't suppose you know how to hot-wire a truck?" he said.

"That's one thing I missed in my education, Cowboy. Why don't you use the key?" she said as she pointed to the key hanging on a chain from the mirror.

He made a face as if saying, "Just my dumb luck, I didn't look up first."

The van started easily. They drove it out of the compound. Cowboy driving around and between the bodies of the four guards Liz had taken out.

"Okay, now that we have the van, where do we hide it so the cops and cartels won't find it?" asked Liz.

"I think we hide it in plain sight, Liz. When we get to the rental, hop out and open the garage door. I'll drive it in, and you close the door. It should be a great hide," he said.

She shook her head and said, "That's the one place they won't look for it. Why didn't I think of that?"

"Don't know and doesn't matter, you found the key," he said, and for the first time, they both laughed. Whether it was from all the stress they had just been through or just the aftermath of all the adrenalin pumping through their bodies, it felt right and good.

Cowboy went out on the pool surround and looked out at sea. He figured that the cenote Hawk was in led to the beach, and D'Arcy had to have a getaway boat nearby. A panga came running full speed across the surf to the south, and he thought that might be D'Arcy making a run for Cozumel. He looked out over the sea and saw a sparkle from the wake of a bigger boat, and knew what was happening. He jumped off the surround onto the beach and headed for the ferry dock. Partway there, he found a panga that was beached and had two outboards. It was sitting on a bamboo pole ramp. He pushed it out and started the engines. He ran both the engines up to maximum RPMs as he raced toward the other panga and the bigger fishing boat running full blast for Cozumel.

D'Arcy had taken the fishing boat out himself. He left the dock with no crew on board. It didn't matter; he could run it himself. When he woke with a start from his sleep under the palapa, he heard the shots being fired. Nacho came running from somewhere and threw the cover off the cenote escape route. He went down the stairs with Nacho following, and ran for the beach outlet. He told Nacho to stay and kill whoever came through the cavern. He was almost to Cozumel and freedom. He didn't want to believe that the raid was the two men Rodrigo had warned him about. It just wasn't possible for two men to wreak all the havoc that had happened in the past week or so. He was so intent on reaching the dock on Cozumel that he didn't think to look back. He turned on his ship-to-shore radio and made a call to one of his men on Cozumel.

When the man who answered D'Arcy said, "Get the car down to dock now, I'm coming over in the fishing boat. It's an emergency. Call Enselmo and tell him to get to the airport and warm up the engines, and don't file a flight plan," he turned off the radio.

Hawk could tell he was gaining on the bigger boat by the brightness of the wake. He was about halfway between the mainland and Cozumel when his engine sputtered, then stopped. He went back to the engine and tried to start it again. He had no luck. He pulled the second gas tank over to change the tanks for gas. He could tell by the weight of the second tank that it was empty. He was out in the middle of the Yucatán Channel with no gas, chasing a psychopathic killer, and he ran out of gas.

He started turning around looking for anything that might help. He felt lost and hopeless, something that he had never experienced in his life. The night was completely quiet, and then faintly he heard a powerful engine running at full throttle, and it was coming closer. The night out on the sea was a pitch black, but for the millions of stars in the sky. He could hear the other boat throttle back, and then over the engine noise he heard a familiar voice say, "Where the hell are you, Hawk? Make some noise or something," called Cowboy.

Hawk called out and turned on the little boat's running lights. He continued calling to Cowboy until the other panga came in and bumped the side of his boat that was dead in the water. He jumped into Cowboy's boat and said, "Hit it. D'Arcy is running for Cozumel, and probably the airport."

When Hawk and Cowboy arrived at the Cozumel dock, there was a Bertram sport fisherman adrift in the water, close to the sea wall. It had to be the one D'Arcy used. It was the most expensive boat there. Hawk knew they had missed him. Both men jumped off the panga as it bumped against the pier, and ran to where the main street of San Miquel, the only town on the island, ran along the seawall, and north to the airport. They hopped in the back of a small taxi waiting across the street at a tequila bar for tourists. They woke the driver from a sound sleep and told him to take them as fast as he could to the private airplane parking area at the airport. The little four-cylinder engine screamed down the street. The driver was hoping for a big tip. They skidded around a corner leading past the arrival area for tourists, and went to the parking area. A small twin-engine plane at the end of the runway was running up its engines. It began to roll, and quickly lifted into the air making a left turn, in case there was other traffic close by.

Hawk watched it, in the early morning dawn, cross over the channel and head west across the Yucatán.

Hawk told the driver to wait for them as they jumped out of the taxi and went to the small office that acted as the FBO for San Miquel airport. There was a young man standing behind the counter. He looked up as the two men walked into the office.

"How can I help you?" he asked.

"That plane that just took off, did it file a flight plan with you?" asked Hawk.

"Why, no, sir, most of the private planes don't. There are only two airports within range that can handle that size of aircraft. Mérida and Mexico City," said the young man.

"Are you in radio contact with the plane now?" asked Cowboy.

"No, sir, they change over to Mérida control as soon as they leave the traffic pattern here."

Hawk told the young man thanks, and Cowboy walked out to the taxi with him, dejected.

Neither man talked on the way back to the ferry pier. The panga had drifted over to the same area where the sport fisherman was resting on the sandy bottom.

Cowboy said, "I guess we wait for the first ferry."

07:41 - 27 AUGUST

TZ R

There was a long line waiting for the ferry ticket office to open. The locals had purchased their tickets the night before and were already boarding. Hawk and Cowboy bought their tickets and boarded the ferry. All the stern seats in the lower deck were taken, so they went upstairs to the open-air deck to find some. In rough seas, the stern seats were a premium. The upper deck stern seats were full also. They went back down and took seats close to the exit in front, planning to get off before the crowd hit the only exit door. During the crossing, several people got sick from the rough ride. They were handed barf bags and left to suffer in silence. The smell was intense. Cowboy was in a bad way too. His color had turned from light brown to whitish gray. He got up and walked out the exit door to get some fresh air. Hawk watched him hold onto the rail and throw up. Hawk felt bad for his friend, but there wasn't a thing he could do for him. The ferry docked, and Cowboy was the first off. He was glad to be on solid ground that didn't roll, rise, or crash down all the time.

By the time they had walked over to the rental villa, Cowboy was back to normal. Liz was outside waiting for them when they walked around the corner of the villa to the pool area.

"What happened last night? I was worried sick about you."

Hawk said, "To make a long story short, we chased D'Arcy to the airport on Cozumel, and he left in a plane, just as we got there. Tell us what's been going on here. We need to put it all together to make a plan."

Liz asked Cowboy, "Did you tell him what we did with the van?"

"Nope, didn't have time. You tell him."

Liz told Hawk, "Come with me. Cowboy and I have a surprise for you."

She walked into the villa, past the kitchen, to the door leading to the garage. Hawk was right behind her. She threw open the door and flicked on the light. Hawk couldn't believe his eyes.

Liz said, "We figured the best thing to do was to hide it where no one would think to look and is handy for us when we want to move it."

Hawk smiled at her and told her, "Great idea. Let's see what's in the back and we'll know better what to do with it."

Cowboy came to the door watching what was going on in the garage. There was a padlock on the back doors hooked to a heavy chain running through the handle on each door. They couldn't shoot it off, too much noise. No crowbar or metal rod to break the lock. No picks to open it.

Liz said, "I guess we wait to see what's in there."

Cowboy had a crooked smile on his face. He walked into the garage to the front door of the van and reached in, getting something from inside. He held his hand closed as he walked back to the two standing at the rear.

Hawk said, "What's the grin for, buddy?"

Cowboy looked at Liz and said, "Long story made short, I was going to hotwire the van but realized I had never done it before, when Liz told me to use the key on the chain hanging on the mirror. Made me feel kinda stupid, but I happened to notice something when I started the van." He opened his hand and held it up to them to reveal the keychain they found earlier to start the van.

Liz said, "You can't use the ignition key to unlock this padlock."

Cowboy held up the key ring and said, "There's another smaller key hanging beside the ignition key. What do ya want to bet it fits that padlock?"

Hawk urged him to try it in the padlock, wanting to know what was in the back of the van. The key slipped in and the lock opened.

Liz said, "Now I know how you felt when I showed you the ignition key, Cowboy." She had a "been there, done that" look on her face.

They took the heavy chain off and opened the doors. There was bundle after bundle of cellophane-wrapped one hundred dollar bills filling the entire back of the truck. The bundles were all stacked on wooden flats so a front-end loader could remove them easily.

All three of them stood in silent awe.

Cowboy was the first to speak. "What the hell do we do with it?"

Hawk continued looking at the money wrapped in cellophane for a minute more, then said to no one in particular, "That van had Texas plates when it came out of the hole of the ship. The money came from the United States. We need to send it back and let the government decide what to do with it. It has to be money from the sale of drugs, that D'Arcy sent to kill our people."

They locked the van doors and went out to the palapa to figure out what to do and how to do it. They needed to deal with the money. They had lost track of D'Arcy. Their mission wasn't over until he was dead. There had to be a way to find out where he went.

"If he flies somewhere internationally, he'll have to use his passport. Could you get whoever you message with the Morse code to check with the airlines and see if he used his passport and where he was going?" asked Liz.

"That's a good idea, Liz. He probably has a Mexican passport and maybe a French passport. They could check for both," said Hawk.

Cowboy went to his bedroom and brought back a notebook to write out the message out they wanted to send. He said, "First we need to do something about the money."

Hawk had a funny look on his face as he said, "Remember those guys flying the C-130s into the dirt strips to re-supply the firebases? They hit the runway and dropped the ramp, then shoved everything off while the pilot hit full thrust on those big four engines and took off as the ramp closed back up. Sometimes they made it and sometimes they didn't," said Hawk.

"Yeah, I remember. What's that got to do with the money and us?" said Cowboy.

"What if we reverse it? We get a C-130 to land on that World War II airstrip that they use for touch and goes, near the San Miguel airport on Cozumel. They stop and drop the ramp, we drive the van on, and they take off. Captain Jack can work on where D'Arcy used his passport and where he's headed. He can get landing permission for fuel at the airport D'Arcy left from. We can leave the plane and start trailing him again. Liz can stay on the plane and get back into the States," Hawk said.

"Well that's all well and good, except the part about me going back to the States. I want that bastard as much you two do. Besides, if he's going to France, do either of you speak French?" Liz said, with her hands on her hips.

Hawk had seen her do the hands on the hips thing several times now and knew it meant trouble. He said, "So now you're going to tell us you speak French, right?"

"That's right. I speak it like you two speak Spanish. My mother was French. My dad married her when he was stationed in Germany, in the army. She made sure I spoke her native language, and after she died I kept taking classes in high school and my four years in college at Texas A&M. You'll need me!"

Hawk looked for help from Cowboy. "It looks like she's got us, if he heads for France," said Cowboy, looking away from Hawk so he couldn't see his grin.

Cowboy went to work on a new day pad, encrypting the new message, and then sent it off. At midnight, the reply came. Cowboy used the pad to decode it. It took him longer than before. It was a longer message. He brought it down to the living room, where Liz and Hawk were waiting, and began to read it to them:

C-130 NO PROBLEM.

TWO DAYS FROM NOW AT DUSK.

WILL GET PERMISSION TO REFUEL.

CHECKING ON PASSPORT USE.

"We're staying here until that afternoon. We take the car ferry in the van to Cozumel. Drive up to the touch-and-go strip, and wait for dusk. Drive to the end of the strip and wait for the C-130. How's that sound?" asked Hawk.

"We need to take the pickup with us. It has all our equipment in it, and the Mexicans or the cartels will have a ball with it," offered Cowboy.

"Liz and I'll take the van. You bring the truck. We get the van on first, and then you drive right on after us."

Cowboy looked at Liz and then Hawk and said, "That's a plan." There were two catcalls at that.

16:05 - 29 AUGUST

TZ R

Two days later they drove the van and pickup to Puerto Morelos. They parked so they would be first for the next car ferry going over to Cozumel, and waited. Some of the men working around the dock keep looking at the van, and the people in it. No one made any move to find out why they were driving it to San Miguel. They had been paid not to notice things like that. When the ferry came, both vehicles went on and were tied down. They stayed in the vehicles.

The seas were quiet, and Cowboy did much better on the crossing. The ferry docked to the south of San Miguel making them drive through the town, then past the San Miguel airport, before they reached the old military runway entrance. There were some old buildings off the runway that looked like they hadn't been used in years. There were large villas on the beach side of the road. Hawk saw a gardener working near the gate to one, and drove the van onto the driveway and stopped. He talked with the gardener and gave him some pesos, and the gate was opened for them. They turned the van and truck around and sat on the pavement of the driveway waiting for the C-130. The gardener told Hawk the owners were in Mexico City and would not return for another week. The gate remained open. The sun was starting to set to the west. The popcorn-looking clouds were turning the brilliant reds and oranges that went with the setting of the sun on Cozumel.

The roar of an incoming prop plane caught the attention of Hawk. He knew that sound by heart. He made a circle in the air, so Cowboy would see it, and then pointed ahead meaning "let's go." They moved through the gate, driving down the beach road to the entrance to the old runway, and turned onto a dirt tract that went to a building sitting almost on the runway. Hawk figured it was the old control building. The wind was coming from the east, as usual. The runway ran east to west dictated by the prevailing wind. Hawk drove over to the west end of the runway and stopped. Cowboy came up beside the van and stopped.

The C-130 roared over them, its tires making a squeak with puffs of white smoke showing next. The props reversed, brakes applied, and the plane made a U-turn while still moving at a good speed. It rolled back to the runup area on the runway and dropped its ramp. The plane started to roll for takeoff. Hawk put the accelerator all the way down, hit the ramp with the wheels in the loading tracks, and shot to the front of the airplane. He set the emergency brake as the crew chief started to tie the van down. Cowboy ran the old pickup onto the ramp and pulled to a stop right behind the van. Another crew member started to tie it down, as the ramp came up. Full flaps and full thrust brought the wheels off the ground a few seconds later. The pilot pulled the plane up hard because the runway was short and it ended in thick jungle right at the beach and the sea. The plane turned to the north and headed out into the Gulf of Mexico.

The co-pilot unbuckled his safety belt and made his way to the van. He told Hawk and Liz they

could turn the van off and get out. It was going to be a while before they landed again. He went to Cowboy in the old pickup and told him the same thing. When they had settled on the folding web seats that came off the wall of the plane, the co-pilot asked which one was Hawk. Hawk started to stand up, but the young co-pilot motioned for him to remain seated. He handed Hawk an envelope with a security stamp on it. It was marked Top Secret.

Then the co-pilot said, "We know where we are headed: Mexico City. But first we need to come in from the Gulf just below Veracruz, then across country to the airport there. We'll fuel up and stop for a minute at the private plane ramp. You guys hop off and get a ride to the main passenger terminal. From there it's up to you. We can't tell you where we're going with the van and truck. I'll come back and warn you when we're landing. No need for the ramp to open; you will get out of the door using the ladder over there." He pointed at a door in the fuselage and then walked back up to the cockpit.

Hawk opened the envelope by breaking the seal, and shook out a folded message form. It read:

MEXICAN PASSPORT USED

TWA FLIGHT MEXICO CITY TO LA GUARDIA

TWA FLIGHT LA GUARDIA TO PARIS

CHECKING PARIS PROPERTY RECORDS

CALL BY PAY PHONE NUMBER AGREED ON

SECURE MESSAGING NOT POSSIBLE

Hawk passed the message to Liz. Then Liz to Cowboy. Hawk looked at Liz and said over the roar of the engines, "Looks like you get to use your French."

09:50 - 28 AUGUST

TIME ZONE ALPHA

Carlos stopped at the immigration desk and got his French passport stamped then walked directly to customs. He didn't have any luggage, so he was passed right through. Two men were waiting for him outside customs. One was a tall skinny man with a hooked nose and bushy eyebrows. The other was stocky, with no neck and beefy arms and hands. They walked to a dark sedan parked at the curb, and all got in. Carlos rode in the back.

He said, "Have you been to the apartment yet?"

The one riding shotgun nodded affirmatively and said, "It is ready for you, Mr. D'Arcy."

"How's my brother these days?"

"He is doing well, sir."

"Were you already here when I called him from Mexico City?"

"Yes sir, we are overseeing the sale of a large amount of your product here in Paris."

"This is a sudden trip. You will be my bodyguards while I'm here. There could be trouble. You will need to stay alert, always."

"It will help us, sir, to know what threat may be out there."

"There are some people that are trying to take me captive or kill me. I don't know much, except they are probably American."

A taxi pulled out from the curb and followed D'Arcy's sedan at a comfortable distance.

08:15 - 31 AUGUST

TIME ZONE ALPHA

The long trip from Playa del Carmen, Mexico, to Paris, France, had taken a toll on everyone. They carried no luggage, but did have their personal weapons with them. French customs wanted to know why they were traveling with no luggage. Hawk told them they were on an emergency trip and would buy the clothes they needed after they checked into a hotel. They wanted to know what the emergency was.

"The president of the United States sent us over to make a final effort to salvage a peaceful end to the Vietnam War," Hawk told them.

Customs passed them through, then they got their passports stamped, and they were out to the taxi line. Liz got in the front seat with the driver of the first taxi in line, and asked if he knew a nice hotel near the Latin Quarter. Hawk and Cowboy didn't understand what she said, but were impressed by how it sounded. The taxi dodged in and out of traffic like they were in a road race, and then they were on narrow one-way streets, with brick or cobblestones as pavement. The taxi stopped at a small hotel on the Blvd. Saint-Michel. The hotel was the Hotel Royal Saint Michel. Liz paid the driver with US dollars, since they hadn't had time to change over to francs. They walked into the hotel, and Liz asked for two rooms with two double beds, that connected. The clerk asked her how long they wanted the rooms. She told him for one week. He nodded approval and gave her the hotel register to sign. She used the name Sabine Bouvier, from the United States. The clerk gave her two room keys for the third floor. He told her the Seine could be seen from the balconies of both rooms. They checked the rooms out and went back downstairs.

Liz asked the clerk if there was a store that sold clothes nearby. He told her across the river: "Stay on Blvd. Saint-Michel, and cross on the bridge Au Change. There are many shops in that area."

They were talking about seeing some sights while they were in Paris as they walked out the front door of the Saint Michel.

Liz grabbed Cowboy's arm and said, "I think that's the Luxembourg Park right across the street. See the big castle-looking building with the long swimming pool in front?"

Cowboy and Hawk acted like they were interested, but both of them started walking in the direction of the Seine. They crossed the Île de la Cité and the Seine on Blvd. Saint-Michel and saw the shops running straight ahead. It looked like a row of clothing shops. Hawk and Cowboy stopped at the first window that displayed men's clothing and checked it out. They needed clothes that wouldn't attract attention, and this store appeared to have those available. They walked in with Liz right behind them. When they had found clothes that fit the bill, Liz asked the clerk if there was a room to try the clothes on. Liz had told them what the sizes were, but the guys wanted to make sure they would fit. The clothes were a good enough fit to get by.

Liz walked up one side and down the other and didn't see any clothes she thought would be okay. She was very exasperated with all the window shopping. She saw a woman coming up the street and asked her, "Is there a department store nearby?"

The young woman smiled and told her, "Walk along the Seine on the right until you see the Louvre. There is one right across the river."

"Thank you," said Liz, as the young woman walked away.

The little group walked along the Seine until they came to the Louvre, and right across the bridge was a department store by the name of La Samaritaine. Liz did a little hop-up-and-down excitement thing. They all went over, but the boys stayed outside watching people go by while Liz went in search of clothes that would work for her. She reappeared quicker than Hawk and Cowboy thought she would, with several store bags in hand. There were small cafés along the way, and Cowboy told them people were looking at him when they passed by because his stomach was growling so loud.

"How about something to eat? We haven't taken the time to eat in a day and a half. I need to fuel up if I'm going to keep this pace up for long," he said while holding his stomach.

Liz and Hawk laughed. "You pick something out, Liz. We won't know what we are eating if you don't order for us, or at least tell us what the menu says, in English."

"So you admit I come in handy," she said.

"Yeah, yeah, I admit you come in handy, sometimes," said Hawk smiling.

They had chicken salad sandwiches with tea. Cowboy wanted to order another sandwich, but they decided to wait for dinner.

They walked the short distance to the hotel and went to their rooms. Hawk went to the bathroom to take a shower, and stopped in his tracks. The bathtub was a third the size they were in the States, and the toilet was a hole in the floor with a peddle by it. Well, he thought, I've been in a lot worse places trying to clean up. He pulled the shower curtain around the little tub and turned on the water. Lukewarm water, at best. He dried off, shaved, and went into the room to dress. Cowboy walked into the bathroom and hollered, "I've seen horse troughs bigger than that." He laughed and turned the lukewarm water on. He shaved with the same razor Hawk had used, and came into the room wearing a towel that was too small for him. He laughed again and said, "I guess Frenchmen are smaller than we are." They went out on the balcony, sat in the two tiny iron chairs, and watched the people and the boats go by while they waited for Liz to knock on the connecting door when she was ready to go to dinner.

Liz knocked on the door, and Cowboy unlocked it for her. When she walked into the room Cowboy said, "Well, howdy. You sure look great, Liz."

"Thanks, Cowboy. I needed that, after what has happened to me in the recent past." She wore nice slacks and a silk blouse. Both fit her well.

Hawk came in from the tiny balcony, and without noticing how good Liz looked cleaned up after the long trip, said, "We need to contact Captain Jack."

Their equipment was in the back of the pickup, wherever it was now. Captain Jack would be able to help them, through the embassy in Paris. They locked the room and took the tiny elevator down to the lobby. It was really small, and Hawk was uneasy being pressed against the side of Liz on the ride down. Liz asked the clerk at the hotel counter where the nearest pay telephone was located.

"On the corner of Blvd. Saint-Michel and Blvd. Saint-Germain. You will turn right when you go out the entrance of the hotel, and walk two blocks. You can't miss it. It's a bright red box."

They left the hotel and followed the clerk's instructions. They crossed a small street only one block long and saw the big red box on the next corner. On the side of the red box, in French, it said *Cabine Téléphonique*, which was easy enough for Hawk to figure out: "Telephone Booth."

Hawk used some of the coins they had received in change when buying their clothes, and dialed 0. A woman's voice came back, almost immediately, speaking French. He asked if she spoke English. She asked him in English how she could help him. I need to make a collect call to the United States. She asked for the number and said, "It will be a few minutes. Please wait." Hawk looked out to find Cowboy and Liz. They were acting like tourists, window shopping down the block. His change dropped into the receptacle that he had used to dial the operator.

"Hello," he heard. "This is a long-distance operator from Paris, France. I have a collect call for you. Will you accept it."

"Yes, operator, I will accept it."

"Captain Jack?" asked Hawk.

"Yes, is that you, Hawk?"

"Yes sir, sounds like we are talking through a pipe. We're in Paris. We will need some equipment, and we're about out of money."

"I will have the embassy bring it to you. Give me your address."

"Hotel Royal Saint Michel, number 3, Blvd. Saint-Michel. Rooms are under the name Sabine Bouvier. Captain Jack, we don't have a clue on how to locate the target. It's a big city."

"When he used his passport to get on the plane to Paris, I contacted a friend at the ASA compound in Baden-Baden, Germany. It's right on the border with France. He drove through the night in his own car. He parked it when he got to the airport, and waited at the taxi line until D'Arcy arrived. Using the description Miss Stillings gave you, he saw him meet two other men. He described him to me as the short, fat man with bulging eyes and puffy lips. He was able to follow them in a taxi to an older hotel in the Latin Quarter, named Hôtel de La Salle. Number 21 Rue de l'Universite at the corner of Rue Montalembert. Are you writing all this down, Hawk?"

"Yes sir."

"Okay, the two men with him parked the car and went into the hotel. They came out to eat that evening, and returned about midnight. My contact has a small room rented across the street that you can equip and use. He will leave this morning. Wait until this afternoon to go there. The room is under the name of Bailey."

"Thanks, sir. Anything else we need to know?"

"One more thing, Hawk. When he was in Mexico he was the only target. Now that he's in France where his half-brother lives, the half-brother will also be a target for you. Is that understood?"

"Yes sir."

"I will gather what information is available about him and give it to you in two days at this same time, and by the way, that number you found in the cartel villa is a private line, not to a Rodrigo, but to a Roger Burns, a deputy director of the CIA. I have an ex-communications monitor tapping the line. Burns has what he thinks is a secret bank account in Zurich. We have traced a deposit from Carlos's Mexican bank to his bank in Zurich. It was sent a few weeks before you came on the scene. The amount was five hundred thousand dollars. I'm certain he will be a target too, very soon. We can't let it be known that a high official in the CIA is a mole for numerous drug cartels.

"Yes sir." The dial tone came on suddenly. Hawk shook his head and left the booth, thinking, as usual for the army, "SNAFU."

He met up with Liz and Cowboy, who had discovered a small café and coffee shop on the corner, a block away. They went there and sat at a small table on the sidewalk facing Blvd. Saint-Germain-des-Prés. Liz ordered coffee and pastries for them. She went to look around the quaint café while they waited for the coffee. She came back in a moment all excited.

She said, "You'll never believe who used to spend time here with friends drinking coffee and talking politics."

Cowboy said, "Mickey and Minnie Mouse?"

"No, Cowboy. It was Pablo Picasso."

"The famous painter?" asked Hawk.

"That's right, Hawk." Liz thought, "He continues to surprise me."

15:37 - 31 AUGUST

TZ ALHA

The coffee came in tiny cups, but the coffee had a real kick to it. Hawk told them about the conversation with Captain Jack. They agreed the first step should be to take over the hotel room across from where Carlos was staying. The embassy would let them know before the equipment was brought to the hotel. They drank coffee and talked about being in France enjoying the sunny, calm afternoon. They left the café and walked to a street vendor, where Liz asked for a tourist map. There were street benches along the boulevard, and they sat on one not far from the café and opened it up looking for Rue de l'Universite. It was on the map running nearly parallel to the river Seine. They walked down the street a few blocks and then turned back to the river. One block from the river they saw Rue de l'Universite. They didn't want Liz to be seen, so they walked on to the river. The Louvre was just up the river, and that gave Liz an idea. She took the guys up to the department store La Samaritaine and went to the cosmetics area. Hawk and Cowboy waited outside.

Liz came out with another bag, and they went back to Saint Michel and the hotel. She went to her room without saying much. Hawk and Cowboy decided to find the hotel on Rue de l'Universite, across from the Hôtel de La Salle. It turned out to be only a few blocks from the Hotel Saint Michel. They walked in, and asked the clerk if he spoke English.

"I do speak English. How may I be of service?"

"A friend, Mr. Bailey, rented a room here, and we would like the same room and another one that has two double beds in it, close by, or better yet, connecting," said Hawk.

"Of course, sir. Let me see. The clerk looked at boxes with keys in them and brought two keys out. The double bedroom joins the one your friend had. Would that suit you?"

Hawk said, "Perfect." He signed the register Peter Higgins, USA, and paid in advance. They got in a wrought-iron elevator, that was so small they barely fit. Both the rooms were facing the street, and they could see the de La Salle entrance. They left the hotel and walked back to the Hotel Saint Michel expecting to see Liz in the lobby. No one was there, not even the clerk. They went up to the room to rest up. A knock on the connecting door brought both of them off their beds. Hawk walked over to the door and opened it up expecting to see Liz.

A young woman stood back from the door. She had short brunette hair with eyelashes to match. Lipstick that made her lips look sort of pouty. She wore tan slacks and a light tan and blue blouse that made her blue eyes shine like the clear blue sky. She put her arms up, and twirled for Hawk. The clothes tastefully showed off her perfectly proportioned body.

Hawk stammered and then choked out, "You look so different, Liz."

Cowboy stood behind Hawk and only said, "Wow!"

Liz beamed at them through long eyelashes and said, "Ya think D'Arcy will recognize me now? I hate not being able to come and go with you guys because someone might notice me."

Hawk continued to look at her with admiration in his eyes, and said, "Liz, D'Arcy will never know you, but I'm afraid every man on the street will be watching you."

"That's okay, as long as it doesn't mess up the mission."

Hawk left with Cowboy. Hawk went to La Samaritaine, hoping to find some luggage. They needed to look like tourists. Cowboy went to the hotel on l'Universite, to start the stakeout of the hotel Carlos was staying in. Liz remained behind, in case the embassy called or came by. It wasn't long before Hawk was back in his room talking with Liz. The room phone rang. He answered, listened for a second, and hung the phone up.

"The embassy is here with the things we needed. I may need your help, if there are a lot of boxes or bags," said Hawk.

They went downstairs together, and Hawk was asked to show his passport. There were three suitcases. The medium-build American had him sign a certification document for the transfer of the luggage and its contents. The three suitcases weren't heavy, just cumbersome. The two of them took them upstairs to Hawk's room and unlocked the suitcases. Hawk checked the contents against the list he had given Captain Jack over the phone. It was all there, including enough ammunition to start a small war and a more than ample amount of francs.

They packed what new clothes they had left in the new suitcase Hawk had purchased at the department store. Hawk called down to the hotel clerk and asked to have a taxi come to the hotel. When Liz and Hawk carried all the luggage to the door of the hotel, the clerk was standing at the curb with a taxi, ready to go. They ended up putting one of the suitcases in the back seat with

Liz. When the driver found out the trip was so short, he started talking to himself in French. Liz leaned up close to Hawk's ear and said quietly, "He's angry about the short ride. The fare will be small, and any tip will be even smaller."

Hawk nodded as the cab turned on to Rue de l'Universite and stopped at the new hotel. The driver went to the trunk and retrieved the three suitcases. Liz asked him to help take them into the hotel lobby. He did so, all the time complaining. Hawk grabbed the one in the back seat. He paid him his fare and then gave a big tip. The driver looked at the tip and said something in French. Liz told Hawk the driver wanted to know if he needed change. Hawk shook his head no, and the driver left, saying something again in French.

"What'd he say? Liz?"

"He commented on how crazy Americans are," she told him with a grin.

Liz went up and asked Cowboy to help with the luggage. The little elevator made it necessary to make two trips to have all the suitcases in the rooms.

They separated out the clothes, but left the equipment cases closed and locked. They would take care of that after dark, when it wasn't so easy to see into the rooms from across the street. They took turns watching for Carlos as each one cleaned up in the tiny bathrooms. Hawk had told Cowboy and Liz one of the things they needed to do was to get the license plate number on the car that Carlos and his two goons used, and where they parked it. He had asked for a low-frequency FM transmitter to place on the car so they could track where they went with the low-frequency receiver that was part of the package. He and Cowboy knew of them because the CIA in Vietnam used them to track Vietnamese generals who the CIA thought might be moles for the NVA.

07:12 - 01 SEPTEMBER

TZ A

Cowboy had the watch for the morning. Hawk and Liz were working on putting some of the gear together from the suitcases. It was early afternoon when the French ate a light lunch. The two goons had brought the car around, and one went into the hotel and later walked out with Carlos. Carlos climbed in back, and the goon took the passenger seat.

The car started down the street, and Cowboy, Hawk, and Liz all three copied down the plate number. They checked the three sets of numbers to make sure there was no mistake. Now they needed to follow the car when it dropped off Carlos and one of the goons later. Cowboy knew more about the electronics end of things, so he would be the one putting the tracker on the car, while Hawk stood guard. They went out for a quick lunch, and returned in time for Hawk to see the car pull up and drop off Carlos and one of the goons. The car took off, and so did Cowboy. He took the stairs at a fast clip, even though the stairs were narrow and steep. It would be faster than the birdcage, as he called the elevator.

He walked as fast as he dared, not wanting to draw attention to himself. He walked through a red stop light and caught a glimpse of the car crossing the sidewalk a block ahead into what looked like an old building, where the guts had been torn out and new concrete floors and ramps were added. He crossed the street and waited for the second goon to come out. Cowboy was looking in a window, watching the reflection of the parking building across the street. The goon came out and walked away toward the Hôtel de La Salle. Cowboy waited until the goon was out of sight for a few minutes, and then went to the street-level ramp and walked up each level looking for the car. He found it on the third level.

He told Hawk and Liz where the car was and which level it was on. It was parked head in, so Cowboy planned on putting the transmitter between the gas tank and the frame of the car, out of sight. Hawk liked his plan. They did without eating dinner, waiting for night to come. Liz took over the stakeout, and Hawk and Cowboy took the transmitter and the receiver in a box that it came in, and walked to the parking building. The car was still there. Hawk went to the support column nearest the car and unscrewed the light that covered the parking area. Cowboy crawled under the car with the box and a penlight. Hawk stood behind a pillar across the way. He could hear noise coming from under the car, but not loud enough to alarm anyone walking by. Cowboy scooted out with the box, dusted himself off, and walked over to Hawk. He took the FM receiver from the box and hit the power switch. Two lights came on: one red for the power, and one green showing it was receiving from the transmitter under the car. Cowboy tapped Hawk on the shoulder, and they went back to the hotel as if nothing had happened.

09:30 - 02 SEPTEMBER

TZ A

The next day, while Liz and Cowboy switched off each hour monitoring the front of the de La Salle hotel, Hawk walked across the street and stepped into its lobby. It was very similar to the hotel they were in. He went up the stairs, and one by one checked the floors for any guards in the hallway. He wanted to know where exactly, D'Arcy was staying. There were no guards until he reached the top floor. There was a small sitting area with a table and chair, next to the elevator. One of the two thugs that were guarding D'Arcy was sitting there. Unlike the rest of the floors, the fifth floor only had one entry door. It was very ornate, unlike the others that were plain looking, with a peephole in the middle. He turned carefully on the stairs, keeping out of sight, and went down, and out of the hotel.

He told Cowboy and Liz what he had found on the fifth floor, and that he thought the whole floor was taken up as an apartment, for D'Arcy. He felt like they needed to get a listening device in the apartment, and if possible, tap the phone line.

Cowboy said, "No problem for me to do that, except I need a way in. I'll walk to the back of the hotel. There may be a fire escape that I can go up and find the phone line outside the hotel for that floor. If it's wired separately from the rest of it, the bug will have to be placed inside the apartment somehow."

Hawk told him, "We're not doing any good sitting here, looking out the window."

Liz had been listening to them talk and said, "Why don't I go there and apply for a maid's job? That way I could let Cowboy in the apartment when D'Arcy and his bodyguards are out of the hotel."

Hawk and Cowboy looked at each other, and then Hawk said, "No. It's too dangerous, and besides, he may recognize you, if you're working around the hotel."

"Okay, with the short dark hair and makeup, neither one of you knew who I was right off the bat. I won't give him a chance to stare at me. Come on, you as much as said we need someone on the inside to make this work. I can do that," she said.

The three of them sat down and discussed the possibilities of Liz working at the hotel. Cowboy and Hawk were against it from the start. The final straw was when Liz said, "You all don't want me to do it because I'm a woman and you'd feel responsible if something happened to me. Well, that's bullshit. I've shown you what I can do, and you need to give me more credit. Besides, if something happens to me, I'll expect you to come to my rescue. That will enable you both to feel really good about yourselves."

That pissed Hawk and Cowboy off. Hawk said angrily, "If you are so hot to get shot, then far be it for me to try to stop you. Go to the department store, and get something to wear like a maid would wear off duty. Get fixed up, and apply this afternoon."

Liz took Hawk's advice, after he got some operation money from the suitcase the embassy had delivered to them. She walked to the Seine and then to the department store. She thought about what she had volunteered to do, and had time to be afraid, and then to get angry that D'Arcy was still walking the earth. She decided she was a strong person and she would be fine as a maid. After all, she thought, I've been kidnapped, done drugs, made to work in a strip club, beaten, and rescued by two great men. Being an insider spy couldn't be that bad.

She bought a simple dress, and shoes, and a small cloth bag for a suitcase. She put the clothes she had been wearing in it, after she had changed into the new clothes at the store. She walked out the front door of the department store in her new plain-looking clothes. But nothing could hide her new self-esteem, or her natural beauty.

She walked to the Hôtel de La Salle. She wondered if Hawk and Cowboy saw her go by. The lobby of the de La Salle was much like the two hotels they had stayed in nearby. She went to the reception counter and asked in French to see the manager.

The clerk said, "Maybe I can be of help."

"No, I am looking for work. I would like to speak with the manager. Is the manager here?"

"Yes, he's in the office. May I give him your name?"

"Sabine Bouvier."

"I'll be right back."

A few moments later the older, balding clerk returned, led by a much younger man with dark hair, a medium build, and a narrow mustache. His light blue eyes ran up and down Liz and stopped on her face.

"Boyce tells me you are asking about work. My name is Gaylord Malmert. I'm the manager. What type of work have you done in the past, Miss Bouvier?"

"I have been taking care of my elderly mother, until recently. Before that, I attended university in Nancy. I have no other work experience, but if you have a maid's position open, I know I could start there."

"I thought I detected an Alsace accent in your French. When would you be available, if I asked you to start as a maid?"

"Tomorrow, Mr. Malmert. I have just arrived by train from Nancy, and will need to find a place to stay, near here."

"That will be fine, Miss Bouvier. Boyce will help you with your uniform, and please be here at seven in the morning. I will assign one of the other maids to be with you during your first day."

"Please, Mr. Malmert, call me Sabine."

"Alright, Sabine, welcome to the Hôtel de La Salle."

Boyce took Liz back to a small room that had the clean linens, and cleaning paraphernalia stored in neat rows, on shelves. In the back, there was a tiny table, a metal coffee pot, a few cups, and the smallest refrigerator she had ever seen. On the other side of the room were neatly hung maid's uniforms. A curtain hung in front of a corner; that was the changing area and the toilet area. She found a uniform that was a bit too large, but would suffice.

Boyce took her back to the lobby, and told her goodbye, until the coming day. She turned to go and saw a thick-set man with no neck sitting back in an alcove watching her intently. He gave her a cold shiver, just looking at him. His eyes were cruel, like those she remembered D'Arcy had. She turned away and walked out to the street. She went down Rue de l'Universite a few blocks and stopped at an antique store like she was looking in the show window. No one seemed to be following her as she glanced over her right shoulder like she was fixing her hair.

She walked around the corner and headed for Saint-Michel Blvd. When she reached the corner, she saw the no-neck man standing on the far side of the street, watching her. She shuddered again. She saw a Métro sign down the street and walked to it. It would take her across the Seine following the Blvd. Saint-Michel. No-neck had to be following her for some reason. She bought a ticket for Sacré-Cœur, the church on the hill overlooking the Seine. She would walk around there as if looking for an apartment, to make sure she lost him.

**

Liz got back to the hotel they were using and went up to the rooms in the tiny elevator. She waited down the hall from the elevator to make sure No-neck didn't come up the stairs or the elevator. Hawk came out of the door leading to the bedroom Cowboy and he were using, and headed to Liz's, stopping when he saw her standing in the hallway.

"What're you doing standing in the hall?"

"A man has been following me since I left the Hôtel de La Salle. He looked mean and tough. I have spent the last hour walking around Paris trying to make sure I lost him before I came back here."

"Hawk pulled his M1911 Colt, pushed the safety off, and walked to the stairs. The pistol held by his leg. He went down the stairs and through the lobby, until he reached the front windows looking out onto the street. He checked right and left and saw no one. He pulled the door open and stepped out to the narrow sidewalk. He looked to his right and saw no one. At the next narrow street to his left the no-neck man backed out of sight. Hawk looked to the left. No one there. He walked back into the hotel putting his pistol at the small of his back, as No-neck walked down the alley-like street and back to the Hôtel de La Salle.

Liz told Cowboy and Hawk about getting the maid's job, and seeing No-neck in the lobby and then again on Saint-Michel Blvd. Then about going to the Métro and taking it to Sacré-Cœur. Then back again to Saint-Germain Blvd., and walking back the hotel. She told them she hadn't seen him again after getting on the Métro.

Hawk said, "We'll have to be on high alert now. He might have been following you with no good intention. Your description of him makes him one of the two bodyguards Carlos has with him. I don't know how he found bodyguards so quickly after entering the country."

Cowboy spoke up, "Probably from his brother. He's mixed up in the drug cartel like Carlos is. He has to have bodyguards to stay alive."

"Good point," said Hawk.

"I think the next move is for Liz go to work in the morning. And, Cowboy, you are the bugging expert. You need to get a room close to the top floor so Liz can get you into Carlos's flat when he and the guards leave. Take your stuff to bug the best area in the flat. I'll set up the noise-activated reel-to-reel recorder to this end of our line, bugging his phone so it's ready to go. We need to check for a fire escape. We can run the phone line from there to this room by following the mass of overhead wires already here.

"I'll take the room for two—or make it three days, to give Liz time to figure things out and get me into the flat the first time they all leave," said Cowboy.

"Liz, make sure you carry your Walther with you," Hawk said.

"The uniform has a small white apron on the front of the dress. I can hide it in a pocket that it has," she said.

"Okay, at dusk, Cowboy, we need to check on an alley, or some type of easement behind that hotel, that the electric and phone company uses to run wire and do maintenance through."

"Right. If I can locate his private line outside the flat, I can go ahead and expose the metal and hook on to it then. The bugging wire is really small. We could run it on the ground and across the street. No one pays any attention to that kind of stuff anymore," said Cowboy.

"To keep us from making too many trips, let's take all the stuff you need with us, when we go tonight," Hawk added.

They spent the rest of the afternoon getting together the things Cowboy would need. Liz and Hawk put together the reel-to-reel recorder, while they talked. He asked her what part of France her mother had lived in before marrying her father. Liz told him that her mother came from an area in eastern France called Alsace, near the German border. Her name was Sabine Bouvier. She went to work at an American PX across the border after World War II. That was where she met her father. She married him, and went back to Texas with him when his service time was up. Hawk didn't tell her much about himself. Some about his father and mother. He still couldn't get over the distrust he harbored deep in his being about what other women had done, that hurt him so terribly. He couldn't tell her about what he had done, what he had seen, the things that had changed his soul during his time in Vietnam. Everything he did was classified Top Secret.

17:45 - 02 SEPTEMBER

TZ A

Liz remained at the hotel to keep eyes on the front of Hôtel de La Salle, while Cowboy and Hawk went down the street and cut across Rue de l'Universite, past the corner buildings, looking for any kind of opening that would lead to the back of Hôtel de La Salle. At the end of the building, there was a white painted gate with a padlock. Hawk pulled out his Kay-bar and shoved the blade under the attachment of the hasp. Each time he did it there was more space, until finally the hasp fell off from the weight of the lock. They closed the gate behind them. It didn't take long for them to walk the length of the corner building. The next building, the Hôtel de La Salle, was built right against it. A few steps past the juncture of the two buildings, the small walkway opened into a park-like square surrounded by tall buildings. There were tables and chairs sitting at the back of each building, with brightly colored umbrellas over each table. Stones had been placed to make small patios and walkways, with benches scattered along the walkways. A number of large old trees grew there, giving shade to the park. The de La Salle had one of the larger patios, and a fire escape, like several of the other tall buildings around the park.

Cowboy was covered with equipment, so Hawk jumped up and grabbed the bottom of the pull-down part of the fire escape. It was rusty from being exposed to the rain. Pieces of paint fell off and dropped to the ground. It made some noise as he pulled it down all the way. He pulled his pistol and waited. No one came to find out about the noise. Cowboy climbed up the ladder and then the metal stairs, to the top floor, where a small landing was suspended off the building. There was a window that looked into the top floor hall. A single telephone wire came from a window that he figured led into D'Arcy's flat. He bared the wire and coupled his wire to it. Cowboy threw the rest of the roll of wire up to the roof and pulled his way up. He trailed the coil of wire across the rooftop, to the corner building, and across it, dropping the remainder down to the ground. He retraced his steps across the roof, and down the fire escape, where Hawk waited, gun still out. They moved down the space between the buildings, that was only shoulder wide. They opened and closed the gate and walked to the coil of wire. There was a low spot in the cobblestones of the street, where they placed the wire, and then Hawk went to their room and caught the wire as Cowboy threw it up the side of the hotel. He walked the end over to the reel-to-reel, and pushed it into the input channel on the front of the recorder. They all felt good about getting D'Arcy's phone bugged, and looked forward to when they would have the room bug in place, in the next few days.

Cowboy had just completed hooking everything up to the recorder and powering it up, when the reel-to-reel and the speaker system activated.

"Hello."

"Carlos?"

"Yes, my brother. How are you tonight?"

"I'm fine, Carlos. I have been concerned about you. Have you had any problems with the men I sent?"

"No, Andre. There have been no problems since I reached France."

"I have news about the boat we had built."

"Yes, what about it?"

"We are to take delivery ten days from now. We will have to pay the remainder of the purchase price by then. I think I will come to

Paris and spend a few days with you. Then we can go to Zurich. We must both sign for the money transfer. I am having the title put in Altamar's name.

"I've forgotten how much the last payment will be."

"Ten million to make a total of twenty million," Andre said.

"After we transfer the money and take delivery, let's take a trip to the Greek islands, and spend some time visiting other ports along the way."

"Sounds great. I'll be up in three days. Keep a couple of rooms open for my security also," Andre requested.

"Consider it done, Andre. I look forward to seeing you tomorrow. It's been a long time."

The reels and speaker stopped. "We need to get Cowboy a room in the hotel and get the room bugged before his brother gets here. We may have gotten lucky with his brother coming up here," said Hawk.

Liz said, "I'll be with another maid all day tomorrow. Better get the room then, but wait till my second day to bug the room."

"I'll come over mid-morning. I'll be a tourist from Madrid. That way if No-neck is in the lobby, he won't have any reason for alarm," said Cowboy.

"Good idea," said Liz. "Try for a room on the fourth floor. Tell them you want the best view possible."

07:01 - 03 SEPTEMBER

TZ A

Liz's first day as a maid started off with a staff meeting that occurred with the maids, three in total, and the day manager, Mr. Malmert. Everyone had coffee or tea, with two of the maids sitting at the small table, and Liz standing by the changing area curtain. The manager went through several complaints with them, that were received overnight. One was a complaint about the way a bed was turned down, and the other about a bathroom floor being dirty. He told Sabine that she would be working the day with the maid for floors four and five. The maid for floors one through three said she should work with her the first day. There were more rooms occupied, so she would get more experience working on floors one through three. Mr. Malmert agreed. He said that if there were no more questions, the maids could prepare for the day. Checkout time was ten in the morning, but there were always early checkouts that they could start on.

Liz had hoped to get the top floor as part of her day of learning, but she jumped right in helping the lower floor maid. She kept her eye out for No-neck as she walked with the other maid from room to room on the first floor, but he didn't appear. The other guard— the tall, skinny one with the hooked nose—came down from the upper floors at about ten and took up the seat No-neck had been in. Liz decided to call him "Hook Nose." She chuckled to herself at the names she had given the two men, but she had no illusions about how mean the two men would be if they figured out who she was. Of course, D'Arcy was the only one that had seen her before.

Right after Hook Nose sat down in the lobby, Cowboy walked in with a backpack and a small suitcase. He asked the clerk for a room on the top floor so he could see the Seine and if possible, the Notre Dame Cathedral. The clerk looked at him and said, "Just a minute. I don't speak Spanish." The manager, Mr. Malmert, came from the office and asked how he could help Cowboy, in Spanish. Cowboy asked the same question to Mr. Malmert. The manager told him the top floor was taken, but there was a single room available on the fourth floor that had that view. Cowboy said he would take it for three days and asked if the hotel had any sightseeing or tourist maps of Paris he could have. Mr. Malmert pointed to a hallway table and said Cowboy could choose from those. He took his key and walked over to the table. He picked two that he thought he might read and went up an elevator that seemed to be the standard small size for hotels in that part of Paris. The room had a single bed, a small dresser, and an even smaller bathroom. It did have a view of the Seine, and barely a piece of the cathedral, but he wasn't going to look out the window anyway.

Cowboy left the room in the afternoon and headed around the block, before going to the hotel where Hawk was watching the front of the de La Salle. Liz came in about three in the afternoon and dropped on a bed, exhausted.

She looked up at Hawk and said, "I never realized how hard maids work."

He said, "It'll be for two more days, and then we need to keep you out of there. Someone may put you and Cowboy together."

"I'm starving," said Cowboy.

"You guys go have dinner. I'm too tired. Will you bring something back for me?" Liz asked.

Cowboy stood up and walked to the door. "You got it."

Hawk opened the door, and they walked out together.

"I saw a place I'd like to go. I'm not sure about the food, but I read about it in a tourist flyer. Do you know about Ernest Hemingway, the author?" asked Cowboy.

"I do," answered Hawk. "What's that got to do with anything?"

"He and his pals hung out at the Café Les Deux Magots, not far from the Café de Flore we ate at two days ago. I'd like to be able to say I ate there," mused Cowboy.

"Let's do this. It doesn't seem fair to leave Liz behind for this. We've got things set up pretty well. I'll go back and drag her along. She'll get a kick out of it," said Hawk.

He took the stairs, which were faster, and knocked on the door. "Liz, it's me, Hawk."

Liz opened the door and let him into the room. "What's got your tail feathers on fire, Hawk?"

Cowboy and I want to go to the café where Hemingway and his buddies hung out. It should be fun. We want you to come with us. We won't be gone long, and the recorder starts on its own. I know you're dead tired, but we really want you to come with us."

Tears started rolling down her cheeks.

"What did I do to make you cry?"

"I'm tired and lonely, and then you and Cowboy do something really nice for me, like share this experience with me. It made me happy to be included."

"Well, ah, take that silly dress off and put something else on. We'll wait down in the lobby for you."

"I won't be a minute." She smiled as she wiped the tears off with the end of her sleeve.

She decided to wear her new slacks with the tan and blue blouse again. She took the elevator down, and as she stepped into the lobby, Hawk and Cowboy both winked at her. They walked the few blocks to Saint-Germain-des-Prés, where they discovered the two cafés were around the corner from each other. They had a bottle of wine while their food was being prepared, and talked about the mission and the fact that D'Arcy's brother was coming to Paris. They were now tasked with taking out both of them. It would have to be a special circumstance to take both targets in a large city like Paris. They could track them fairly well with what they had put in place, but Paris was a concrete jungle, not the kind they were used to working in. It might be better to take them out on the trip to Zurich, depending on what transportation was used. They must keep connected and be ready to make the move when an opening appeared.

Their orders came, and they ordered another bottle of wine. Like little kids, they tasted each one's orders, and took a vote. Liz won, with her sautéed escargot in red wine sauce, braised rare filet mignon served on a bed of whipped cream, buttered mashed potatoes, and roasted asparagus with chips of almond. They were so full, and their taste buds were worn out. They decided to come again, if they could, and have a desert.

06:00 - 04 SEPTEMBER

TZ A

Cowboy left them to go to his room at the de La Salle. The recorder hadn't picked anything up while they were gone. They turned in and slept like logs until Liz's alarm went off. She got ready to go back to the de La Salle, and banged on Hawk's door to make sure he was up and ready for the day. She and Cowboy were planning on putting the bug in the flat if D'Arcy and his men would only leave long enough for her to get Cowboy into the flat. Hawk answered the knock by knocking back. Liz left for the de La Salle in her maid uniform, her Walther tucked in the pocket of her apron.

The morning meeting for the maids went quickly. There were no complaints to worry about, and the top floor maid didn't come to work. Liz figured she took the day off knowing Liz, the new girl, would be there. Mr. Malmert looked at his watch and said that Liz should take the fourth and fifth floors for the day. She wanted to jump up and down with joy, but held it down as she pushed her cleaning cart to the elevator. She got off on the fourth floor and knocked on Cowboy's door. He opened it slightly and told her he would wait for her in the room and that he was ready.

Liz cleaned several of the fourth-floor rooms, and left the rest. She went up to the fifth floor and knocked on the door, saying, "Maid service."

The answer came, "We'll be leaving in fifteen minutes. Come back then."

She went back, to clean another fourth-floor room. After the fifteen minutes were up, she returned to the flat on the fifth floor. She knocked again. No one answered, so she used her pass key and went in. The living room and kitchen were open and well decorated, like some decorator had done the entire flat. She ran out the door and down the stairs and knocked on Cowboy's door. He came out with his suitcase and backpack immediately, like he had been standing by the door waiting. They took the stairs two at a time and ran down the hall to the apartment door. They burst into the flat, and Cowboy began looking for the best place to put the bug. There was an end table by a large brown leather sofa that was close to the island that divided the kitchen from the living room. He took off the shade from a lamp sitting on the end table, unscrewed the bulb, and placed the two fine wires to the bug in the socket. Then he replaced the bulb and wedged the bug between the socket and the support for the lampshade. It was nearly invisible. He looked at Liz and said, "It's ready."

Liz told him, "Get out of here and back to the other hotel. I'm going to stay and clean up. It will be better if I stay working here until we leave, I think."

"Good idea. I'll see you this evening."

10:22 - 04 SEPTEMBER

TZ A

Hawk watched as D'Arcy and his guards left the de La Salle hotel. He was sure that Cowboy and Liz were in the top floor flat already. Hawk had been ready to follow the three men since before Liz knocked on his door. He had his 1911A1 tucked in the small of his back, and his silenced .22 tucked behind his belt, with his shirttail out to cover it. If he had to protect himself, he would use the .22, so any bystanders wouldn't hear the shot and raise an alarm.

He hoped the three didn't go to the garage and use the car. Cowboy had put the FM transmitter on it, but he and Hawk still hadn't rented a car in Paris. He ran down the stairs to the lobby and watched as they headed away from the garage and toward a Métro entrance on Saint-Michel. Hawk stayed well back on the other side of the street as he started to follow the three men. There was no way to stay at a safe distance behind them once they went down the steps to the station. He had to take his chances that he wouldn't be spotted following them. One of the bodyguards went to the ticket window and came back with tickets for them. Hawk waited a minute, looking at an ad on the wall, that was out of date by two months. He walked over to the same window and asked the clerk if he could buy a ticket to the end of the line. She sold him one. The underground train came into the station a minute or so after he bought the ticket. D'Arcy and his men were busy looking at the map on the platform wall. They got on the train that was going north, and Hawk followed by stepping into a car next to theirs.

The subway stopped several times after it went under the Seine, but the men stayed on the train. The sign at the last stop said Gare du Nord was the next stop. All three men stood up and held on to the rail that ran overhead. Hawk figured they were getting off at North Train Station, so he stood up and held on to the overhead rail looking back, trying to not let them see his face. The subway slowed to a stop. The three men got out and started walking up the stairs and through the big open area where the ticket windows were. The trains were behind a gated wall where you had to show your ticket and were told which track your train was sitting at, if you didn't already know. Hawk watched them, through the throng of people, walk to the Switzerland ticket window. D'Arcy stepped up to the window and talked with the woman behind the glass. The two guards stood looking around. Watching anyone near D'Arcy, eyes darting here and there, not stopping on any one person unless they felt something was wrong about the people they were looking at. Both had their right hands under their shirts close to their backs. Hawk knew that's where the guns were. The short one's gaze, the one Liz called No-neck, stopped for a second on Hawk, and then moved on. Hawk walked over to a fountain and got a drink of water, waiting for D'Arcy to finish.

He waited until D'Arcy and his henchmen had walked away. He figured he would lose them when he went to the counter, but they were traveling somewhere. He needed to know where and when. He went to the Switzerland window and said, "My friends just bought tickets. I was late getting here. I need three tickets, the same as they bought."

"Yes sir. Three to Zurich. Do you want the club car like they bought, or coach?"

"I'll take coach. I need rest, not drinks." He smiled. "By the way, how long is the trip to Zurich?"

"Only four hours."

Hawk paid for the tickets and saw they were for three days in advance. When he looked up, he saw No-neck watching him intently. He didn't see D'Arcy or the other guard. Hawk figured No-neck had been left behind on purpose. Somehow, he had been spotted. He looked around for someplace to confront him. There was a men's room a short distance away. He walked over to it and went in. He quickly went to each stall to make sure they were empty, and then walked back to the wall blocking the entry from sight. No-neck, if he was any good, would wait a minute, and then carefully come past the blocking wall and into the toilet area.

First the right hand, then the rest of the right arm, moving back and forth, as his eyes moved around the toilet area. No-neck moved farther into the sink area, and Hawk walked quickly up behind him and knocked the gun from his hand. No-neck turned suddenly with a short stabbing knife in his left hand, and thrust it toward Hawk's body. With his left forearm, Hawk shoved the knife and his arm farther out to the left and pulled the silenced .22 from his belt. The knife went flying as he pushed the .22 hard against the soft spot under No-neck's chin and pulled the trigger, blowing the top part of No-neck's head off with the hollow-point bullet. No-neck flopped down like a wet rag. Hawk quickly pulled him into the first stall and searched him. He found his wallet and passport and left him sitting up on the seat with what was left of his head leaning against the stall wall. There were blood and brain matter all over the sinks and floor, but he couldn't do anything about that. He put the .22 back where it had been and walked from the men's room, toward the stairs leading to the Métro that would take him away from North Station.

He ended up by the Eiffel Tower. He caught a taxi that took him to Café la Flore, and then walked to the hotel on Rue de l'Universite. Cowboy and Liz were already there, waiting on him to return. He told them what happened at the North Station as he threw the passport and wallet on the bed.

He said, "I took those"—pointing down to the wallet and passport— "to hopefully make the police and D'Arcy think it was a robbery."

"How do you think No-neck picked you out as trouble?" asked Liz.

"I don't know for sure, unless it was last night when you came in and told us about him following you. Remember, I stepped out of the front door to the hotel, looking for him. He could have been hiding somewhere and tied you and I together, and then when he saw me at the Gare du Nord today, he decided it was time to find out who I was."

Cowboy said, "That's kind of a long shot, if you ask me. I don't think we need to worry about him anymore. We need to find out if he talked to D'Arcy about you and Liz."

"Maybe, we'll pick something up from the bug you planted today," said Liz.

"We better hope so, or Cowboy will be the only one clear to be seen by them, without compromising the mission," said Hawk.

15:12 - 04 SEPTEMBER

TZ A

"I have to know what happened to Claude. Was it an accident, or not? It couldn't be the people from Mexico. Is he in Paris somewhere, or at a hospital?" asked Carlos.

"Maybe he will still contact us, sir," said Hook Nose.

"Turn the radio on to the Paris news channel. Maybe they will have something about him," said Carlos. "In the meantime, I'll call my brother and make sure he is coming to Paris tomorrow and tell him to bring another man with him."

D'Arcy went to his phone and called his brother's number in, Marseille. His brother answered on the first ring.

"Andre, one of the men you sent to me has gone missing. I'm trying to find him. If I don't, bring another man with you to replace him."

"Do you think it was foul play?" asked Andre.

"I don't know yet."

"I didn't tell the two men what our plans are. Did you?" Andre asked.

"No, of course not. Just bring another man with you along with the two men who normally guard you," said Carlos angrily as he slammed down the phone. "That brother of mine gets on my nerves, sometimes," he said, to no one in particular.

In the hotel room across the street, they were listening to the bug in the room and recording the phone call. After it got quiet in the flat, they rewound the tape and played it.

Hawk said, "It sounds like we may have been lucky. He doesn't seem to know what happened to No-neck, and that means we're in the clear. No-neck must have stayed behind on his own, thinking he would get a reward or something when he brought me to Carlos and told him my connection to Liz and that I was following them."

"Let's keep listening to the bug for tonight, and turn the radio to the Paris news station, like Carlos is. That should cover all the bases, for now," said Cowboy.

Liz walked over to the nightstand by her bed and tuned the radio to a news station. She told them, "I'll listen to the Paris news while you two take care of the bug and the phone."

Hawk and Cowboy each took up position next to the room bug speaker and the recorder. Nothing happened until Liz pursed her lips for them to be quiet. They had started talking to keep from being bored out of their minds. She pointed to the radio and translated as the reporter said, "There was a police call to North Station for a robbery and murder earlier today. The police haven't released the victim's name, and they have no suspects at this time. The man was found by a bathroom cleaning person. According to the police report, when they got there the victim had been dead for about fifteen minutes."

She turned the radio off as Hawk said, "Let's see what, if anything, Carlos has to say, now that the police have released the information to the news."

All three listened intently to the room bug until Carlos spoke to the guard that was still with him. "Sounds like Claude went to the men's room and got mugged then killed. That how it sounds to you?"

"Yes sir, just a very bad accident. It's a good thing you asked your brother to bring up another man to help me."

Liz said, "Boy's I'm going to bed. I'll let you know if the speaker or the recorder start up. Good night."

07:15 - 05 SEPTEMBER

TZ A

The next day, Liz pushed her cleaning cart to the fourth-floor elevator door and hit the button for the fifth floor. She waited for the elevator to come up from the lobby. The elevator cleared the third floor with two men in it. One of them gave her a shock. It was D'Arcy. She started to turn away, and stopped. There was something different about him. He was taller than she remembered, and less fat. More on the medium weight side. Still, he had the bulging eyes and bulbous lips that D'Arcy had. By this time, the elevator had stopped, and the cage door rolled back. The man that looked like D'Arcy spoke to her in French, with an accent from Southern France. D'Arcy would have a Mexican or Spanish accent. This had to be his brother, Andre.

"Pardon us, miss. We're going to the top floor, and there is no room for your cart. I'll send the lift back down when we get off," said Andre.

He closed the cage door and turned to his guard as the lift ascended, and said, "She is very beautiful. Much too beautiful to be just a maid in my hotel. Keep that in mind when I am making plans for travel with Carlos. I may want to take her with us."

Liz opened the elevator door and pushed her cart into it. She pushed the button for the lobby. She took her cart to the maids' room and went to Mr. Malmert's office. The door was open.

"May I speak with you, Mr. Malmert?"

"Yes, of course, Sabine. What is it?"

"I'm not feeling well—something I ate last night, I guess. I have finished cleaning the rooms on the fourth floor. May I go to my apartment and rest for a short while? I'll come back and clean the flat when I feel better.

"Is your apartment nearby?"

"Yes sir, it is but a short ride on the Métro."

"Make sure you are back in time to clean the owner's flat, and Sabine, don't let this be a habit. Do you understand?"

"Yes sir. I'll be back in plenty of time to clean the flat."

She went through the lobby and out to the street. She turned toward Saint-Michel Blvd., where the Métro entrance was, and walked around the block in case someone was watching her. She went to her room, and found Hawk and Cowboy there listening to a conversation on the speaker.

"I took a short time off, to make sure you knew that his brother, Andre, has arrived. He looks like D'Arcy, but taller and less fat. Same eyes and lips though."

"We heard him talking to someone new, but didn't know who it was. His accent is more French. Carlos's accent has a Spanish sound to it."

She waited for an hour before returning to the hotel, following the same route she had taken to get to their hotel, but in reverse. She checked in with Mr. Malmert and took the cart back to the top floor. She knocked on the door and was asked to come in. It surprised her, but she knew she had to confront D'Arcy at some point. The two brothers were standing together, talking with four guards sitting around the living room. Andre told her she could start with the bedrooms and baths. Both men looked her over from head to toe and back again as she moved to the first bedroom. She wanted to scream, but got control, and realized even though the brothers had visually undressed her, Carlos didn't seem to recognize her. She realized she had left her cart out in the hall. She pulled sheets from both bedrooms, and towels from the one used by Carlos. Then she had to cross the living area to get her cart. She went out and got the cart, hoping she was invisible, like most maids. She could hear the men talking softly when she reached the bedrooms with the cart. She cringed again and let her hand drop to the reassuring feel of her pistol in her apron pocket. She heard the entry door open and close. She continued cleaning and changing bed sheets until she had finished the bedrooms and baths. She pushed her cart down the short hall and into the living area. All the men were gone. She quickly looked around the kitchen and living area to find anything that might be helpful. There were newspapers spread about the sitting area. She looked through them quickly and put them in her cart's trash bag. Liz finished cleaning the kitchen, which didn't look like it had been used, and straightened up the living area.

***

When she got back to the hotel, Hawk and Cowboy told her about the conversation the brothers had while she was cleaning the bedroom area.

Hawk said, "They both admired you, after you went to clean the bedrooms, and then discussed travel plans. Carlos didn't recognize you. It seems like Andre wants to take his car to Zurich. That leaves Carlos to take the train, or use a car. If that happens, hopefully he'll still use the one parked in the garage, with the radio beacon attached. It would make it easier for us to follow. Then they decided to have lunch, and left."

Hawk didn't tell her exactly what they had said about her, physically, or what they would like to do with her, or to her. Cowboy and he had talked it over and thought it better not to get into the nitty-gritty of the foul-mouthed ideas the brothers shared.

"I'll take the Métro out to the airport in the morning and rent a car for us. We'd better be prepared for any contingency," offered Hawk. "Cowboy, you keep watch on the electronics. Liz, are you up to being a maid one more day? It might help us to know how many men we're dealing with, plus any information you can pick up that we don't get from the electronics."

"I'll be there bright-eyed and bushy-tailed, as we say in South Texas," she said.

Andre was standing on the little balcony overlooking the interior park when he asked, "Carlos, I don't see why we can't leave early in the morning. There's nothing keeping us from it, is there?"

Carlos, standing by him drinking scotch, said, "No, I suppose not. I'd like to get the banking finished and head down to Marseille and start that trip on the new yacht."

"I'll tell the men to get ready. Are you taking the train or driving?" asked Andre.

"I can change the train tickets to today. It's only four hours to Zurich, compared to six by car. Do you want to stay at the Widder Hotel like we normally do?" asked Carlos.

"It very nice, and close to everything, including our bank," said Andre.

"The Widder it is," agreed Carlos.

They walked back into the living area and told the bodyguards to prepare to leave for Zurich. Andre took his main bodyguard out to the little balcony so his brother wouldn't hear his instructions. He asked him if he remembered the small wooden gate on the narrow alley that opened on to the park, at the back of the hotel. The guard said he did. "I will have the manager keep the maid in the office. When I go out to the car, you will go to the office, and if necessary, bind and gag her, and carry her out to the street, in front of the gate. We will pick you up there and drive to Zurich. Don't speak of this to anyone. I want her to be my companion on the new yacht." The guard told him he understood completely.

07:06 - 06 SEPTEMBER

TZ A

Liz went back to the maids' room in her uniform. The maid that had been absent the last few days was having a cup of coffee and talking with the other maid. She told Sabine good morning and that she appreciated her covering the top floors for her. Mr. Malmert came in and told Sabine she would be taking the ground-floor rooms, and after that help out where she was needed most.

Hawk took the Métro out to the airport and rented a car. He used his fake passport and driver's license in the name of Peter Higgins, as ID. He drove back to the garage on Rue de l'Universite and paid the man at the chained driveway, to park for a day. He walked back to the hotel.

Cowboy was excited when he came into the bedroom and said in a hurry, "Something is up. I only got a bit of the conversation, but it sounds like they have changed their plans and are leaving today for Zurich."

"Today?" asked Hawk. "Are you sure?"

"I'm sure. I don't know if they are going together, or one by train and one by car."

"Here's what we'll do. I don't like the idea of splitting us up, but it looks like the only way. If Carlos takes the train, you'll have to keep track of him. I'll pick up Liz, and we'll follow Andre in the rental car, since it is rented under my alias and Carlos and his crew may know me or recognize Liz. You good to go with that, Cowboy?"

"I'll put some clothes in a backpack, and keep my weapons on me. You'll have to take the rest of the stuff we may need, in the car. I can help you do that right now."

They hurriedly packed and took all the suitcases, including Liz's clothes, down to the car. Cowboy took his suitcase and a train ticket to change, and waited by the bedroom window. Hawk wanted to go tell Liz what was happening, but thought better of it. If he went over there it could blow the whole mission. They still hadn't seen an opening to take the brothers out. They had to continue to track them until the opportunity came. Hawk would get her as soon as they left in the car, if they left in the car.

Andre sent his driver down to get his car and park in front of the hotel to load the luggage. They were taking Carlos's and his men's luggage in the car. It would be easier that way. When the driver came back up, the luggage was taken down all at one time. Andre had talked with the manager, and he knew what to do. He was to call Sabine in and keep her there until Andre's man came in the office. Malmert was to leave, and Andre's man was to tape her mouth closed and her hands together, then carry her out the back door of the office to the little patio, and then to the gate, where Andre would be waiting with the car. His brother would never know about the kidnapping, until they reached Zurich. The hotel Widder was an 1800s hotel that had many ways to enter. He knew he could keep her in his hotel room for the one or two days they would be there, no problem.

The luggage was in the car. Carlos shook hands with Andre in the lobby and went out, with his two guards following him, to the Métro entrance. Andre turned and gave the signal to Malmert to call Sabine into his office. When she came in from cleaning a room on the lobby floor, he told her to take a seat. He started to tell her that he liked the way she did her job, when the office door opened and a man she had seen acting as a bodyguard for the brother Andre walked in and motioned for Malmert to leave. She stood up and faced him. He hit her hard on the side of her face. She fell to the floor, out like a light.

09:50 - 06 SEPTEMBER

TZ A

When she came to, she was in the back seat of a car moving through the streets of Paris. Her mouth was dry, and she tried to lift her hands to touch them. When she lifted her hands, they were taped together at the wrists with duct tape. She figured her mouth was duct taped also. She saw Andre in the back seat with her. Watching her, like an owl watching a field mouse. One of his guards was driving the car very fast in the Paris traffic. The other guard was turned so he could see her in the back seat. Her mind was going a mile a minute. What did Andre have planned for her? Did Hawk and Cowboy know she had been kidnapped? She was sure when they knew, nothing would stop them from coming after her, and the people that had taken her. Then she remembered her apron pocket. She carefully felt the button. She could move it. Her Walther was cocked and locked like Hawk had told her to do. She would wait for the right time to use it. Knowing she had access to the pistol gave her hope and courage.

Cowboy left the hotel and followed Carlos to the Métro and bought a ticket for North Station. The train came right on time. He went into the car behind them, like Hawk had done before. Carlos and his men didn't seem to be concerned about anyone following them. Cowboy left the car at North Station after Carlos and watched from the top of the steps while Carlos changed tickets. When they walked to the entrance of the train loading area, he walked over and changed his ticket. Carlos had gone into the loading area looking for the correct train number. When Carlos boarded, Cowboy went to the closest coach car and sat down. He could see into the club car through the windows of the train cars. The train started to move. Cowboy watched the men in the club car to make sure no one jumped ship.

Hawk ran over to the Hôtel de La Salle, looking for Liz. He looked around the lobby and then went to the clerk. The clerk acted rather strange. He told Hawk he would have to talk to the manager. The manager told him she had quit her job and left.

Hawk went around the desk where Malmert was sitting and jerked him out of his seat. He hit him as hard as he could in the face, breaking his nose. Blood splattered everywhere.

"Where is she?" he demanded. "I'll hurt you badly if you don't tell me."

"I can't tell you. They will come back and kill me," Malmert said while trying to wipe some of the blood on his white shirt sleeve.

Hawk said, "You will tell me now, or you will die now." He pulled his silenced .22 from under his shirt and pressed it against Malmert's forehead.

"The owner, Andre D'Arcy, took her with him in his car. He took her to Zurich with him. That's all I know." He looked down at his pants as a large wet spot appeared in front.

Hawk ran to the table he had seen in the lobby and grabbed a road map of France. He ran to the garage and jumped in the rental car. He wound through the streets until he reached a street that went east and west. He headed east weaving in and out of traffic. A road sign indicated a highway ahead, going to Zurich. He didn't know if it was the same one Andre was on, but any one that led to Zurich was the right direction. The traffic continued to thin, and his speed came up accordingly. When the highway left Paris behind, there was a *Y* in the road. Both went to Zurich, but the one to the left had a higher speed limit. He drove with the gas pedal all the way to the floor, toward the faster road. Further down, the highway ran through a small village. But he didn't slow down. There was no traffic going west. After another village went past, he could see a car going in his direction. It suddenly dawned on him he didn't know what kind of car they were driving. He raced up on the car and started to pass it. There were three men in it. One in back and two in front. As he started to pull around the rear of the car, the man in the back looked back at him. Hawk had never seen Andre, but he knew it couldn't be Carlos. The way Liz described Andre with the bugged eyes and the bulging lips, he was looking at Andre. Hawk pulled up even with the other car, looking at the back seat as he did. Liz was in the back, with duct tape over her mouth. She saw him as he passed, and nodded her head at him. He pulled ahead and moved into the right lane. He started to slow down little by little, not using his brakes. Just letting the inertia of the car slow itself down. The car with Liz in it started to pass him.

Liz felt the car slow down. Hawk was trying to stop Andre's car. Hawk was weaving back and forth across the road to keep Andre's car from passing. All three men were looking at the crazy driver in front of them. Liz slowly slipped the button through the button hole and reached into the shallow pocket, grasping the handle of the Walther. She pushed the safety off and prepared herself for what she had to do. She pulled the Walther out and shot the bodyguard in the right front seat. The shot hit him in the face, blowing it apart. She turned the gun to Andre, who had an astonished look on his face. She shot him in the right eye. The driver looked back, trying to see what was happening, when she shot him in the side of the head. Brain matter, bone fragments, and blood hit the inside of the windshield. The car pulled to the right, hitting dirt and gravel on the side of the road, and swerved down into the ditch, rolling over, and stopping right side up.

Hawk saw what was happening in the other car. He continued to slow, until the car Liz was in went into the ditch and rolled over. He slammed on his breaks and jumped out of the car, leaving it running. He pulled his M1911 from his back and ran to the car, trying to open Liz's door. He couldn't open it, no matter how hard he pulled. He had to get to her and make sure she was alright. He pulled on the driver's door, and it came open. The driver was over on top of the man riding in the front seat with him. Hawk yelled Liz's name and heard a moan. He saw her lying on top of the man, Andre. Hawk reached into the back and pulled gently on her arms until she was upright. She opened her eyes and made a small smile. She still had her pistol in her hand. He took it from her as she resisted, and put it in the front of his pants. Hawk pulled her to the front and picked her up. He took her to his car and put her in the back seat lying down. He got in the front seat and started to drive off. He had to get away from the wreck and carnage in the car before anyone came by and saw the car he was driving pulling away from the death and destruction.

14:02 - 06 SEPTEMBER

TZ A

The train stopped in a huge terminal in the middle of Zurich Old Town. It had passed over a bridge to an island surrounded by two rivers. Cowboy followed D'Arcy and his men from the terminal on to Bahnhofstrasse. They walked down the street, and in a few minutes, a huge old hotel, with the name Widden Hotel, appeared on the right side of the street. The men went into the lobby. Cowboy waited until he was sure they were staying there, and went looking for the hotel the clerk in Paris had recommended. He went back to the train station and walked across a bridge connecting the island and train station to the mainland. The river Limmat ran swiftly under the bridge. One block from the bridge, he saw the Central Plaza Hotel. It was located in the middle of the Old Town shopping area and close to all the various business centers and banks. A tram ran down the middle of the street. He went through the nicely done lobby to the reception counter. He booked two rooms for a week. The clerk asked about his luggage. He told the clerk it was coming with the other people using the second room. He went up to the double room. It was bigger than any they had used in Paris. The beds were comfortable, and the bath was twice the size they had in Paris. He stretched out and soon fell asleep.

Carlos had taken four rooms with two adjoining. That would keep the bodyguards close at hand. He couldn't possibly imagine a problem happening in Zurich, but he was still jumpy from the things that had happened in Mexico. He made a call to their bank, the UBL Switzerland bank, and told the manager that he and his brother would need an appointment for the next day to transact some private business. The manager gave him a three in the afternoon time.

Hawk drove on for another hour, even though Liz was making all kinds of noise in the back seat. He saw another village coming up, and pulled off the highway to a rest area, along the side of the road. When he took the tape off Liz's mouth, a torrent of yelled cuss words blew from her mouth.

"Why the hell didn't you stop and take this tape off my mouth, you son of a bitch! I could have choked to death, you bastard!" she screamed at him.

"I needed to get us away from the crash scene. You killed three people back there. You want to live in a French prison for the rest of your life?" He continued to take the tape off her hands and pointed to a restroom. "You can clean up in there. Make it quick. We still need to put distance between all the dead men back there and us."

When she came back to the car, much cleaner and calmer, Hawk was sitting in the rented car waiting. Liz took the shotgun seat and looked straight ahead.

Hawk said, "That was a hell of a thing you did to those assholes. Tell me how you decided which one to do first."

He pulled onto the highway and headed East for Zurich.

"I don't want to talk about it right now. Let's just say, they kidnapped me, and I wasn't going to let that happen to me again. Thanks to you and Cowboy, I was able to take care of myself, and I knew one, or both, of you would find me. Because of that, I wasn't ever really scared."

Hawk didn't look at her when he said, "You're one of the best I've ever seen!"

"What'd you mean by that?" she asked.

"You're a natural. Most need years of training, but you think on your feet, don't get flustered when something goes wrong, and have steel nerves. You're a natural-born assassin."

"I guess that was a backdoor compliment. Let's not tell anyone else about the nice things you just said about me, alright?" she said with a crooked smile at him.

"No problem," said Hawk.

It took them seven hours to reach Zurich and to find the train station where they parked the rental. They carried three suitcases across the bridge and found the Central Plaza Hotel with no trouble. The clerk gave them the key to the other room Cowboy had reserved, and they went up in the elevator, a real one this time, to the second-floor room. Hawk knocked on the connecting door, and a sleepy-eyed Cowboy opened it. Hawk walked in and looked around. It was bigger and nicer than any they had in Paris. He asked Liz if she liked her room. A quiet yes came back, and then she said, "I need to take a bath and a nap. Wake me when it's time to eat." She closed the door on him.

"Cowboy, were you able to tail those guys to the hotel they are staying at?" asked Hawk.

"They're in a place named the Widder Hotel. It's down from the train station a few blocks on Bahnhofstrasse Street."

"Let's walk down there so I know where it is, and while we're walking I have something I need to tell you about."

They walked across the bridge to the station and went down Bahnhofstrasse to the Widder Hotel. Hawk told Cowboy about Liz being kidnapped and what happened after that, while they walked. When he finished, Cowboy said, "She did all that without help from you?"

Hawk nodded his head up and down. Cowboy said, "That's one tough lady. I'm glad she's on our side. Do you think she's doing okay with it?"

"I think she's having some questions about the whole thing. I mean, she's not jumping up and down about doing all three of them. I think she realizes she had no alternative and the 'them or me syndrome' is helping her remain stable. I don't think we should treat her any differently or ask questions about it. She'll talk with us when she has it straight in her head, and not before, I think," Hawk said.

"Well, I have to tell you I'm damn proud of her!" Cowboy said strongly.

"Me too! We need to find us some hides to watch D'Arcy and his men come and go. Let's walk around for a bit and see what's available," Hawk said.

There was a café directly across the street from the hotel, and a coffee shop on the corner. Both looked like places they could use. Since there were three of them they would rotate from place to place and change times throughout the day.

By late evening Carlos was wondering where Andre was. The train took four hours to get to Zurich. Driving took six or seven hours depending on which highways they were using. He should have been in Zurich by at least three or four in the afternoon. Maybe they had a flat, or an accident. He called the headquarters of Altamar Shipping and asked for the CEO, Jean-Paul Durant.

"This is Jean-Paul Durant."

"Jean-Paul, this is Carlos D'Arcy. Andre and I are in Zurich, about to take care of some private business. I was planning on coming down to Marseille with Andre and having a business meeting with you about the continuation of our special shipments program. I am considering cutting this trip short and returning to Mexico. There is a possibility of increasing our special shipments program to Mexico by at least double in the next few months with the closing down of our biggest competitor. Would you be able to come up for a day or two in the company plane and discuss the possibilities with us?"

"Of course, Carlos. I'll clear my appointments for the next two days. I'll plan on being there in the morning. Are you at the Widden again?" asked Durant.

"Yes, we are. I will make a reservation for you. Will there be anyone with you that needs a separate room?"

"No, I'll make the normal reservations for the pilot and co-pilot."

"Good, we'll see you in the morning, then."

Carlos called the reception desk and made a reservation for Jean-Paul Durant, on the same floor as they were on.

Durant told his secretary to make a reservation for two rooms at the Central Plaza Hotel in Zurich, for the company pilot and co-pilot for two nights, and to call them and tell them they would be flying to Zurich early in the morning for two days, and then return to Marseille.

Cowboy and Hawk returned to the hotel and took turns cleaning up. They left a note for Liz, under the connecting door, and told her they would be in the lobby lounge when she was ready to go out for dinner. Liz noticed the note when she was going to knock on the door. She was hungry, and could use a drink after the happenings of the days, so she rode the elevator down to the lobby and looked for the lounge. It was separated from the main lobby by a low wall and etched glass. A waiter stood by at the opening to the bar and offered to seat her. She saw the boys at a small corner table, with their backs against the wall, both facing the bar and other tables. They saw her talking with the waiter and waved her over. They had a couple of cold beers in frosty mugs in front of them. When she sat at the table, a waiter was beside her with the drink and snacks menu.

She looked up at the waiter and said, "Do you have tequila here?"

"Yes, we do."

"Sauza?" she asked.

"Yes. Which one would you like? Extra or Conmemorativo?"

"Conmemorativo, please."

"How would you like it served?"

"I'd like it chilled in a tumbler. No salt, no lime."

"As you wish," said the waiter.

Hawk and Cowboy watched this exchange and then laughed out loud. "We should have known you were a tequila drinker. That fits right in with all the other events of the day. Enjoy yourself, Liz. The party's on us," said Hawk.

07:22 - 07 SEPTEMBER

TZ A

Hawk took the first watch at the restaurant across from the Widder Hotel. It was barely past daybreak, and the early risers and early workers crowded the counter wanting a coffee to go. Hawk sat with his back to the wall, facing the street. No one entered or left the hotel until ten in the morning. Businessmen were going to meetings, and salesmen went to talk with shop owners. There was one man that walked to the hotel with an overnight bag and a briefcase coming from the direction of the train station, or the airport, which was just past the station to the north of town. He was better dressed than the average businessman. He walked with authority, not looking down or around, but like he was on a mission. He disappeared into the hotel. A waiter came by, and Hawk ordered another coffee.

***

Durant checked in and was given a key for a room near the two rooms the D'Arcy brothers had. He had been upset all the way up from Marseille. Late last night, there was a call from the Zurich police asking if he knew an Andre D'Arcy. He told them he did. He was the co-owner of Altamar Shipping, the company he worked for. They told him Andre was dead, had been murdered along with two other men just inside the Swiss border from France. He had a business card, with Durant's name on it. They wanted to know if there were relatives they could contact. He told them no, he had no relatives. He knew Carlos wouldn't want the police asking him questions about family, of which, there were none. But also about their business and why his brother had been shot in the head. Execution style. He was going to tell Carlos in person. He was certain it would upset him.

Durant knocked on Carlos's room door. A bodyguard asked who was there. He told him his name. The guard opened the door and stepped aside so he could enter the living room. Carlos was sitting on the sofa having coffee. He didn't stand to shake hands. He didn't ask Durant to sit down. He simply said, "How good to see you cousin Jean-Paul."

Durant nodded and cleared his throat. He began by telling Carlos about the late-night call, and about his brother, ending with, "I didn't mention you as the nearest relative. I thought if you wanted to do that, you would."

Carlos sat still for a moment and told him he did the right thing. With the company doing the special shipments program, there couldn't be any type of police involvement. Carlos didn't miss a beat. He told the guard to prepare to leave immediately. He told Durant that he was still running the company, and the special shipments were to continue. He would let him know if the shipments needed to be increased. He told him there was a rival company in Mexico that had been trying to stop him, and the special shipments. With Andre now murdered, he had to go back to Mexico and put a stop to the rival company. Durant knew what they were shipping and received special bonuses several times a year that allowed him to keep his mistress happy, and his wife too. They discussed other business while the guards were packing. Durant asked what Carlos would like to do about his brother.

"I can't have any connection to him. You take care of it. Cremate him. Where he's going it'll be hot anyway." Carlos laughed at his little joke.

Durant couldn't believe how callous Carlos was about his own brother. He told Carlos to let him know if he could be of any further assistance, and walked to the door.

Carlos called him back into the room. He told him about the yacht and the money they were going to transfer. He then told Durant to go to the bank and cancel the appointment. Then when he reached Marseille to stop the delivery of the yacht. He would have no need for it in Mexico, and he could use the $10 million in other ways, now that his brother was dead. Carlos said as Durant walked out the door, "We never had this meeting, Durant!"

***

Hawk noticed the well-dressed businessman leave the hotel. He thought it odd that he wasn't there for long. It wasn't long before Cowboy came to relieve him. He moved a chair so he had his back to the wall and could see the hotel also.

Carlos walked from the hotel, with his two bodyguards carrying suitcases, behind him. They walked toward the train station. Carlos thought, "I have to get out of Switzerland and get back to Mexico where I'm safe. No one must know Andre was my brother." Hawk and Cowboy stood up at the same time.

Hawk said, "We'll follow on opposite sides of the street. When we know what he's up to, one of us cuts to our hotel and gets Liz. If it's the train, I'll get tickets and wait for you at the main gate to the loading area. If he heads to the airport, we'll both have to follow to know where he is flying, and then get Liz."

"Well, I followed that, sort of. Let's follow him to the train station and then re-think what we want to do," said Cowboy as he moved at a fast walk toward the far side of the street.

"I can't believe this is happening. He had to have some meetings set up for a day or two. He must have found out his brother was dead this morning. Wait a minute. The guy in the nice business suit. He had something to do with Carlos leaving suddenly," thought Hawk as he walked along Bahnhofstrasse.

Carlos and his guards went to the *hauptbahnhof*. Hawk stayed with them, and Cowboy ran back to the Central Plaza Hotel to get Liz. He told her what had happened while they repacked everything. They saw a tram in front of the hotel and ran to catch it. The tram didn't stop again until it reached the train station. They hopped off, and fast walked into the ticketing area, where they found Hawk standing at the main boarding gate. He held out three tickets to the man checking tickets and was told by him the train to Paris was on line four and about to leave. They hurried to the last coach car, resting against the stopping barrier, and hopped on with backpacks only.

Hawk told them Carlos was again in the club car and seemed very agitated by the time he went past the ticket agent at the gate. He told them what he thought about the man in the nice suit, and ended by saying he didn't have a connection between the two men. It was just a hunch.

They settled in for the four-hour train ride back to Paris. Carlos and his guards went to the taxi station in front of the train station north, and left in a cab. Hawk, Liz, and Cowboy did the same. Hawk felt a little silly about telling the driver to follow that cab, but that's what he did. After following the taxi for a short distance, the driver looked in his rear-view mirror and said, "It's going to *aéroport de* Paris Nord."

Hawk tipped the taxi driver for following the other taxi, and they all walked into the ticketing area for the North Paris airport. They wandered around looking at the signs with various flights and times for cities all over the world. Carlos went to the TWA counter and bought a ticket. The two bodyguards went with him to the waiting area. Hawk went up to the counter and asked the clerk to give him a ticket for the same flight as his friend just bought.

"Do you want first class also?" the ticket agent asked.

"No, coach will be fine," said Hawk.

The ticket agent gave him two tickets. One was for a flight to La Guardia, and the other was to Mexico City. He paid for the tickets. He thanked the agent and walked back to where Cowboy and Liz were standing.

He told them, "He's headed home. La Guardia then Mexico City. I have tickets on the same flight. I don't know what you guys want to do. I'm going to finish this mission. It's all volunteer, so Liz, if you want to go back to Texas, this is a good time to go. Cowboy, what's your choice?"

Cowboy looked at him in a disgusted way and said, "You couldn't find the seat of your pants if I didn't help you. I'm in."

Liz said, "After what that asshole did to me, you think I would miss out on the end of the hunt? I'm in for the whole deal."

"I'm going into the gate area. You two buy tickets for the same flights tomorrow. I'm afraid we might overexpose ourselves if we all go on the same flight with him. He only bought one ticket, so the goons will leave him when he goes to the gate area. They will probably go to the Hôtel de La Salle. Follow them and stay at our old hotel across the street. Listen to what they say there, or what is said on the phone. Catch the flights tomorrow, and I'll meet you at the airport in Mexico City when you land. Unless some special opportunity comes our way, we probably won't finish the mission until he is back in the Yucatán."

Cowboy and Liz's flight was delayed by an hour, due to storms along the east coast of the US. They had their backpacks with them, so they didn't stop at the luggage area. Hawk was waiting for them by the entry/exit doors in the ticket area. He told them he had a rental car, and a couple of rooms near the airport to rest up in, and to make plans. On the way to the hotel, he told them he had checked with the FBO where private planes parked. The manager there told him a twin-engine plane filed a flight plan for Cozumel early in the morning and took off as soon as the one passenger boarded. He told them that the manager was sure about only the one passenger. The flight plan, the co-pilot filed had the number of souls on board as three. The pilot, co-pilot, and passenger. It had to be him.

They each got a key for the two rooms, and called down for room service for dinner. While they waited, Cowboy told Hawk about the information they had picked up from the two guards, who had stayed at de La Salle as Hawk had hoped. The talk between the two of them was about how scared D'Arcy was when he got the word from the head of Altamar Shipping that his brother had been murdered. He wasn't concerned about his brother. He was highly worried he would be caught up in a police investigation about it. They talked about how callous he was about his brother's death, even to the point of making a joke about cremating him. Carlos had told the man running the shipping company for him that the special shipping program would continue, and could double in volume if a rival company went out of business. A Mr. Durant called to let them know they were needed back in Marseille. He told them Mr. D'Arcy had gone back to Mexico to make sure the other company failed in its attempt to take over Mr. D'Arcy's company. Hawk picked up on the man named Durant. He told Cowboy and Liz about the well-dressed man that had come and gone, in a short amount of time, from the hotel where D'Arcy stayed.

Room service came, but they continued to talk as they ate. Hawk thought they should rent a pickup, or something like one, to use on the way to the Yucatán. Cowboy wrote out a list of things they would need. The truck with their equipment was somewhere in the United States. Hawk told him to put down a spotting scope and an M14 with a scope, with plenty of ammunition, and a new Kay-Bar. Liz needed more ammunition for her Walther. Cowboy wanted a pair of prick sixes. When the list was complete, they all went for a walk, stopping at the first pay phone they saw. Liz and Cowboy walked around looking in windows along the street watching out for Hawk while he made the call and read off the list of things they needed. After what seemed like an hour to the window watchers, Hawk hung up and walked over to them.

He said, "The stuff will come in on a private plane to Mérida in two days around eight at night. It'll park away from the FBO, in as much dark as possible. The pilot's code name will be Wild Bill. He'll help us load, and then take off, without filing a flight plan. We'll try to find a pickup in the morning. Captain Jack has added Roger Burns to the target list. There was a presidential finding made to cover us in the United States, for this type of mission. The president can't afford to have Burns's traitorous behavior become common knowledge. It could tear the county apart. His death will have to look like an accident. It'll take a day and a half to drive to Mérida from here. We all need to pick up new clothes too."

Hawk went down to the reception desk and asked if there was a car rental nearby that had pickups to rent. The desk clerk said he knew of such a rental company, but it was on the other side of the city. He asked when they would need it, and Hawk told him in the morning early. The clerk said, "No problem, senor. I will have one brought over tonight. They will leave the rental papers at the desk for you to sign."

They were all worn out from the travel of the last week, along with the stress of keeping track of D'Arcy and company. Liz went to her room yawning. Hawk and Cowboy collapsed on their beds, fully dressed, and went to sleep. The phone started to ring at seven in the morning. Hawk fumbled around to pick it up. A cheery female voice said, "This is your wake-up call, as requested. Good morning."

07:05 - 08 SEPTEMBER

TZ SIERRA

Hawk slammed down the phone, rolled out of bed, and shook Cowboy until he said he was awake. A few bangs on the connecting door, and Liz said, "Alright, alright already. I'm up."

Cowboy hit the shower while Hawk ordered up breakfast for three, and a large pot of coffee. The breakfast came quickly and was eaten quickly by three ravaged people that hadn't eaten for a whole day. They dressed in the clothes they had worn for the last two days, and went down to the desk, hoping a pickup would be waiting for them. The paperwork was there—that was a good sign—and after all three signed as drivers, they walked out expecting another dump. Sitting under the hotel portico was a new Ford F-150. It was tan and white, and the front said it had a V-8 engine. They couldn't believe their luck. Hawk and Cowboy flipped to see who would drive first. Cowboy won the toss, and then the female of the group said, "How about me? I know how to drive too."

So, Cowboy took her on. Each flipped a peso in the air and let it land on the ground. The side with the snake and eagle was decided in advance to be heads. All three walked over and looked at the coins. Liz let out a whoop, and did a little dance as she took the keys from Hawk and said, "You guys can fight over who gets the middle part of the seat." She jumped up in the truck and fired up the engine. When the two men were in the truck, she dropped it into low gear and peeled out, leaving two fishtailing black lines on the portico driveway.

Cowboy yelled, "WAHOO!" as loud as he could.

Hawk acted like he was pissed, but inside he was going, "WOW, she can drive too."

The traffic in Mexico City was a nightmare. They talked it over and decided not to stop to buy new clothes in the city. The streets were packed with cars, side by side, all stopping and going at stop lights. Each block of cars moved one block and then had to stop again at another red light, except the Mexican drivers kept running the red lights, and stopping in the middle of the intersection, stopping the cross traffic from moving. There was a sign for the highway going to Puebla at the corner, where they were stopped. The light turned green, and before Liz could move, a taxi drove up on the sidewalk and tried to cut in front of the truck, hitting the right front fender. Hawk got out with horns blaring from everywhere. The taxi driver got out shouting and waving his arms, saying Liz had hit his taxi. A police car pulled up, and two policemen got out. They talked to the taxi driver and then talked with Hawk. They wanted Hawk to pay the taxi driver for the damage to his car. Hawk refused. One of the cops used his car radio and then came back to talk with Hawk. Hawk shook his head and walked over to the truck.

He said, "The cops want us to pay the taxi for his damages. I told them he was the one driving on the sidewalk, and he caused the wreck. They have called a wrecker, and are going to impound the truck if we don't pay the taxi driver."

Cowboy said, "How much does he want?"

"Fifty USD," he says.

"Pay him and let's get going," said Cowboy.

Hawk went over and talked to the taxi driver, and gave him some money. The cops walked over and told Hawk they were going to give the driver of the truck a ticket and tow the truck anyway. Hawk told Liz and Cowboy what they said.

Cowboy said angrily, "They want *mordida*." He told Liz, "That translates to 'the bite.' It's a bribe to let us go. Cops down here do it all the time, especially when they see rental license plates on the offending car. How much do they want, Hawk?"

"One hundred USD," said Hawk.

"Pay it and let's get out of this crazy place," said Cowboy.

Hawk paid the cops off, and at the change of the light Liz went straight ahead to the turnoff for the highway to Puebla, with the cops following them until the city limit sign went by. The highway went by the city of Puebla, where Cinco de Mayo started, and through the volcanic hills near Veracruz with its lime tree orchards going up the sides of the mountains. The high planes between Cordoba and Villahermosa were covered in pineapple and agave cactus fields. Liz pulled off the highway at a pineapple stand under an overpass bridge for some fresh, cold juice. There was another stand right next to the juice stand, selling fresh-made tamales. Those two together made a good lunch for everyone. Cowboy took over the driving. They spent the night in Villahermosa, and in the morning Hawk drove to the Gulf Coast road headed for Mérida. They reached Mérida in the early afternoon and went down Avenida Montejo to the hotel they had stayed at the last time they were in Mérida.

They were given two adjoining rooms with balcony views to the patio and pool. They all opted for an afternoon siesta, and then went shopping for new clothes. The private plane with their equipment was due in at eight in the evening, so they had an early dinner and drove out to the airport.

18:35 - 08 SEPTEMBER

TZ S

Hawk was looking for a way into the FBO area that wasn't closed off to traffic. He drove around the airport perimeter checking for an opening, or hole in the fence that surrounded the entire airport. The airport was north of the city, and in the middle of the jungle. There was always a chance for wild animals to cause a plane crash, on landing or takeoff, thus the fence. Not far from the FBO gated entrance where there was a guard, was the maintenance area. The gate there was open and no guard. Hawk told Cowboy and Liz they would park in the main terminal area until dark, and about eight they would drive down the perimeter road with the lights off and park near the maintenance building. When the plane landed and taxied toward the FBO, he would flash the truck lights. They would meet the plane and unload in the dark.

According to the plan, Hawk drove out of the main parking area for the terminal, and drove slowly down the perimeter road, with no lights. The gate to the maintenance area was still open. He pulled the truck past the building and parked just off the taxiway to the FBO area. It was pitch black, with the only light coming from landing lights on the runway. There weren't any lights on the taxiways for some reason. Cowboy thought it was because the airport was off the power grid. They had heard the big generators running when they were parked at the terminal. The terminal and the one runway were lighted, but that was all. The planes that taxied at night had to use their own lights on the plane.

The twin-engine plane came down, without getting in the traffic pattern. The windsock was hanging limply on a pole in front of the FBO. The wind indicator at the end of the runway was hanging down also. The plane landed at the short end of the runway and taxied toward the FBO.

Hawk hit the truck lights, and blinked the high-low switch until the King Air turned toward them. He wondered if it was the same King Air he had been on when the mission had first started. The plane stopped with a little rock back and forth, and the lights went out. The steps dropped down, and two men started bringing down boxes and suitcases before the props stopped spinning.

Hawk drove near the plane, and then backed the truck up to the stairs and got out, with Liz and Cowboy running around the other side. They started helping the two men load the bed of the truck. The bed was loaded, the plane was emptied, and the steps were retracted before anyone came to check on what was happening. Liz and Cowboy were already in the truck when Hawk opened his door, started the truck, and pulled away from the plane, through the gate, and down the perimeter, going the long way around the airport. He was still driving with the truck lights off when the King Air roared over them as they passed the end of the runway. It didn't have any lights on either.

At the first exit they came to, Hawk turned the lights on and got on the highway leading back to Mérida. He pulled the truck into the gated parking of the Montejo Hotel. He showed his room key to the man at the gate. They put a tarp over the gear. Hawk took the first watch. Cowboy would wake him, and early in the morning Liz would relieve Cowboy.

Hawk knew the man at the gate had seen some of the gear in the bed of the truck. If he was connected to a gang or cartel, Hawk would find out, he knew, later in the night. Hawk, like Cowboy, was used to staying awake for long hours or even days, when it was required. He had stretched out on the bench seat with his head barely showing above the rear window edge. He was on edge, every sense alert. It was hot in the cab. He had closed the windows to keep the mosquitos out. As he fell asleep, he could feel the abyss nearby. He fought to win over it, but lost.

***

The elephant grass kept any breeze from reaching him. His jungle fatigues were soaking wet from perspiration and from crawling his way through a rice paddy on his way to the enemy. Days before, a swift boat crew on the river next to the rice paddy had seen enemy activity beyond the rice paddy, up in the jungle and low hills. His orders were to recon and advise HQ of the strength and makeup of the enemy in the possible camp. He had been watching the footpath for a few hours, and all he had seen were VC. He crawled up a small embankment and saw the camp. The VC that were pulling guard duty were very lax. One slapped a mosquito. Another was standing with his weapon leaning against a tree trunk while he was looking into the camp and the fires spread around the area. He crawled for what seemed like hours around the camp, until he saw some officers talking at a campfire in front of a larger tent. The camp ran all the way up another hill and around it to a ravine. This was a main camp with NVA and VC both. They had to be planning an attack on one or more of the nearby outposts or fire support bases. He had to disobey his orders. He knew he could take out the command structure of the largely hidden camp. If he did, it would take a lot of time to regroup. He waited until the camp quieted down and the officers were in the large tent. He hadn't moved an inch for hours. He worked his way to the back and then the side of the large tent, setting up two Claymore mines he carried in his ruck. He moved an inch at a time until he was in the ravine. He left the clackers there, and moved down the ravine to the river, and back. The guards were sleeping, or not paying attention along the ravine. When the Claymores went off they would run to the camp to see what had happened. He went back to the clackers and set the Claymores off. There was nothing left of the large tent with the officers in it. He scrambled down the ravine, past the elephant grass, running full tilt along the rice paddy dikes, headed for the river and safety. A man stood up from the edge of the rice paddy with his ancient rifle pointed at him. He didn't have time to do anything, but run full tilt into him. He pushed the man's head underwater. The enemy thrashed with arms and legs until he drowned. There shouldn't be any noise. He was dead. The noise was louder. More crashing and pulling, metal on metal. He moved his legs to run to the river, but he couldn't move them.

He woke up in a sweat, realizing what had happened. He found himself all the way down on the floor of the cab. The noise was coming from the bed of the truck. He pulled his M1911 and opened the door. There were four men taking the gear out of the bed and putting it in the bed of a small truck, like a Datsun. The guard was one of the men. Hawk told them to stop what they were doing and lay on the concrete drive of the garage.

Two of the men ran down the ramp, weaving as they went. Hawk let them go. The guard went to the concrete, and the last one pulled a revolver from his pants and fired. The shot hit the window of the door by Hawk. The big .45 roared in the cement cave, and the thief's head blew apart. He heard a heavy-caliber pistol fire twice down the ramp. He didn't have time to check it out. He pulled the guard over on his back and asked him who he worked for.

"I work for myself," he said.

Hawk shot him in the right knee.

"Do you work for a cartel or some street gang?"

"I work for a cartel," he said through gritted teeth.

"Give me the name of the leader."

"It was Senor Peneda, until he was killed. The man that killed him has taken over the cartel and made it part of his cartel. He is Senor D'Arcy."

"Where is he now?"

"I don't know; he moves around now. Too many people want him dead. I've heard there will be a big meeting of the men who help run the two cartels. They will become the Peninsular Cartel. Much more important, much bigger. I thought if I took all these supplies, I would get to be a big man in the new cartel."

Hawk shot him in the heart.

Cowboy ran up to him with his .357 Smith and Wesson hanging by his leg.

"What the hell's been going on, Hawk? It looks like another ambush."

"They were trying to steal the gear for a new cartel. We need to move the truck and make it look like a shootout. Was that you shooting a minute ago?"

"I was coming to take over the watch, and I saw two guys running at me. I heard you shoot, and I took them down."

"You take the Datsun with the bodies in the bed. I'll follow you and help put them in the Datsun like they had a wreck, and burn it. We take what gear is in the bed of the Datsun and put it in the Ford. Then come back to the garage, and park up higher so it won't be near the blood on the cement."

Cowboy told Liz what happened when she came to the truck to take over the watch. She sat on the low wall of the parking garage with her Walther in her lap. No way was she going to be taken by surprise. Hawk came to get her after the sun had come up fully. They went together to meet Cowboy for breakfast at the restaurant in the hotel.

Hawk went over what the guard had told him, for Liz. They talked about any ideas they had. Finally, Hawk said, "We know for sure that D'Arcy is back and trying to put together Peneda's old cartel and his own cartel to have more protection, more distribution, and use of the drugs he can bring into Mexico and the United States. He is moving frequently, to keep other drug cartels, and us, from finding him. I don't think he knows about us, at this point. He is having a meeting of all the top men from both cartels to try to unite them into one larger cartel. Give me your ideas on where we go and what we do next."

Liz said, "I think if we run all over the Yucatán Peninsula trying to anticipate where he will be, we'll be wasting our time. The place to get him, and as far as that goes, a lot of other drug people, will be at that meeting. How do we find out where and when the meeting is going to happen?"

Cowboy spoke up, saying, "It looks to me like we have to take one known member of either gang at a time, and make him or her talk. We gather enough information, we will be able to figure out the where and the when."

Hawk asked, "What's the best way for us to do that? Where do we start? I'm open to suggestions."

Liz said, "Let's go to D'Arcy's strip club, the one that I was taken to, and take the manager, or one of his men, to question. We learn a bit and use it to question some other member at some other bar or club to make the thread shorter to follow. Maybe another of his guards later on. How about that idea?"

"I agree, Liz, we have to ask enough questions and get enough answers to put the time and place of the meeting together. What do you think, Cowboy?"

"It appears to be the only way. We need to move today because of what happened last night. I think recon on the club where Liz was, and then tomorrow night we hit someone. Liz should be able to help with taking the right guy."

"I have his face burned into my brain."

"Let's pack up. Liz, you check us out. Cowboy and I will load the truck, and meet you in front of the hotel. We need to stay along Avenida Montejo tonight for security. We'll pick one of the other hotels that have lighted and gated parking, and do the same watch as we did last night. Hopefully with quieter results," said Hawk.

They drove up and down Avenida Montejo, and finally decided on a small hotel on the main plaza near a police station and the American Embassy. The hotel was built in a square, with the parking in the interior garden area. There were very few cars there when they parked the truck. The two rooms were on the interior court, and the truck could be seen from both rooms. At least the one watching could stay in the room, and not fight the mosquitos. The rooms were very clean and done in the Mexican style. The floors were polished Saltillo tile, and the baths were clean, with showers. The café had an indoor part and a part in the courtyard. They ate in the courtyard part where candles were lighted to keep the insects at bay. Last night had taken a lot out of Hawk and Cowboy, so Liz took the first watch on the truck.

10:21 - 09 SEPTEMBER

TZ S

The next day, after having a good Mexican breakfast and plenty of sleep, they walked over to the place Hawk and Cowboy had rented motorcycles before. Liz hadn't used one before, but soon got the hang of it. They rode down to the street where all the bars and brothels were, and rode around the area where the strip club was. The alley that ran behind the club was still open, and the same buildings were there to use as hides waiting for the manager to come out. They rode the bikes back to the shop and then walked back to the hotel.

There were two ways to come and go at the strip club. The front door, and the back door. Hawk figured that when they locked up, the front door would be locked from the inside, and then they would use the back door to leave. Liz didn't remember which one was locked first. Tonight, would be the watch night. All of them would be in the corner of the building down the alley or on the roof of the building that was closed and being used as a drug house. They needed to make sure the manager was the same guy as before. Liz was the only one that could do that. Hawk and Liz took the inside corner of the building, next to the club on the alley. She would be able to see anyone leaving by the back door. If she spotted him, they would leave, and go back to the hotel, make their plan, and execute the next night. When Hawk and Liz took him, Cowboy would have the truck at the corner they had used before, with the pickup. Hawk felt like the planning for this snatch was good. He and Cowboy had done a very similar plan when they were going to snatch Liz, but all hell broke loose when Peneda's cartel took her to the ranch house on the beach.

Liz and Hawk were in place by two in the morning. Cowboy was in the truck parked at the corner of the alley, and two streets up from where Liz and Hawk were located. Cowboy heard the click of Hawk's prick six indicating they were set. He clicked once to let them know he was set. Liz had told them the club closed around three every night. There was no talking between Liz and Hawk. They were both concentrating on the back door of the club. A bare bulb cast low light and shadows on the door area.

At first some clients came out the back way, hoping to keep their visit to the strip club a secret. The girls started to come out, two or three at first, with a handler to keep them from running, and then the rest, around three o'clock, came out with another handler. It was a while before the door opened, and a man stepped out with his back to Liz. He locked the door. He was putting the keys away when he turned to walk up the alley, to where the employees parked their bikes and cars. Liz grabbed Hawk's arm tightly and said in a whisper, "That's him!"

"Are you sure?"

"Yeah, I'd know that son of a bitch anywhere," said Liz.

Hawk clicked the radio twice, letting Cowboy know the manager had been spotted. They waited until he had passed them, and Hawk stepped out with his M1911 in his hand. He hit the manager on the back of his head and picked him up in a fireman's carry as the manager dropped. Liz walked to his side with her pistol out, as the guard. Hawk dumped him in the front seat and quickly taped his mouth, wrists, and his ankles. A trick he had learned from the bodyguards of Andre D'Arcy. He got in beside the taped-up manager as Liz climbed into the bed of the truck and lay down on top of the tarp. They drove out of town on the same road they had taken to the ranch house on the beach. Hawk remembered there was an auto hotel outside of Mérida. It was walled, with only one way in and out. The rooms were against the outer wall, with a drive going around the central business building. Each room had a private parking area, and the rooms were charged by the hour. It was where men brought prostitutes. Hawk paid for six hours, and they drove into the parking area of their assigned room. Liz climbed out as Hawk pulled the manager from the truck and Cowboy opened the door to the room. There were a large bed and a small kitchenette. Both the nightstands had ashtrays loaded with condom packages.

Hawk put the manager in a chair he had positioned in the middle of the room, and taped him to it. Liz filled a glass with water and splashed it in the manager's face. With a bunch of spluttering, like he was drowning, he came awake.

"You are here to answer questions. When I take the tape off your mouth, if you yell out, you will be killed. Nod your head if you understand. The manager nodded his head. When the tape was removed the manager said, "What's going on? I haven't done anything."

"You don't ask the questions. I'll ask the questions. If I think you're lying, I will kill you," said Hawk.

The manager stared bug-eyed with his mouth open around the room, and at the men and the woman that stood around his chair.

"What's your boss's name?" asked Hawk.

"Carlos."

"What is his last name?"

"D'Arcy."

Hawk knew he was telling the truth for the first few questions, so he started on what he didn't know.

"Where's your boss now?"

"I don't know for sure. He moves every day."

"Why does he move so often?" asked Hawk.

"He thinks there are people from the United States after him."

"Why would he think that?"

"I don't know. Some say he has a *topo*, a mole, there."

"When is the meeting between Peneda's cartel and D'Arcy's cartel?"

"I don't know. I've heard it will be at a hotel on the beach, near a place called Majahual. I'm not included."

Hawk walked into the kitchenette and motioned for Cowboy and Liz to do the same.

"Anything I've missed? Anything you want to know? Ask him now, before we go," said Hawk.

Liz walked back to the manager and asked, "How many men will be at the meeting?"

"I don't know exactly. There will be all the middle leaders of both cartels, and their bodyguards. Maybe thirty or so, I guess."

Cowboy asked, "Have you ever been to this hotel in Majahual?"

"Yes, once. I was there with the other managers of all the clubs in the Yucatán."

"Tell us about it. How big is it? Is there more than one building? Are there other people living nearby? Do they have electricity?" asked Cowboy.

"It was two stories tall, where the meeting was held. A kitchen and a restaurant both lower level and a meeting/party area with a large bar on the entire upper floor. The rooms are in a separate building running along the beach. A swimming pool is between the rooms and the main building, with a patio around the pool and running to the edge of the palm trees on the beach. The closest town is about ten kilometers inland, and north. It is called Limón. The electricity is supplied by two large generators."

"Are the generators gas or diesel?"

"Gasoline, I think."

Hawk looked at Liz and Cowboy. "That about it?"

Cowboy said, "I think we're good to go. How about you, Liz?"

"I'll be out in a minute. You guys get the truck ready. Okay?"

Hawk said, "No problem."

Cowboy started the truck and backed it out of the little garage. Hawk waited with the other door open. There was a single shot from the room, and Liz walked out putting her pistol away.

"We couldn't very well leave him to tell Carlos about us and what we look like. Could we?" she said.

Cowboy and Hawk looked at each other while she was getting in the middle on the bench seat. Both nodded as if to say, "She was right, and besides, she owed him."

They drove back to the hotel, and parked in the courtyard as they had the day before. Breakfast was being served in the courtyard. They picked up a coffee pot and three cups and walked out into the garden area to a table and chairs to talk over what they had learned, what they still needed to know, and what plans they could make with the information they had. Hawk talked with Liz and Cowboy about getting more information about the meeting place and the hotel. Cowboy was concerned about not knowing how many people would be there. The estimate they had wasn't good enough. Liz put in that they didn't know if there would be tourists or other guests there at the same time the meeting was to be held. If they took down the generators, were they for sure gasoline fueled?

Hawk brought up the big question that no one was talking about. "If there are thirty people there and all or most are carrying, how does that factor in on us getting D'Arcy, which is what our mission is about. We are good, really good together, but we're no match for that many guns, and who knows what other weapons they might have."

"Okay, we have enough information to get started, but we're running out of time. I think we need to move to a location closer to Majahual and make it our base of operation. We are too far away now, and we have all the info we're likely to get here in Mérida," said Cowboy.

"I'm going to the wife of the owner here and ask if she knows of a place near Majahual that we could stay at on our trip from here," said Liz.

Cowboy and Hawk watched as she walked away. They continued to talk things over, hoping for an easy way to accomplish their goal, but not coming up with anything positive. Liz came back and sat down at the table. She told them the wife of the owner told her there was a place between Chetumal and Majahual that they loved to go to in the summer. "It's a huge fresh-water lake called Bacalar. There are nice hotels on the shore and plenty of restaurants too. It is about an hour drive around the lake to Majahual, but there is a little ferry that runs during the high season to the other side of the lake. Its dock is on the far side, between Majahual and the last town on the beach, at the end of Mexico. Its name is Xcalak. She told me the town of Limón is small, and the only people that live there are the orchard owners and families that pick the limes."

Hawk suggested, "I'll go to the truck and get the Mexican road map. I'll be back in a minute."

Hawk came back and unfolded the map on the table in front of Liz. Cowboy moved over and looked over her other shoulder. From Mérida, they knew the route to Playa del Carmen. There was a road that cut off to the southeast, that ran along a train track to a town named Phillipe Carrillo Puerto. It was about an hour north of Majahual, by the measurement on the map. There was another road that ran directly south and joined a road between Chetumal and Escárcega. That one looked best, with the least amount of traveling time. They went to their rooms, packed up, and drove away from Mérida on their way to Chetumal, the capital of Quintana Roo State.

11:14 - 10 SEPTEMBER

TZ ROMEO

Carlos sat at his desk in Playa del Carmen. The villa had been cleaned, and the bodies disposed of while he was in Europe. There was a pattern to the killing and death that had been following him. The girl had been taken from his club in Mérida by Peneda's cartel. Peneda was killed, and the cartel thought Carlos was responsible. Then the attack on his villa. His brother was killed, as well as several bodyguards, and his majordomo, Nacho, was killed. Rodrigo, his mole in the United States, had told him there were people coming after him. He grabbed his phone and called the number in Washington, DC.

"Hello."

"Rodrigo, this is Carlos."

"Yes, Carlos, how can I help you?"

"I am worried about the killings that are happening all around me. Could this be the American you told me about?"

"It is very likely, Carlos. I don't know his background, except that he severed in Vietnam. You are the one that sent your people to kill him in Colorado when I first called you about him. Why have you not killed him? He is only one man."

"I am planning a reception for him now. It will be a big surprise to him. I have forgotten. What is his name?"

"As I recall, it was Diego Black Hawk."

"In a few days, I will make sure he bothers me no more."

Carlos hung the phone up and called for Mario. He was Carlos's new majordomo.

When Mario came into the room, Carlos told him to have the army send men that had knowledge of explosives and booby traps to his hotel near Majahual. "Two should be enough. I will be there in a few days to direct them in what I want done."

"Right away, Senor D'Arcy," said Mario.

***

It took all day to drive to Chetumal, and then another hour north, to the town of Bacalar. As they neared the town they began to see the huge lake on the east side of the road. There was a little sign saying "Blue Hole" in Spanish and English, at the beginning of the town. There was a steep cliff that fell off the highway, down to the clear turquoise water. At the edge of the lake, there was a large round cenote opening, that was almost a perfect circle. The water coming from the underground river was a deep blue, really a purple color. The cenote supplied the entire lake with fresh water.

They quickly found a hotel with a dock, on the lake. On the bluff above the hotel was an ancient Spanish fort. Cannons and all. The clerk at the hotel told them pirates used to come from the Caribbean Sea, through an inlet, to resupply and get fresh water. The Spanish fort would shell them and drive them off. The Spaniards were afraid the pirates would try to take the fort and whatever was in the treasury. Hawk asked if the ferry was running. The clerk told him not today. The motor was broken.

The two rooms were both on the patio, next to the lake and a long wooden pier. People were fishing off the pier. The water was so clear it looked like you were looking through glass. Dinner was being served, under a high palapa roof. It was open to the lake, and the refreshing breeze that came from it. After dinner, they ordered a local beer from the bar and walked out on the pier to relax from the long day's drive, and the hectic days that went before. It was quiet on the lake. The pier had little colored lights strung along it that gave the clear water different colors, as the low waves came into the sea wall, at the end of the pier.

07:13 - 11 SEPTEMBER

TZ ROMEO

In the morning, the sun cast its golden colors on scattered clouds that were moving from the Caribbean to the shore in waves, like the waves on the lake. They too were coming from the east, upon the easterly wind blowing stronger than it had been the night before. Coffee and pastries were breakfast for the trio. They were on the way to recon Majahual and the hotel before the sun had a chance to fully rise above the jungle canopy. Cowboy was taking a turn at driving. The intersection of the road to the hotel came up in half an hour, to the right. He turned onto the one-and-a-half-lane, oil-topped road and slowed down. The road was covered in holes that would stop a tank. He was busy weaving right, and left, and off the road to miss most of the holes and bumps. Then suddenly, after a mile or so, the oil topping ended and the trail was gravel and dirt topped. Then they could see a breach ahead where the road, such as it was, ended. There were ruts in the deep, soft sand, but that was it. The tracks went right on down the beach, moving in, and out, and around clumps of palm trees. The trail stayed on the beach. Past the palms, the sand turned to mangrove and swamp. There were shacks, once in a while, made from flotsam and driftwood that came ashore. The surf was breaking in rows of three, and in the distance the low roar of the waves breaking over a barrier reef could be heard easily.

When they came up to the hotel, it was as the manager had told them. One-story rooms running along the beach, pool, and patio, and the two-story building with the meeting room upstairs. The ruts in the sand went behind the buildings onto more solid ground between the building and the mangroves. They passed slowly, taking in everything they could. Cowboy spotted the generators sitting on a concrete slab, with a palapa over them. It would be easy enough to get to them. There were several fifty-five-gallon drums sitting away from the generators labeled Gasoline. Hawk reached across Liz and tapped Cowboy's leg. Hawk said, "Over there, sitting in the shade of those palm trees." There were two men in uniforms, sitting in the shade, drinking what looked like bottles of beer. Hawk, Cowboy, and Liz drove on down the beach watching the surf roll in and wishing they could use one of the hammocks strung between coconut palms. Coconuts were lying everywhere. Cowboy turned around before they made it to Xcalak. They drove more slowly when they came back to the hotel, looking for the men again. Now the men were working on something near the pool. There was no way to tell what they were working on. Hawk thought it was something to do with the meeting. Liz called attention to the roof. It was made entirely of palm fronds, in the palapa style. The roof for the long, low beachfront rooms was made the same way.

When they reached the turnoff from the beach, they decided to continue going north along the beach looking for a good hide, to watch the road for traffic coming to the beach hotel for the meeting. The beach they found was totally deserted, except for some really large iguanas. On their way back, they found a hidden trail made by cart wheels. They stopped, and Hawk went to investigate. He came back from the brush looking back at the cart trail, and over to the sand with the ruts in it that led to the oiled road. He told Liz and Cowboy there was a small thatched hut back in the brush, with a two-wheeled cart and a *panga* stored next to it. Some fishermen that didn't want to take their work home with them left the boat and cart by the hut. The mangrove was right behind the hut, and they had been cleaning their catch there and letting the animals clean up for them.

"I could see the whole road from the gravel and sand part, all the way up to the turn to go to the hotel. This would be the best hide, so far. Let's go toward the town called Limón. Maybe there will be something worthwhile around that intersection."

They made it back to the oiled part of the road, and then to the intersection. They turned right, and headed north, toward Limón. When they reached Limón, it wasn't anything but some huts along the road with a rope across the road, to slow down traffic. They returned to the intersection and walked around. Despite looking behind low trees and brush to cart paths running into the jungle, there wasn't a single place to watch the intersection from that gave views in every direction, like the one Hawk found at the corner of the beach and the wheel ruts in the sand. They drove back to Bacalar.

Cowboy had seen a little café on the way out of town, and he stopped there to try the food. It was hot and spicy, the way Texans liked it. Hawk, on the other hand, had beads of perspiration on his forehead as they left the little hut by the highway. They went back to the hotel on the lake and called it a night. The plan was to go back to the hut in the brush, with plenty of water and snacks, and take turns watching the corner where the road ended and the ruts in the sand started.

07:55 - 12 SEPTEMBER

TZ R

The morning was bright and clear as they prepared to leave for the hut. Cowboy had found a store with local supplies, near the highway. He bought bottled water, sandwiches, a bag of ice, and a Styrofoam box to keep the water and ice in. He picked Liz and Hawk up at the hotel, and they drove as quickly as they could to the hut and parked the truck. There were two chairs and a stool in the hut. The stool went outside, behind some brush and palm trees. There was a clear space through which they could see the corner. There was shade there too. It was really getting hot during the day, and the insects, including the ever-present mosquitos, were swarming over the mangroves.

The time passed slowly, and they changed watch often. Hawk thought back to the heat and sweat that he and Cowboy had endured on some of their missions. It seemed like yesterday sometimes, and many years ago at other times. He couldn't lose track of where he was and what the mission was now. He could feel it getting closer to being finished. It was his watch coming up. He had to get that spaced-out feeling he got, when he went back in time, out of his system. He didn't want Liz to know what happened to him sometimes. Cowboy knew. He had it happen to him, but not very often. Cowboy figured out his trigger was the sound of a helicopter going over. He had learned to fight it when it started. Hawk hadn't been able to stop it, yet. He kept working on it, like right then.

He walked down the cart path and stood still for a minute watching Liz as she sat quietly on the three-legged stool, sweat staining her blouse through. She had a hat on, but it wasn't giving her much shade. The palms weren't good shade trees, and the heat seemed to seep through everything. He tapped her on the shoulder, and she jumped. She was really concentrating on the corner area.

He sat on the stool and began his watch. A four-wheel red jeep came down the road. It surprised him, but he was able to get a look inside. Two men were in front and one in back. The man in the back had bulging eyes and fat lips. It was Carlos D'Arcy going to his hotel with two bodyguards. He continued his watch, and when Cowboy came, Hawk told him what he had seen.

"Keep a sharp eye out, Cowboy. This may be the start of the people coming to the meeting."

Cowboy took over the three-legged stool and took a swig of water from his bottle. His time watching the corner was a waste of time. Not a single car or SUV came down the trail to the corner.

Liz and Hawk came out to the hide and watched with Cowboy for a short time, and then Hawk said, "Let's call it a day. It's getting into late afternoon, and I doubt there will be a sudden flood of cars or trucks coming along at night."

They drove the truck from behind the hut and onto the gravel-and-sand trail to the oil-paved road. Cowboy was driving, and he pushed the Ford's speed up. There weren't any police to catch them speeding, and the breeze felt great.

They drove back to the hotel on Lake Bacalar. There were more big sedans and jeep SUVs parked in the lot. Hawk had an idea and asked Cowboy to turn around and drive up and down the lakefront road.

"Watch for big sedans and four-wheel drive SUVs that are parked in the hotels along the lakefront. If I'm right, they may be staying here and going to that meeting tomorrow at the hotel."

There were a number of them at the hotels around Bacalar. Some just pulling in or unloading had families that were there to enjoy the lake, but most of them had a second car or jeep with one or two obvious bodyguards watching over the men, or families.

Cowboy said, "I think you're right about the cars and SUVs. Let's make another circuit and count the big cars or SUVs and multiply by three. That should give us a comparison for the number the manager figured."

They came up with seven SUVs and five large sedans. That was more than the manager had guessed. Liz suggested, "I bet some of those sedans are for the wife and kids. The SUVs are for going over rough roads and beach sand. They're all four wheels too."

Hawk said, "That makes sense. So twenty-one for three times seven. Let's play safe and make it twenty-five going to the meeting. There might be some that want to stay in the beach rooms at the hotel."

They went back to their hotel and had lunch on the patio. The lake wasn't as calm as it was the night before. The clouds in the sky were moving around as if they were angry for some reason. The lake was rough because the wind had picked up. They enjoyed the time spent on the patio, but decided to all take a siesta. No telling when they might get the chance to rest again.

Hawk and Cowboy had their window open with the screens drawn closed. Hawk woke first; he always woke when there was heavy rain. It brought back too many hard times to him. It wasn't a few minutes, though, before Cowboy was up and looking out the screen at the lake that was now in a low turmoil. Gray clouds were starting to roll over each other, from the southeast. The rain slowed, and then would speed up again. A palm frond blew across the patio and into the palapa area. Hawk saw Liz running to their room, and opened the door in time to let her dash in, out of the storm.

Cowboy threw Liz a beach towel to use to dry herself. Hawk kept looking out the screen, as if in a trance. Liz and Cowboy sat quietly at a small table. There were only two chairs. They looked at each other as if to say, "What the hell is up with Hawk?"

Hawk finally stopped looking out and sat on the edge of one of the beds. He said, "I need to go talk with the owners of the hotel. No use you both going. I'll be back shortly."

He got up and walked out the door into the wind and rain starting to come down hard enough to sting when it hit his skin. He found the owners in their office listening to Radio Cuba. Hawk smiled at them and motioned for them to continue listening. He pulled a chair closer to the big console radio and listened to the weather warning coming from Havana. After the announcement was over, Hawk asked them if it pertained to the eastern coast of Mexico also.

"Yes, senor, the warning is for a hurricane to travel along the east coast of Mexico and turn across the peninsula somewhere below Bacalar. It could be very bad for us here," said the husband.

"I didn't hear a prediction of when it might make landfall. Did they give any information about that?"

"Yes, senor, but not very exact. The radio said within twenty-four to thirty-six hours," the husband said.

The wife looked at Hawk and said, "Our guests that just came in are planning on leaving in the morning. They told us they were here for a meeting but they weren't staying for it. It was to be near Majahual, and that is right on the beach. That would be very foolish and dangerous."

Hawk thanked them both and told them they would be staying on. The wife told him that if the water became too high at the hotel, the town would open up the old fort on the bluff. It had never been bothered by hurricanes.

Hawk walked back to the room where Liz and Cowboy were and told them what was happening.

"This may be the break we've been looking for," Hawk said.

"You must be crazy," said Liz. "I've been through a hurricane when I was a teenager. My dad and I stayed in a condo in Port Aransas, when one came ashore there. The beach was gone, the dunes were gone. The town was flattened, and it took three days just to get power again. What exactly do you think the big break is, Hawk?"

"Look, Liz, you don't have to come. Cowboy and I can handle this. You can stay here and go up to the old fort, like the owner told me. We are used to working in this kind of weather. Not the wind, but the rain, yes. We lived in it and came to be friends with it. The rain covered our tracks. It covered any noise we made. It helped us hide. It helped us take down the target by keeping the enemy from maintaining good perimeter security, and it helped us get back to our outfit safely. We like bad weather!" said Hawk.

Liz looked at Cowboy for help, but all she got was a nod of agreement with what Hawk had just said.

"Well, hell," she said. "I'm in if you two are in, but it better not mess my hair up," she said with a grin.

The boys watched her to make sure she was kidding, and then broke out laughing. Cowboy ended on the floor. Hawk on the bed. Both laughing so hard it hurt.

When the laughter stopped, Hawk and Cowboy went out to the pickup and rummaged around in the bed under the tarp getting the things they would need. There were three rucksacks there, and they filled them up with gear and went back in to sort it all out and make sure they hadn't forgotten anything. All three cleaned and oiled anything metal. They dried everything and put it back in the rucksacks, evenly divided.

The rain kept increasing as the evening turned into night. Liz went to her room next door to catch some sleep. Hawk told Cowboy that it would be a good idea to get one of the four-wheel-drive jeeps parked at the hotel, and hide it. They would need a four-wheel drive when they hit the beach in the morning.

05:00 - 13 SEPTEMBER

TZ R

Cowboy and Hawk took turns sleeping. There was no alarm clock in the room, and no rooster outside, so Cowboy woke Hawk up at five in the morning. The storm was raging. The skies were dark gray and angry looking. The temperature had dropped, and combined with the rain, a jacket would have felt good. They put on T-shirts and jeans along with jungle combat boots with drain holes and fabric sides. Each had a floppy jungle hat on, with a strap under their chins. Hawk had his M1911 tucked in the small of his back, and his silenced .22 in a shoulder holster under his left arm. His new Kay-bar was taped on, upside down, on his left ruck strap. Cowboy wore his S & W .357 Combat Special in a shoulder holster under his left arm. He had two speed loaders on his belt. He walked through the driving rain and knocked on Liz's door to make sure she was up and getting ready.

A few minutes later Hawk and Cowboy stood under the eve of the tile roof over the office at the hotel. It was still too early for guests to be stirring. It was an early-bird-gets-the-worm day outside. They didn't know if the men would all leave at the same time, or one by one. The storm was getting bad enough so only fools or crazy people would head for the beach. The palms around the hotel were bending over toward the ground. A frond or coconut would fly by once in a while. A window at the side of the office was already broken out. There would be no morning light. It was going to stay partially dark until the storm passed, in the next day or so.

The first person to go out to a four wheel and start it up looked like a bodyguard. Medium height and build, with no fat showing. Short haircut, and eyes that were always moving. Cowboy waited to see if he was going to go back to his room and help his boss, or wait in the car. The bodyguard turned on the lights and backed out of the parking slot he was in. Cowboy's hopes for a quick, easy steal went out the window. He stood back in the dark of the office roof and waited for another driver to come out. The four-wheel jeep that had backed out went down the row of SUVs and sedans. At the end, it pulled in, and the guard got out and went to the end room. He knocked, and the door opened, and closed after he went into the room. Cowboy ran to the jeep and jumped in, slamming the jeep into reverse, then into first gear while he turned the lights out. He hit the gas and drove off as the door on the last room opened, and a shot was fired as the jeep disappeared in the dark up the bluff road.

Hawk saw Cowboy take the jeep and walked back to Liz's room. When he knocked on the door, it came open, like she had been standing behind it waiting for someone to come get her. She had on jeans that fit, a long-sleeved blouse, and a hat like Hawk and

Cowboy. Her Walther was in a shoulder holster under her left arm. There were two full clips on the leather strap at the front of the holster. She had on a smaller version of the jungle boots Cowboy and Hawk were wearing. She grabbed her ruck, putting it over her right shoulder, and walked toward the office with Hawk.

"Cowboy went up the bluff road with the jeep. I want to leave the truck at the little hut on the beach. I'll take you up, and you can ride with Cowboy," said Hawk.

She got in on the shotgun side and waited quietly while Hawk pulled the Ford out, drove up the bluff, and looked for the jeep. It pulled out from behind the old fort and blinked its lights.

Hawk drove the truck over, and Liz changed trucks. Cowboy knew that Hawk was taking the truck as far as the mangrove hut, and got behind him as he hit the highway. The wind was blowing hard enough that it continually pushed the truck and jeep on and off the road. The wipers didn't do any good. It was like driving blind. Turning on the lights didn't help. The rain was too heavy. Liz held on to the door handle and gritted her teeth. It was the scariest thing she had ever done, she thought. Instead of one hour to make the drive, it was two hours to the intersection. There was no way to go fast in the storm. Hawk hit the gravel and dirt, now mud, first. The rear end of the truck started sliding around, like it was on ice. He slowed to a crawl. Cowboy reached down and pulled the lever up to engage the four-wheel drive on the jeep, and stayed behind the Ford a good distance so they didn't hit each other.

The truck made a very slow turn in the sand and moved to the cart path. Hawk backed the truck in, as far as he dared. He got out and walked, leaning into the wind, from palm tree to palm tree, for stability. Liz was in the left-side seat, so he opened the back-right door and slid in, with a torrent of wind and rain blowing in with him.

Cowboy sat there for a few minutes, until Hawk had caught his breath and relaxed a little from the work it had been to cross the short distance from the truck to the jeep. Their plan was to park at the end hotel unit and move toward the main two-story building, one on the backside, and one on the front. Liz was to keep the jeep running and wait. When she found that out, there was no stopping her. She was going with Cowboy, the back way.

They were standing in front of the jeep making last-minute changes and adjustments to their gear, when there was a huge explosion down the row of hotel rooms, by the swimming pool.

Cowboy asked, "What the hell was that?"

"I don't know for sure, but it sounded like a landmine of some type going off," said Hawk.

"Let's take cover and see what happens," suggested Cowboy.

They all ran to the side of the last room and hunkered down. The rain and wind with the surf breaking were enough to make it impossible to hear.

***

Carlos jumped from his easy chair and spilled his scotch. He looked to the guards sitting across the meeting room and yelled, "What the hell was that!"

One of the guards said, "It sounded like a bomb going off, senor."

Carlos said, "Go out there and see what happened."

The guards looked at each other, and one said, "Senor, you had the army booby-trap the whole area around the kitchen, bar, and meeting room. We don't know where the mines are. Do you have a copy of the way they laid them out?"

"Yes, yes! Here it is. Now go out and see if that American killer has come here. If it is him, he must be stopped. I'll give the man that kills him ten thousand USD."

Both men stood up and adjusted their pistols, and one grabbed a new-looking AK-47 with two clips taped together. First, they went out on the balcony overlooking the pool. The doors to the balcony were blowing in and out with such force the panes of glass in them broke into a thousand pieces. The lighter, smaller pieces flew in the wind all over Carlos, making him even angrier. The two guards came back in and tried to get the doors closed, but they had no chance with the glass out of the frames of the doors; the doors acted like wings on a plane, and flew first in and then out making a horrible racket.

"The swimming pool is gone, senor."

"What the hell do you mean the swimming pool is gone?"

"There is a big hole where it was. One of the bombs must have exploded."

Carlos was to the point of hysteria. "Bombs don't explode by themselves. That man must be here, getting ready to kill me. I pay you to protect me. Go out there, find him, and bring me his head."

The guards left the second floor. They went slowly down the stairs to the ground floor, and stood looking out the storm windows. The pool was just a hole in the ground quickly filling with sand and water. They walked outside in the dark with the rain beating down on them and the wind blowing hard enough that they had to hang onto anything heavy to keep from being blown over.

***

Hawk and Cowboy went carefully out to the front of the end room, trying to see what had happened. The sand from the beach was being washed and blown up to the front of the rooms, and was at least two feet deep, right at the front wall of each room. With the sand gone from the beach, the roaring surf was tearing up everything in its way. Palm and coconut palms were being tossed around like they were matchsticks.

Hawk said, "We need to get back in the jeep and go wait this out by the truck."

They ran to the jeep and got in. Liz was squatting next to the wall of the last room and couldn't believe her eyes when they came running back and jumped in without calling out to her. Then she realized Hawk was holding the front door open for her. She took off at a run. She was wet to the core, and it didn't matter, she realized. Everything in the line of the storm was saturated to the core.

"Where we going now?" she asked.

"We're going to sit this one out for a while," said Hawk.

When they reached the truck, Cowboy backed in as close as he could. He wasn't sure he was on the cart path. It was all sand and mud, and the surf had torn up the beach sand and brought it in shore, to cover up the front of the pickup.

"Did you all figure out what the explosion was about?" Liz asked.

Hawk answered, "I know what happened now, and what will, undoubtedly, happen again. You both remember the two men sitting under the palm trees when we drove by the first day we were here." They both nodded. "I'm betting Carlos had the army send them out to lay patterns of land mines around the area. They probably didn't have all the types we have. I'm guessing they had pressure mines. We called them 'Bouncing Betties' in Vietnam. You step on a pressure sleeve, like a piston, that triggers the main fuse, and then the mine blows up to about three feet and explodes, throwing shrapnel all over the place. It's an antipersonnel mine. I think they buried a bunch of them in the sand not thinking about or not knowing about the hurricane coming. The high surf brings the beach sand in and dumps the wet sand ten feet high in flat areas and against anything that'll stand up to it. The wet sand piling over the pressure switch of the Betties is making them go off, by themselves. Let's watch for a while and see if I'm right. No need to go running around getting killed, if we don't have to.

***

It wasn't long before another bomb exploded, not far from the generators. The lights in the two-story building went out. Carlos started yelling for his bodyguards, but they were out front in the storm and couldn't hear him ranting on the inside. Carlos watched the wind and rain blow in the two destroyed balcony doors. The storm was just starting to crank up. He had been in more than one hurricane, but never right on the beach, never alone in the middle of a hurricane. What little nerve he had, he was quickly losing. A huge gust of wind, the strongest so far, hit the front of the two-story, building, and blew off most of the palm fronds that made up the palapa-style roof. The torrential rain and hurricane-strength wind came tearing into the meeting hall, upsetting chairs and tables, blowing over glasses, and blowing out the rest of the windows as it made a vacuum in the room. Another huge boom went off. This time where the outside staircase used to be. Carlos ran down the interior stairs to the dinning and kitchen area. His room was between the two. He ran in and grabbed his overnight bag, and a pistol he had placed on his nightstand. He ran to the front door and called out for his guards. He saw them standing up under the roof overhang of a room, halfway down the beach rooms. They were hanging onto a post that had supported the roof. The palapa roof was gone. He waved them to him, yelling, "Let's go. The storm is too strong to stay here."

The guards left the security of the post and ran out into the sand and around the hole that was the swimming pool. There was another horrendous boom. Carlos saw both the guards thrown up in the air. Body parts were flying in every direction. He shuddered in the rain and wind and walked into what remained of the meeting building. He had the jeep keys in his hand. He was afraid to go out the front door. He stood there for a moment and looked at the hole where the pool used to be. There couldn't be another bomb at the pool, or the generators. The jeep was parked in the jungle, behind the meeting building. He ran past the hole and past where the generators were. There were mangled pieces of metal, and burned parts everywhere. He made it across the sand and dirt that led to the narrow parking lane and the jeep. He jumped in, threw his gun into the right seat, and started the engine. He pulled up the four-wheel lever and put the jeep in reverse. He swung it around in an arc and drove ahead trying to see where the turnoff for the beach road was. It wouldn't be this bad up north in Playa del Carmen. He would go to the villa and see if it was safe. He saw the turn. He had to slow down to get across the sand that was piled up like a sand dune. He took the jeep over the side of the dune and started again for the intersection.

***

Hawk, Cowboy, and Liz had heard three Betties go off and had seen the roof blown away. The generators had to be affected, or the lights would still be on. The storm was starting to get its act together. The winds were gusting strong enough to push the jeep off two wheels. Then it would drop again and rock and throw the three of them around in the jeep. Hawk was about to say they should try to take the meeting building, when all of them saw another jeep pull up to a dune that was forming on the sand-and-gravel intersection of the road. It didn't go over the top, but to their side, with all four wheels digging and spinning until it topped out and got traction again. It sped away to the big intersection of the coast highway.

All three of them had seen who was in the jeep. Hawk sat quietly while the hurricane roared outside the jeep, and said, "Well, shit!

Here we go again. You want to drive, Cowboy, or do you want me to?"

"I'll drive for now. I should be able to see better going with the storm than against it. We need to see which way he goes."

"Yeah, I don't know if he has anything in Chetumal. I'm figuring he'll head to Playa del Carmen and the villa, or maybe to Cozumel and his airplane, if it's still in one piece."

Liz was really upset that Carlos was on the run again. She wanted him stopped, before he could hurt anyone else. She hung tight and watched the road with Cowboy. In the hurricane two sets of eyes were far better than one set, she figured.

Cowboy was following Carlos by his red lights. Cowboy slowed when they got too bright, and sped up when they were becoming dim. The rain was still torrential, but with it coming down in sheets from the east, it was easier to see going west, like they were. Liz caught the brake lights go on before Cowboy did, and touched his arm and said, "He's going to turn in a second." No turn signal was used. All three of them saw the right turn, and it gave them hope. Even if they lost him in the storm, they knew where he was headed. They stayed back now, and after hitting a tope in the middle of Limón, they turned on the lights. The lights weren't much help, except for missing chuckholes in the road or topes running across the highway to slow traffic down. The town of Filipe Carrillo Puerto was vacant. No lights, no one out along the road, and in town the wooden huts and shacks were torn apart and thrown by the high winds every which way. People were huddled together wherever they could find cement structures strong enough to resist the rain and the wind.

The main street, part of the coastal highway, of Tulum was under water, up to the undercarriage of the jeep Carlos was driving. He was concerned the road ahead would be the same. There was a turnoff before leaving Tulum for Coba. That road, he knew, would take him past a Mayan pyramid and on to Mérida. That would be a safer place to stay during the hurricane than the villa in Playa del Carmen. Mérida was across the Yucatán peninsula. The storm would lose a lot of its power going across it. He would stay there until the storm had passed, and then go back to the villa, that he called home. He noticed the wind and rain were less severe when he made the turn to Coba. He was going west to the Mayan ruins and then cutting north to Mérida.

Hawk in the truck, still leading the jeep with Liz and Cowboy in it, drove into the submerged main street of Tulum at a slow pace trying not to cause high waves or to let the tailpipe of the truck to go underwater. He had learned not to cross the swollen creeks and rivers in the Colorado mountains during spring. If water got to the engine of a car or truck, it would stall, and the driver would be stranded in the middle of the stream. They continued on, driving carefully while the wind and rain tried to stop their progress. The highway past Tulum was on higher ground and wasn't flooded. Their progress went faster as they neared Paamul, the village on the bay they had stayed at on their trip from Mérida to Playa del Carmen. Hawk looked down the road that led to the beach, and Paamul. The road and mangroves were underwater, and the little village on the bay was gone. Just debris and sand stuck in the brush and jungle gave any sign that there use to be a village there.

When they reached Playa del Carmen the town was under sand and water from the beach, and the ferry dock was torn apart. Hawk parked the truck as far as he could in the jungle, hoping it would be there when he came back. No one would venture out in the jungle during a hurricane. There were too many snakes, scorpions, and other species trying to stay alive in the flooded jungle and mangroves.

Cowboy pulled up behind him, and Liz opened the jeep door for him to hurry and get in. The water was deep in what used to be the sand, and dirt street. Cowboy drove with two wheels on what was the board sidewalk, until they turned in front of the line of pilings that supported the dock. Hawk thought of a book his mother had made him read when he was young. It was about a man that made war on windmills. He couldn't remember the name of the book. It was Don something.

Hawk still had the key to the villa with the garage that they had stayed in earlier. The front of the house was taking a beating from the surf, and sand was piled up over the sea wall and into the swimming pool. They drove the jeep into the garage and went into the house through the entry door from the garage. The main floor was wet and had a layer of sand throughout the villa. Upstairs was wet around the windows, but otherwise in good shape. They went back downstairs and talked about how they would get to Carlos at his villa on the jungle trail.

It was decided that Liz would go to the exit inside the tree line of the beach, where Carlos's dry cenote escape tunnel came out, while Hawk and Cowboy would enter the villa through the gate, like they did before. That settled, Cowboy went to the garage and started up a small generator that sat there, and hit the switch to power up the villa. He opened the garage door slightly so no buildup of carbon monoxide would occur. Liz checked the fridge. The food needed to be thrown out, but the beer they left was still good. She brought out three cool bottles and sat down at the island in the kitchen, where they had been making their plan. There was the sound of three beer caps being popped, and then quiet while the first swings were taken.

Cowboy and Hawk left to do a recon on the villa at the circle. They stayed close to the jungle in case a car or person started to use it. The heavy rain and wind gave them immediate cover. When they reached the circle, they went together into the jungle, which smelled of wet and decaying plants. It was an odor they both had smelled before. They watched from the edge of the jungle and moved slowly closer to the gate and wall when they saw there were no guards at the top of the arch. The parking area inside the compound wall was empty. The jeep Carlos had been in wasn't there. They kept watch for another hour, but there was no activity of any kind inside the walled compound.

Hawk said, "Let's go inside and see if anyone is there. Maybe we can find someone that has some information we can use. There was a gate door on the right side of the larger car gate, that they found unlocked. Hawk drew his pistol and pointed to the left. Cowboy did the same, but went to the right. Both men made for cover behind the garden trees and plants. Hawk pointed at himself and ran for the front door. Cowboy covered him, and then ran to the near side of the door. Cowboy tried the door. It was locked. Hawk made a circle with his hand and went to the left, moving around the villa to the patio and pool area. Cowboy did the same on the right side.

Hawk checked out the pool and its surround, while Cowboy went to check out the palapa area. The palm frond roof that made up the roof of the palapa had been blown off and was scattered around the garden area. Hawk signaled that he was going to the floor-to-ceiling windows and doors. The rain and wind were still as strong as ever. One of the windows was shattered, and the silk curtains were blowing in the villa at a horizontal level. Cowboy had gone to the poolside entry to the cenote escape cave that Carlos had used earlier to get away from them. The wood limb cover was gone. The entry was open, and rain and wind blew down the opening, like an open chimney for a fireplace. He could see water lapping at the lower step of the circular staircase.

When Cowboy got to the broken window, Hawk stepped sideways into the open living room. He stood to the right as Cowboy went to the left. The curtains were saturated with rain water, but the wind was still strong enough to have them blowing out into the living area. All the rugs on the tile floors were soaking wet. Hawk took the right side of the villa, and Cowboy the left to clear. They met back at the broken window, and compared notes. The staff had fled the villa when the storm started to become strong. Carlos had not come to the villa. They decided to work their way back to the villa on the beach and figure out the next best move.

Liz was waiting for them with hot coffee and dry beach towels. Hawk and Cowboy went upstairs and changed clothes. When they came down, Hawk told Liz about the recon of the sand trail villa.

Then Liz suggested, "Like you said, Hawk, we need take one of the higher-up employees of Carlos's and squeeze him or her for info on where Carlos might be hiding and when, if ever, he might come back to his villa here. We need to make a trip to get supplies, and then watch for people to come back as the storm moves away from the coast. I'll be the watch again from my bedroom. One of you could go to the villa and wait. Or do you think it would be foolish to expose one of us to returning staff or guards?"

Hawk though for a minute, then said, "That would be a good idea. We could use a hide in the villa and use the prick sixes for contact. If we tried to change people when one got tired, it would be too much exposure. It might scare everyone off, including Carlos."

Cowboy said, "I like the idea. I don't care about staying over there. Something will give in the next twenty-four hours. When the rain eases and the wind quietens, the staff will start coming back to clean up the mess. I think we can switch off every eight to ten hours. If someone comes, we just hunker down until it's time to make our move."

***

Carlos reached Valladolid and stopped. The town's location right in the middle of the peninsula would not get the brunt of the big hurricane moving onshore above Chetumal. The main part of the storm would move to the south of Valladolid into the southern mountain area of Mexico. He found a place to stay for a day or two at a ranch that rented rooms, in the main building. The rental even included meals. He was very frustrated by what happened at the hotel on the beach. The hurricane had temporarily stalled his plan to incorporate the remainder of the Peneda Cartel into his own. He couldn't believe the stupid army people that placed the land mines around the hotel had used mines that blew themselves up. He couldn't get a grasp on what had been happening to him. When he got back to the villa he was going to have his men go all out to capture or kill the man Rodrigo called Hawk. He sat in his room brooding and angry.

17:00 - 13 SEPTEMBER

TZ R

Cowboy left the villa on the beach, with his rucksack and one of the prick sixes. It didn't take long for him to reach the villa on the circle and work his way into the house itself again. He went directly upstairs to the front bedroom with a balcony overlooking the front garden and the gate into the compound. He took off his sopping wet clothes and rung them on the furniture around the room. He then settled in with a comfortable chair and desk facing the gate, and clicked once on the prick six.

Liz walked in the rain with Hawk until they found the exit of Carlos's escape cenote. The cover was still off when they walked up to it. Liz wanted to go down the ladder and see what the cenote looked like, but Hawk asked her not to go. He told her what she would find down there. One of Carlos's henchmen, dead. That he had killed, trying to keep up with Carlos. The body had been there since his escape, over a week ago. She told him she appreciated his concern, but she needed to see the area if she was to be the only stopping force against Carlos using the escape route. Hawk agreed and told her to be careful going down the steps, they were really steep. She went down slowly. Halfway down she turned on the field flashlight from her pack. She swung the light around the open area at the bottom of the staircase, seeing for the first time the limestone walls, stalagmites and stalactites the size of gigantic granite columns in a Roman theater. The cavern was flooding. The water looked to be knee deep, and there were traces of motion hitting the far wall. She was about to go back up the staircase, when her light hit the corpse of Nacho on the floor of the cave below the staircase. It had washed up against the stairwell. She took a deep breath and forced herself up the stairs. She wasn't going to let Hawk she her upset, after he had warned her.

That night, after Hawk had taken over the watch from Cowboy, the rain started to abate. The wind died down, and a speck of the moon peeked through the gray angry clouds. Liz and Cowboy made dinner, and ate in silence. That's how waiting sometimes went. She went back to her room after they had cleaned up from cooking, and sat by the window looking out at nothing. There was no electricity, so no lights anywhere, unless there was a generator handy. She heard someone walking in the jungle at the edge of the sand trail. She couldn't see who it was, but knew it was a man, or woman. It didn't sound like an animal. The noise was from someone walking in a straight line determined to get somewhere. It wasn't a wandering here and there noise. She picked up the prick six and clicked twice. A single click came back, and Liz said, "I hear someone moving in your direction, along the edge of the trail."

"Roger that," came the reply.

The noise subsided as the movement turned and went toward the villa where Hawk was waiting. A few minutes later a man walked out from the edge of the jungle. He walked to the small gate. He took out a key, and there was the grating sound of a lock being unlocked and the gate opening. Hawk watched as the man walked around the side of the house and disappeared. Hawk went to the window at the end of the hall and watched the man walk around the pool and look at the torn up palapa. The man went to the broken window downstairs and slipped in sideways like Hawk had done earlier. Hawk watched him from the open hall that opened on the living area as he looked at the damage the storm had left. It was like he was inspecting it. He looked around the downstairs and came up the stairs to finish his inspection. Hawk had moved behind the door in the front bedroom, waiting. Soon, the man opened the door and walked into the room. He saw the chair and desk Cowboy had moved, and started to turn to leave quickly. Hawk slammed the door closed and pointed his .22 at the man's head.

"Do you have a weapon?" Hawk asked in a conversational tone.

"No, senor, I don't like guns."

"Turn around and let me search you," Hawk said.

"Yes, senor." The man complied. Hawk didn't find any weapons.

Hawk told the man, "Go over to that chair and sit down."

"Yes sir." The man went to the chair Cowboy had used, and sat down.

"What is your name?"

"Mario Contreras."

"Why are you here?"

"I'm the administrator for senor D'Arcy for Playa del Carmen, mainly the house, but other things too."

"What other things?" asked Hawk.

"I make phone calls for him. I hire and fire people. I make sure, when he is here, his stay is a good one. Things like that."

"Are you a member of his cartel?"

"No, senor, I only work for him here."

"Do you know about the cartel?"

"Yes, senor, we all know about it, but this is a good-paying job in Playa. So I work for him."

"When is he coming back, Mario?"

"Today or tomorrow, senor; it depends on a meeting he is to have in Majahual, and the storm."

"Mario, I'm going to have someone come take you to a safe place, and you can tell them all you know about this place and about Carlos. You will not be harmed, and you will be free to leave this place in a day or two," Hawk told him.

"Yes, senor. I will be allowed to leave in one or two days," Mario said.

Hawk clicked twice on his prick six, and after a single click, he told Liz to send Cowboy to the villa and take D'Arcy's manager back to the villa and find out all he can from him. She said okay and shut the six down.

Cowboy took Mario by the arm and led him blindfolded to the villa on the beach. Cowboy and Liz talked with Mario through the evening, but didn't get anything else from him. He did say that the other workers at the villa would not come back until the power came on. Liz told Hawk that, and that she would come up to relieve him around two in the morning. She went to bed then, trying to get some rest before it was her turn at the other villa. Cowboy kept Mario talking for a while, and then locked him in Hawk's bedroom for the night.

02:00 - 14 SEPTEMBER

TZ R

Liz went up and took the watch at two, letting Hawk go back to the villa. He told her he would sleep with the other prick six, if she needed him. His room was locked when he got to the villa. Figuring that was where Mario was, he went into Liz's room and crashed. The night was quiet, and the morning broke with a bright sunny sky, and no clouds to speak of. The seas had regained their normal wave height, and the surf was barely making a sound. The blue sky was spectacular. Cowboy and Hawk couldn't believe the tons and tons of sand the storm had moved from the beach to the fringe of the jungle in a day and a half.

Mario was let out of his room and seemed to be enjoying himself. Cowboy checked with Liz and went to relieve her. She walked back to the villa and went right to bed. Hawk took over the window watch, and Mario sat in the room with him.

The rain and wind stopped early in the morning at the ranch in Valladolid. Carlos waited until the sun was up to leave for his villa in Playa. He had breakfast at the ranch since it was paid for, and drove down to the highway and headed back to Tulum via Coba. From Coba to Tulum. And then Playa was an hour-and-a-half drive, normally. It took about three for him because of all the debris on the roads left by the hurricane. He drove to the turn at the ferry dock and was shaken by the amount of destruction the storm had caused. The road to his villa was impassible. He parked by the beach road and started to walk to it.

***

Hawk watched as a man walked by on the sand trail. He didn't register at first. The guy was walking down the road like any other person, without a care. Mario shook Hawk's sleeve and said,

"That's him, that's Carlos D'Arcy." Hawk picked up the radio and clicked once. That told Cowboy Carlos had just gone by the villa. Cowboy clicked back.

Hawk forgot all about Mario and ran to Liz's bedroom. He woke her and told her that Carlos was going to the villa.

She had slept in her clothes. She came out of bed, put her shoulder holster on, grabbed a bottle of water, and ran out the door going for the beach exit of the cenote cave. Hawk gunned up, and left Mario sitting at the kitchen table drinking coffee. Hawk went for the jungle and quickly caught sight of Carlos. He was going through the small gate.

Cowboy saw Carlos cut across the cleared circle on foot and enter through the small gate. He stood in the front garden and walked around the house. Cowboy went down the stairs, two at a time.

Hawk ran through the small gate, and around the house, looking for Carlos. Cowboy came out the broken glass window at the same time Hawk rounded the corner of the house.

Carlos saw Cowboy first and turned. He saw Hawk blocking the other way. He drew his pistol and shot at Hawk. Cowboy fired and hit Carlos in the arm, making him drop his weapon. Carlos whirled around like he had practiced the move a thousand times, and dove for the stairs in the cenote hole. He got halfway down and hit water. He didn't take time to think. He started to swim for the beach outlet. Hawk went after him, telling Cowboy to go for the other opening, where Liz was guarding the beach outlet.

Hawk could hear the splashing of Carlos swimming in the chest-deep water. Hawk chose to walk through it, and not make any splashing noise.

Liz heard the shots from the villa and figured the boys had taken Carlos out. She didn't give up on her assignment though. She drew her Walther and checked to make sure it was cocked and locked. Her heart was beating a mile a minute, but she chose to go forward. She went to the staircase and started to climb down slowly. When she got to water it was higher than it had been the day before. She stopped on the steps when she was chest high in the water. She stood still with her pistol up in front of her with a combat grip.

Cowboy called from above, but she didn't answer. She had just heard the sound of someone splashing in the water. The noise wasn't like someone swimming; it was like someone thrashing around in brush trying to escape from something terrible. She stood quietly waiting. Carlos came around the little corner that had a pillar on each side, and stopped in his tracks. The sun shining through the escape hole above let him see Liz standing on the steps with a gun pointed at him.

"Get out of my way, bitch," he said in Spanish, and started forward.

Liz kept her stance and said in English, "I've been hoping for this chance."

"What the hell are you talking about? Get out of my way," he said in English as he aggressively moved forward.

"My name's Liz Stillings, and you bought me like a piece of meat," she yelled at the top of her voice.

Carlos stopped. He looked at her, and his bugged-out eyes grew bigger in recognition. There was the noise of someone coming up behind him. One of the men, he thought. Maybe the one called Hawk. He thrashed forward, saying, "Give me that damn gun, bitch, and get out of my way."

The Walther bucked in her hands, and Carlos's right buggy-looking eye exploded and the top and right side of his head blew off, hitting the water in splashes. He sank under the water, not far from the body of Nacho.

Cowboy looked down the stairs to make sure Liz was the one that shot. Hawk came around the corner and stood still looking at Liz. She stood still with the Walther hanging at her side, staring into the distance. Hawk moved toward her and saw the body of Carlos floating next to Nacho, by the steps. He stood at the bottom of the steps and looked up at Liz.

"Sometimes it hurts you to do the right thing. You just did the right thing," whispered Hawk.

She shook her head and said, "He was a plague on the world. I just stopped a plague."

Cowboy said, "I'd like to know what's goin' on down there. What're you all whispering about. What'd you shoot at, Liz?"

Hawk said, "This part of the mission is complete. Let's go to the States and make an accident happen to the deputy CIA director. Then the mission will be over."

Cowboy helped Liz up the steep steps, and Hawk followed. They went by the villa and told Mario he could go home, but unfortunately he needed a new job.

They left the jeep where the truck had been hidden, and buried all the unused gear in the trap out in the mangroves. They drove through the night to get to Mexico City. They stayed at the same hotel close to the airport after getting tickets to fly into San Antonio, Texas. Hawk left the banged-up truck with the clerk that got it for them. He told the clerk about the damage, and after looking at a copy of the rental agreement, the clerk said, "No problem, senor, you checked the box for full-coverage insurance."

The flight to San Antonio was smooth and quick. They checked into a hotel near the airport, and Hawk called Captain Jack. Hawk talked for a long time, while Liz and Cowboy went shopping on the river walk in downtown San Antonio, not far from the Alamo. When they came back to the hotel, Hawk had a frown on his face.

"What's the trouble?" asked Cowboy.

"Well, you know what they say: there's good, and then there's bad."

Liz jumped in and said, "Just tell us; don't keep us guessing."

"For you, Liz, Captain Jack told me the DEA and the FBI have taken their info on your ex-boyfriend to the state's attorney's office. They have filed charges against him for possession of drugs and intent to distribute drugs, as well as conspiracy to commit kidnapping. He is resting in the Austin jail, awaiting trial. He could get up to thirty years, if convicted."

"That makes me feel better," she said.

Cowboy said, "Anything else, Hawk?"

"Yeah, but it doesn't have anything to do with you guys," Hawk said. "You can go see your dad, Liz. I'm sure he wants to see you. And you, Cowboy, can head home and go back to ranching with your dad. When you get there tell him I appreciated him looking after Eliot, and would he mind if I pick him up later. I have some unfinished business to take care of."

"Who's Eliot?" asked Liz.

"What other business have you got to take care of, Hawk?" asked Cowboy.

"When they started bugging Rodrigo's phone and trailing him, they found out Carlos was just the tip of the iceberg. Captain Jack wants me to take him out so it looks like an accident. It seems he's giving out government secrets faster than the government can make them up. With him being a deputy director of the CIA, he hears about them all. It seems he lives way out of his means. Drives a new sports car, and has a home on a lake in the Virginia hills, about an hour out of DC. Captain Jack didn't say anything about you two helping me."

"I say we go do this while we're still all together," said Cowboy.

"You want me to go home to my dad while you go finish the mission. I say, I'm in to the finish," said Liz. "And who's Eliot?"

"Eliot's my cat," said Hawk.

"I'm glad I got that straightened out," said Liz.

Cowboy said, "Call Captain Jack back and tell him we'll take care of it. We need his information, and then we'll let him know what equipment we will need. By the way, I hate to ask this question, but we're in the United States now; will this be considered murder?"

"I asked him the same thing. His answer to me was that the president needs some people to get things done that can't be done the proper way. He told me the president had my back. I guess that includes you two also."

"Better get that clarified for us, and not just you," said Cowboy.

Hawk went back in the room and made the call. He came back out in a few minutes and told them they were all covered under the presidential finding that he told them about before: "Captain Jack said they were normally used in conjunction with the CIA. This finding is totally covert, and only the president and Captain Jack will know. I told him to give us the information on this guy as soon as possible."

***

The next day Captain Jack called and told Hawk to go to Lackland Air Force Base. The guard at the main gate would have a pass for him to pick up a security package from the base security office.

Hawk drove over to Lackland and picked up his pass at the gate. The guard told him where to find the security office. He went in and presented his passport. The clerk went into an office where an officer was working, and brought out a large package and a book to sign. He signed it, meaning he had received the numbered package, and it was unopened.

He stopped at the gate and gave the pass to the guard, and then drove back to the hotel, where Cowboy and Liz waited.

Hawk opened the package on Cowboy's bed and pulled out the papers on Roger Burns. The photo showed an average height, balding, forty-five-year-old male. His description said he had blue eyes with sandy-brown hair. The picture showed him in a business suit with the coat open. He had a gut on him. One big enough that he had his belt below his belly, making his suit pants look like they were shorter in front than in back. He was listed as single. He had a brother in Maine. No other known relatives. He had a condominium in DC, and a summer place near Occoquan, Virginia. About forty-five minutes from DC, on a river with the same name as the town.

They took a taxi to the San Antonio airport and bought tickets to Dallas, and from there to Dulles International Airport. They each brought their favorite weapon, but if need be Captain Jack could easily supplement those. When they arrived at Dulles they rented a non-descript car and drove to a hotel near where the target owned a condo. The condo was within walking distance. They rested from the whirlwind travel they had done in the last week, before walking down to check out the location of the condo.

The condo was located in a high-rise building, that was fairly new. Liz went in to check how many floors there were and if there were any easy accessways to get into the building. She came bac and told them that the condo number 2020 was half the top floor. Condo 2010 was the reverse two-story condo, taking up the other half of the top floor. There was an elevator to the top and a larger freight elevator for residents to move furniture and appliances in and out. They could see from the outside that there was a large balcony off both the condos on the top floor. Smaller ones went with all the other condos. A stairwell went all the way up, and there was an underground parking lot with enough places for one car to each condo. An emergency door came into the main foyer. There was a large lobby area, a swimming pool on the tenth floor, and a rec room.

Hawk looked at Liz in askance and said, "How did you get all that information in ten minutes' time?"

She smiled at him and said, "Easy, I went into the real estate office on the first floor and told them I was interested in buying a condo." She held up a brochure and waved it at Hawk and Cowboy. "This shows all the different condo configurations, including the top two. How about that?" she said.

"Are both the top ones owned now?" asked Hawk.

"No. I asked that while I was there and made an appointment for me and my husband to take a tour of the one not sold yet," she said.

"When's the appointment?" Cowboy asked.

"In the morning at ten o'clock."

"Hawk, you going in as the husband?" asked Cowboy.

"I guess I'd better; you wouldn't be able to find your way out without me showing you." Hawk smiled at Cowboy and slapped him on the back.

"Liz, those places look mighty expensive to me. How much are they?" Hawk asked.

"In the half-million range, they said."

"We better find a suit for me to wear in the morning. I need to look the part. Right?" asked Hawk.

"Right!" she said. "Let's go the other way. I saw a shopping area on the other side of the hotel."

10:00 - 15 SEPTEMBER

TIME ZONE ROMEO

The next morning, they took a taxi to the front of the condominium building. Hawk opened the door for Liz, and they walked over to the sales office. A young woman met them at the door and introduced herself to Hawk as Ella Griggs.

She had the keys to the top-floor condo and asked if they were ready to see it. Liz nodded, and Ella took them to the elevator, where she tapped in the condo number, 2010. She explained as it went up that each side door opened on alternate floors, except the top floor. There, one side opened for each condo. When they reached the twentieth floor the left door opened into a foyer where the stairs joined in. The door to the condo was right in front of them. Ella opened the door to the condo and showed them in.

The condo was breathtaking. Wide-open rooms with columns for roof support. A large kitchen, and living room, with two walls of floor-to-ceiling glass. Past the main wall of glass was the large outdoor balcony that had a full view of greater Washington, DC.

Liz said, "The view at night must be awesome."

"It is really wonderful," said Ella. "If you think you're really interested I can make a showing appointment for you in the evening so you can see it for yourselves."

Hawk told her that would be nice. They had an earlier engagement for the evening. "Could you make it for tomorrow evening?"

Ella told him that she would be glad to do so. She asked, "How's eight o'clock sound to you?" and she looked at Liz.

"I think that would be fine," Liz said. "How about you, honey?"

Hawk stood for a minute, then looked at Liz, who winked at him. He said, "Oh, oh sure. That'll be great."

They looked around the rest of the condo, then went down the elevator to the lobby and made their goodbyes and departed.

They were walking over to a taxi stand when Liz said, "You about blew it there. You know that, right?"

"Why the hell did you have to call me honey? I wasn't prepared for that. Don't ad lib on me, ever again!"

"Why so touchy, Hawk? I was just kidding."

"Just drop it, okay. We have a lot of work and planning to do. If we can come up with a plan, we can finish the target tomorrow night."

"That's kind of quick, isn't it?"

"Depends."

They walked past the taxi stand and on down the street, to the hotel where Cowboy was waiting for the news.

They sat in the boys' room as Hawk and Liz told Cowboy how the viewing of the condo went. When they finished, Cowboy told them he thought the first thing to do would be to establish any routine that Burns had. And that would include when he went to his condo. No use starting a mission if the target wasn't at home.

"Starting in the morning, we start rotating in and out, at a hide we still need to locate," said Hawk.

"If we decide to take him in his condo, we're going to need a lock pick. We'll need a rope and grappling hook to cross the space between the two balconies," said Hawk.

"Are you crazy? You can't cross that open space twenty stories up. You must have a death wish or something," Liz said.

Cowboy told her, "We've been trained to do those things. We won't do it unless we know we can accomplish the task."

She sat quietly and looked down at the carpet in the room.

"Okay, here's how I see it happening. We pick the lock. Liz pulls watch at the front door. Cowboy and I make the throw. Cowboy protects the connect. I cross, and terminate the target. Then reverse everything. We should be in and out in ten minutes or less," Hawk said.

"We prepare, then things go well. Get the guy in the condo. Pick the lock. Cross the space. Terminate. Reverse. Sounds right to me," said Cowboy.

"What about the appointment at eight?" asked Liz.

"You have her card. Call her in the morning and tell her we've been called out of town and will check back with her when the business trip is over. Something like that," said Hawk.

Hawk called Captain Jack and told him what he needed. He told him to get it all into one ruck. Hawk gave him the address of the taxi stand in front of the hotel and told him he would be near the stand at ten in the morning.

09:00 - 16 SEPTEMBER

TZ R

Cowboy left early to watch for the target to leave the building. Liz waited until Hawk left for the taxi stand, to call Ella at the sales office and cancel the appointment. Hawk waited by a telephone pole near the taxi stand, watching the traffic. A white van stopped by the pole, and a backpack was handed out by a guy in the van. Hawk left for the hotel as the van pulled back into traffic. He went to his room and started making the rope connection to the grappling hook. The lock pick set was a good new one. The rope was heavy, but not too heavy to toss over the space between the balconies.

Liz left to change with Cowboy. He told her the target had left at eight thirty and had not returned. Cowboy went back to the hotel and checked Hawk's work. It was like checking each other's chutes before a jump. The rope was a good one. The knot to the hook was a strong one. He had used the type of lock pick in the class he had taken at Fort Devens.

02:10 - 17 SEPTEMBER

TZ R

Hawk went to relieve Liz. She hadn't seen the target come back. She went back to the hotel. Hawk stayed on watch. At two in the morning, Liz and Cowboy walked to where Hawk was watching the condo building. He told them the target was in and the lights on the top floor had gone out at ten thirty. Cowboy gave the ruck to Hawk. They went in the building and past the guard, who was asleep, to the elevator. They rode up to condo 2010, and Cowboy worked with the picks for about two minutes, when the door clicked and swung open. They all walked in, and Liz locked the door. She stood off in a corner so she could see anyone coming from the elevator.

Cowboy coiled the rope around his shoulder and whirled the hook. He let the hook fly in a nice high arc. It fell to the balcony across the space, beyond the balcony railing. He pulled it back to him until the hook clamped on the bottom of the railing. Then he and Hawk pulled it taught and tied it off. Hawk went over the side and wrapped his legs around the rope and slowly pulled his way across, until he could get both his hands on the rungs of the railing. He pulled himself up and over the railing, and went quietly to the balcony doors. He had the pick out that Cowboy had used, and put it in the lock. He pulled on the door before he spent lots of time trying to pick the lock. The door slid open. He put the lock away and walked through the living area to the master bedroom. The door was open, and he could hear soft snoring from the far side of the bed. He stood in the door and put on a pair of surgical gloves. He walked to the edge of the bed. He reached down and pulled up the man's head. The target's eyes came open, but he didn't comprehend what was happening to him. Hawk pushed his head to one side and got behind it. Hawk made a quick, hard twist, and he heard the neck crack like a dry stick breaking. He pulled the man out of bed and put his slippers from the side of the bed on the man's feet. He carried him into the living room and put him on a rug by a large high coffee table. He went to the kitchen for a glass of water. He came back and moved the body over. Hawk stood still and kicked up the edge of the rug, and at the same time spilled the water and threw the glass. It broke past the end of the coffee table. He picked the target up and let him fall beside the coffee table. Hawk brought his head up and hit it hard on the corner of the table, waited for some blood to accumulate, and dropped his head down beside the corner. He walked out the balcony door and closed it, went back to the rope, and crossed the space again. Cowboy untied the end and pulled sharply on the small cord connected to the hook. The hook collapsed on itself making it lose contact with the rail. It fell a short way as he coiled it up on his shoulder. They closed the balcony door as Liz unlocked the front door, and they rode the elevator to the second floor. They left the elevator there and walked down the stair. Hawk checked the counter where the guard was sleeping. The three left the condo building and walked back to the hotel. They got in a taxi and rode out to the airport. Hawk threw the ruck with everything in it into a trash container before they went inside, and bought tickets to Dallas Love Field and then to San Antonio.

Hawk talked it over with Liz and Cowboy while they were on the flight from Dallas to San Antonio. They decided to stay at the hotel near the airport again, to give Hawk and Captain Jack time to make sure all that all went well with the last mission, before they split up and went back home.

Hawk called Captain Jack from the hotel.

Hawk said, "Our end of the mission went as planned. Any problems on your end?"

"Nothing has been reported about a death at the condos. I doubt the cleaning people have been to the condo yet."

"We're getting ready to head out. Any last request, Captain Jack?"

"I need a bank account number for you, before you go. You should get the same information for the other two and keep it for the time being. You will understand later."

Hawk gave him his account information. He told Captain Jack that the balance was very low. Captain Jack laughed softly and told Hawk it wouldn't be low for very long.

Hawk told Liz and Cowboy what he had said about getting their account information.

"I have a checking account, is that okay?" asked Liz.

"That's what I gave him, so I guess that's good," said Hawk.

Cowboy gave him the ranch account number, which was the only one he had.

Hawk told them he didn't know what was going on, but would keep them posted. The next day Liz rented a car to go back to her father's ranch. Cowboy and Hawk did the same, to make their way to Cowboy's ranch near Del Rio. They said their goodbyes in the parking lot of the car rental agency. Liz hugged the two men and told them they had changed her life for the better, and if they ever needed her, to let her know. She would be there to help. Cowboy and Hawk got to the Double D Ranch that evening. Paco was thrilled to see his son back safely again, and Eliot rubbed and purred at Hawk's legs until he picked him up and carried him around like a little baby.

Hawk and Eliot drove back to the camper in the mountains of Colorado and started to pick up where Hawk had, so suddenly, left off. He didn't have a job, or any money. He figured he would take a few days to get his head on straight again and then go job hunting in the towns close to his camper. He sat in his beat-up lawn chair, with Eliot in his lap, taking in the quiet and peaceful surroundings, when he remembered what Captain Jack had said. He didn't have a phone in the camper. He put Eliot down and drove into Frisco to check his bank account. He gave the clerk at the tellers' counter his account number and his driver's license. She pulled up his account and told him she would be back in a minute. Hawk figured that he was overdrawn or something.

When she returned the president of the bank was with her. Hawk couldn't figure why he would be necessary to tell him his account had been closed for insufficient funds. The banker said hello to Hawk and asked him to come to his office. Hawk had never been in a bank president's office.

The office was full of real leather furniture and the smell of money.

The bank president said, "Mr. Hawk, your account has an extremely large balance. What we would like to do is set you up some CDs and a savings account. We also have some very good investment accounts. Would you be interested in any of these opportunities?"

Hawk stared at the banker and said, "I've been out of pocket for some time. What exactly is the balance in my account, sir?"

The banker cleared his throat and said, "Just a few dollars over three million, Mr. Hawk."

Hawk sat there not believing what he had heard. "There must be some mistake. Did you get the wrong account number?"

"No, sir, everything is in order. You received a bank transfer two days ago from the US Treasury Department in the amount of three million dollars."

Hawk started to understand, but still couldn't believe what the banker was telling him. He asked the banker if he could use his phone for a private call. He waited until the banker was out of his office and called Captain Jack's number.

"Hello," said Captain Jack.

"Captain Jack, why do I have a three-million-dollar balance in my checking account?"

Captain Jack laughed out loud. "I was expecting this call, Hawk. Remember the Dodge van that you sent back in the C-130 from Mexico?"

"Yes sir, it was full of one hundred-dollar bills."

"That's right. It went back to the Treasury Department and was counted. It added up to thirty million dollars in cash. It was considered 'found money.' The treasury gives a ten percent finder's fee to whoever returns money like that. Government employees aren't allowed to get finder's fees, so you qualified for the finder's fee. Your finder's fee was three million dollars, Hawk. Congratulations!"

"You really mean that money is mine to do with whatever I want. What if I want to give it away? Can I do that?"

"Yes, you can. I thought you might want to do something like that, but keep some for yourself, Hawk. And by the way, it's all tax free."

"Yes sir, I will, and thanks."

Hawk hung up and motioned for the banker to come back to his office.

"Sir, the first thing I need to do is transfer some money to several different accounts. Can you do that for me?"

"Give me the names on the accounts and the amounts, and it will be done in a few minutes."

"After I take care of the transfers, I will want to talk with you about how best to invest the rest."

"We'll be glad to help you, Mr. Hawk. Now, about the names and accounts."

Hawk pulled out his wallet and gave the banker the account numbers and the amounts of one million dollars each, for his only two friends: Elizabeth Stillings and Juan Luis Diaz Villalobos.

Made in the USA
Columbia, SC
11 May 2024